THE KEYN

Dr Phillips

A Maida Vale Idyll

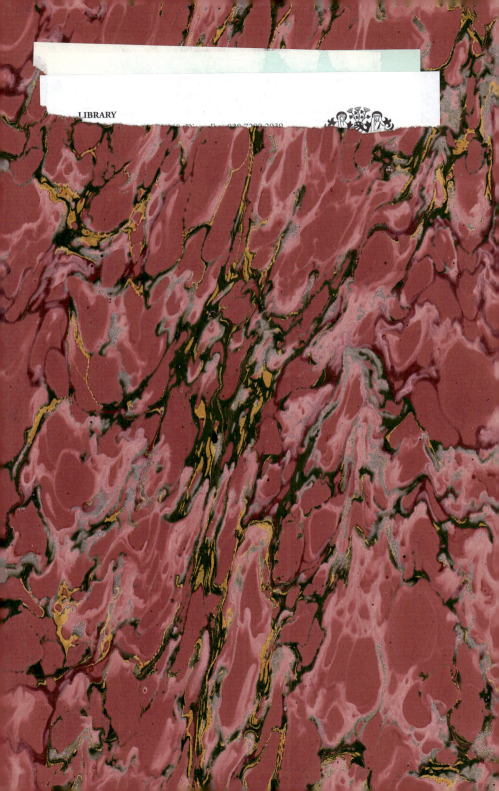

FRANK DANBY

Dr Phillips

A Maida Vale Idyll

THE KEYNES PRESS

BRITISH MEDICAL
ASSOCIATION

© Copyright in this format The Keynes Press 1989
ISBN 0 7279 0167 2

First edition (1887) published by
Vizetelly & Co
Published in 1989 by The Keynes Press
BMA House, Tavistock Square, London

Illustrations by Tabitha Salmon

Printed in Great Britain by
the University Press, Cambridge

Introduction

At first sight *Dr Phillips* might seem an odd choice for reprinting in the Keynes Press: the plot, it might be alleged, is pasteboard, subplots are lacking, and there is none of the depth encountered in the great Victorian moralists—George Eliot and George Meredith, to name but two. Yet we do not accuse Tissot of shallowness because his pictures lack the compassionate earthiness of van Gogh, and Frank Danby's novel has many virtues. Compared with novels written only 20 years earlier it is pithy, with none of what the critic Walter Allen called "remplissage"—rubble thrown in to make up two or three volumes for the Victorian circulating libraries. Its characters are sympathetic and believable, and at this stage in the nineteenth century there is no longer a need to ensure that the villains get their deserts. Nor is it really a novel of sensation: there is no sudden shock, as in Wilkie Collins—indeed, the murder of Mrs Phillips, the climax of the book, when Phillips gives his wife an injection of a grain of morphine after she has had an ovarian cyst removed, is terse and low key. And two other positive features must be added to all these: the depiction of a particular segment of society at a particular time, and the story of a physician/medical editor who murders his wife, a *roman-à-clef*, some think, based on rumoured events in the life of Ernest Hart, a great but undervalued editor of the *BMJ*.

At the beginning of the book we encounter Dr Phillips as a busy doctor. Now a valued general practitioner, he was formerly a surgeon of promise as well as a subeditor of a weekly medical journal. Bored after six years of marriage to a barren wife—who lives only for food, cards, and gossip with a small circle of well-off Jewish friends—Phillips has taken a mistress. Their child, Nita, provides the element of goodness that will be overcome by evil: neglected by her mother she dies of croup, and on the same day her mother, "Mrs" Mary Cameron, deserts Phillips for a younger man, even though Phillips has killed his wife so that he can marry her.

We hear no more of the mistress but throughout she is the most rounded character of them all. We also sympathise with her the most, given that the daughter, Nita, is largely brought in to evoke pity (though one would hardly go as far as Oscar Wilde, who could never read of the death of little Nell without being convulsed with laughter). But who faced with the drudgeries of a poorly paid life as a governess would not settle for being a kept woman in the luxury of Brunswick Place, and why should we moralise or be surprised when she leaves for married respectability with the young if vapid man about town? (And I suspect that 40 years on the former Mary Cameron will have become a censorious old matron in some cathedral town.)

At the end of the book there is a description of Dr Phillips 10 years later as both a public and a private figure; an aging idol of his clinic with a large and eager following of medical students, a lonely widower whose only consolations are luxurious surroundings and a pretty parlour maid. If ever there was an author who fulfilled Wilkie Collins's injunction to novelists to "make 'em laugh, make 'em cry, make 'em wait," it was Frank Danby.

"Frank Danby" was the pseudonym of Julia Frankau, born Davis in Dublin in 1864, who was educated by Mme Paul Lafargue, the daughter of Karl Marx; publishing three novels under this pseudonym as well as two non-fiction works under her own name, she was also a prolific reviewer. She was married to Arthur Frankau, a cigar merchant, and had a daughter and

vi

three sons, one of whom was the celebrated novelist Gilbert Frankau. She died in 1916.

Though Jewish herself, Frank Danby was attacked by some critics for what was described as "the most uncompromisingly honest presentation of Jewish life in English fiction" in *Dr Phillips*, her first novel. To be sure, her publishers did promote the book by advertising it as "A novel of Jewish life"—which helped to sell out the first edition. Yet the accusation is unfair: it was meanness, affectation, ostentation, and snobbery that were Frank Danby's real targets rather than any particular religion. To attack all of these she chose a masculine pseudonym rather than using her real name, adding a preface in the second edition denying that *Dr Phillips* was aimed at Judaism. No less a person than Israel Zangwill was later to praise her novel, *Pigs in Clover*, for its realism and depiction of the problems of British Jews striving for social equality with gentiles. And we have only to compare Danby's milder mockery of life at the Detmars or the Levys with Anthony Trollope's savage treatment of Ezekiel Brehgert in *The Way we Live Now*, published only 14 years before *Dr Phillips*, to realise how different the attitudes are: as John Sutherland has commented in his introduction to the Penguin edition, "parts of *The Way we Live Now*...would be practically unwritable today because of the proscriptions of the race relations laws."

Trollope's novel was published only 10 years after the passing of the full Jewish Emancipation Act of 1858, while the first Jewish judge was not appointed until as late as 1873. Thus, had his father not had him baptised and brought up in the Christian faith, one person who would have been affected by the previous laws was Trollope's *bête-noire*, Benjamin Disraeli (who became MP for Maidstone in 1837 and Prime Minister in 1867). But a figure who concerns us more and who was affected by such laws was Ernest Hart, the future editor of the *BMJ*. Because he was a Jew, Hart was not allowed under the University Test Acts to take up the Lambert-Jones scholarship at Queens' College, Cambridge, having to study at St George's Hospital Medical School instead. Even so, Hart's progress was rapid. Taking his MRCS in 1856, he successively became house surgeon at St Mary's Hospital, an anatomy demonstrator at its associated institution, Lane's School, and ophthalmic and aural surgeon at St Mary's, with consulting rooms in Queen Anne Street. In 1863 he was appointed dean of St Mary's Hospital Medical School and a year later part-time assistant editor of the *Lancet*. The editor at the beginning of his time there was the great Thomas Wakley, but subsequently Wakley's son James took over and thereafter relations were never very happy. In 1866 Hart moved to the *BMJ* as editor, a post he was to hold until his death in 1898.

Hart was undoubtedly one of the great medical editors of all time, to be included in the small pantheon that contains Thomas Wakley, Theodore Fox, Hugh Clegg, and Francis Ingelfinger. Less known than any of these, surprisingly few records and documents survive about any aspect of his life, while his difficult personality must have had a major role in making people forget his important positive qualities. Boastful, querulous, and self-righteous, Hart can hardly have surprised his American audience in 1893 when he declared his creed: "An editor needs, and must have, many enemies: he cannot do without them. Woe be unto the journalist of whom all men say good things."

Yet Hart's qualities far outweigh his defects: he left life different from how he found it, surely the touchstone of immortality. Among other things, he campaigned successfully against infanticide, air pollution, and the condition of workhouses, and for medical services for the armed forces, compulsory vaccination, and vivisection. As well as placing much more emphasis on original scientific communications in the journal Hart also introduced reports of medical events from all over the world, and the *BMJ* was chosen to report the proceedings of the International Medical Congress in 1881—which was attended by Pasteur, Lister, and Virchow, among others. The reports of conditions of the wounded during the Crimean campaign and the inadequacy of the medical care were to start a tradition of reporting such arrangements for medical care in wartime that was to continue through the Franco-Prussian war, the Boer war, as well as the first and second world wars.

Given all this, the journal lost all semblance of being a BMA newsletter, and its circulation rose from 2500 when Hart took over to over 20000 at his death, helping a poverty stricken BMA achieve financial security. By 1887 Hart could claim that the second volume of the *BMJ* for that year was the largest of its kind ever published. Some in the association feared that it might become a "mere appendage" of the *BMJ*, but Hart was also active in the BMA—and as chairman for 25 years of its most important committee, the Parliamentary Bills Committee, he was well placed to push his campaigns into the political arena, often successfully. Nevertheless, two events ensured that the association and its journal and editor stayed strong but separate. The first was in 1869, when Hart suddenly resigned, to disappear for a year before he was reappointed; the second, in 1888, 10 years before his death, when he survived censure for breaking confidentiality over the case of the dying Emperor Frederick of Germany.

No explanation has ever been given for Hart's resignation and inevitably legend and speculation have substituted for fact. It has been said that he had misappropriated some BMA funds, had got a friend to cash a worthless cheque for him, and had had to flee the country. Certainly in the year Hart ceased to be editor there was a debate at the Annual Meeting of the BMA at Leeds about a payment of £802 by the *BMJ* to unknown contributors. The editor had control of this sum, the names of the contributors were never made public (though they were said to include some of the most eminent in the land), and the implication must have been that Hart himself had appropriated most if not all of it. And when the next editor, Jonathan Hutchinson, was appointed it was arranged that future contributors would be paid by cheque issued by the treasurer of the BMA. Yet a year later Hutchinson resigned and Hart was reappointed editor from among several distinguished applicants.

Hart just escaped having to leave his post in 1888 when he published a handwritten note by the dying Emperor of Germany alleging that his German doctors had maltreated him. This was the culmination of a long story of bungled diagnosis and treatment of the emperor's cancer of the larynx, in which Sir Morrell Mackenzie had been concerned, and accusation followed counter-accusation with eventual writs for libel. The reaction in Britain to the publication of the document in the *BMJ* was swift: a memorial signed by many prominent medical men, including Lord Lister, stated that it was a violation of professional confidence and discreditable to the profession, asking the Council of the BMA and its president to take immediate action to clear the association's name. At a special meeting of the council on 1 December Hart apologised: while regretting its appearance in the *BMJ*, however, he justified the action by pointing out that there were good reasons for believing that the document was genuine, and that it was hardly a breach of confidence given that the topic had already been discussed.

Hart's statement did not satisfy those who had signed the memorial, and some resigned, but it did placate the BMA Council, which thereafter defended Hart and reiterated its confidence in him. So, a bit like Thomas Mann's trickster Felix Krull, Hart survived yet again—to continue as an authority in medical journalism (he was consulted by the American Medical

Association on how to make its journal better), to travel, to write, and to push his Parliamentary Bills. He died in harness in 1898 from gangrene of the leg, a complication of his longstanding diabetes, and the journal for the following week had no fewer than 11 pages of tributes from the good and the great, which, even by the more extended standards of the time, must say much for his contemporary reputation.

However Hart comes out when weighed in some sort of moral or journalistic balance, how far was he used as a model for *Dr Phillips*? There are several obvious parallels: his religion, his joint appointment as medical editor and fashionable London physician, and his love of luxury (he had a house in both London and the country, kept a good stable, and collected Japanese works of art avidly well before the artistic movements of the 1880s and 1890s made these all the rage). More importantly his first wife, Rosetta, died in November 1861 under mysterious circumstances: in the night she mistakenly drank some tincture of aconite instead of the intended "black draught." The resultant vomiting worried Hart, but she seemed well by the morning when she was examined by her general practitioner; on his second visit two hours later, however, she was dead, having been given three doses of hydrocyanic acid to check the vomiting. A verdict of accidental poisoning by tincture of aconite was recorded at the Coroner's Court presided over by none other than Thomas Wakley, Hart's former employer, but it seems that there was some tittle-tattle about the circumstances. Indeed, a legend grew up subsequently in the *BMJ* office that Hart had had to flee the country to avoid being tried for murdering his wife. This seems unlikely given that she died in 1861 and Hart did not absent himself for a year until 1869. And much later in reply to Edward Muirhead Little (who wrote the history of the BMA) the editor of the *Lancet*, Sir Squire Sprigge, stated: "When I came to look into the crime story, which was more or less traditional in the office, I came to the conclusion that it was without foundation." Yet that there was some reason behind all this is shown by the well-authenticated story of a dinner party in the early 1870s at the Thatched House Club in London. A Dr Fisher was having dinner in a private room with a friend and a friend of his, and the talk turned to a barrister who had recently had to leave the country in a hurry because he couldn't pay his debts. Fisher said it was a similar case to Ernest Hart's, except that Hart had fled to escape prosecution for murder. The unknown friend of the friend present was none other than Mr Rowland, the brother of Hart's second wife to be, and a few days later Fisher was told that Hart was to bring a slander action against him. As it happened, Fisher had been told the facts of the case by Lambert, an eminent lawyer who had been present when the question of whether Hart should be prosecuted or not had been raised with the Attorney General. Fisher put this fact down in a deposition to his solicitor and never heard another word about a possible action for slander.

Equally mysterious is how far Frank Danby based *Dr Phillips* on Ernest Hart. Some accounts say that it was pure coincidence—yet the publishers altered the book's title from its initial one of *Dr Abrams* (Hart's middle name was Abraham) and in later life Gilbert Frankau often stated that his mother had based her protagonist on Hart. But *sub specie aeternatatis* does it really matter? Frank Danby's novel is worthy in its own right, Ernest Hart is one of the great medical editors of all time, and if the one draws attention to the other then we should all be grateful.

September 1989

STEPHEN LOCK
Editor
British Medical Journal

Book I · Chapter I

The staircase was hung with Gobelins tapestry, vases on malachite pedestals stood on the landing, and on entering the drawing-room your feet were surprised by the softness of the carpets. There were gilt chairs and satin draperies; marble figures upheld the red shaded lamps; exquisite china lay on inlaid tables. The clock on the mantelpiece was a work of art. But this large and beautiful house was filled with floating suggestions of a Bond Street showroom; the furniture looked as if it were on view.

Far away in a distant corner stood a piano, draped with an Indian shawl and hung with photographs. Near by was a card table, round which were seated four women; and in the crimson light the aquiline features and strongly marked brows of the players were sharply modelled.

Mrs Montague Levy called "Abundance." It was an anxious moment! Would she or would she not make the nine tricks and take the contents of the pool, besides ten shillings each from Mrs Collings, Mrs Lucas, and Mrs Jacobs?

Mrs Collings and Mrs Lucas looked at each other with questioning eyes and unsuccessfully endeavoured to telegraph "play trump." Mrs Jacobs maintained a calm demeanour that gave hope to the sisters. One, two, four tricks fell to the opposition. It was now or never. Where was the knave of spades? Mrs Levy looked alarmed, miserable, agitated, and was almost unable to hold her cards. Seven rounds passed in pregnant silence. Three hearts were beating with pleasure, one with anguish. Mrs Levy played the ten of spades and Mrs Jacobs put the knave upon it with a triumphant air.

1

Then Mrs Montague Levy paid her debts and restrained her tears.

"Did you ever see anything so unlucky?" she asked, looking round for sympathy with a tremble in her voice. "I had eight trumps with the ace. I never saw anything like it."

The party was composed exclusively of Jews. During ten months of the year they met about four times a week and played cards at each other's houses, their favourite rendezvous being Mrs Detmar's. This lady, in whose house we now are, was the most popular hostess of them all. She is seated a little out of the light of the card table. Her face is lost in the shadow, but you can see she is a woman of about forty, with bushy eyebrows, heavy jaw, and thick underlip. Her husband is in the bric-a-brac trade, from which he derives an income of about ten thousand a year. Mrs Detmar, by virtue of her exceeding riches, was a leader in her set. She was gushingly intimate with all her dear friends, and delighted in the evenings when they met and played cards in Northwick Place. She liked to provide a sumptuous supper for them and to hear afterwards of the success of her entertainment.

Mrs Collings and Mrs Lucas were big, handsome, untidy looking Irishwomen living in two adjoining houses in Sutherland Avenue; and whenever either of them had any little family difficulty to adjust, which was often, she would run round without gloves, and with an old bonnet on, to tell Mrs Detmar about it. Neither of them was young and their peculiarities and their accent seemed to have grown with them; moreover, Mrs Collings's children, although they had never so much as seen Ireland, all spoke with a slight brogue.

Mrs Montague Levy was the second wife of a prosperous advertising dentist and Mrs Jacobs was a young bride from Birmingham, but quite able to hold her own with the others, even in solo whist.

2

There were no men in the room. In their parties, as in their synagogues, the men and the women sit apart.

When Mrs Detmar moved away Mrs Jacobs asked, with her Birmingham accent: "What is the matter tonight? Why aren't they playing?"

As usual, Mrs Collings and Mrs Lucas began to speak both together.

"Oh, don't you know," they chorused. "Dr and Mrs Phillips are coming and they are going to bring a friend."

"And she is not one of us," snapped in Mrs Levy in an aggrieved tone; she suffered from indigestion, and it spoilt her temper.

"Not one of us!" reiterated Mrs Jacobs, her soft eyes wide open. "Why, what is she coming for?"

"I wouldn't have had her if I'd been Mrs Detmar," said Mrs Collings; "I don't believe in mixing with Christians."

"Bah!" said her sister contemptuously. "It's all véry well for you to say that, because you don't know any except those you've met at my house."

"And I would never have had them in mine, my dear. I'm too particular about whom I let my girls associate with."

"You may say what you like, Mrs Lucas," interposed Mrs Levy as she leaned back in her chair, "but I don't believe in Christians. The men drink and the women are bad. It's all very well for Dr Phillips to visit them; he has no children to set a bad example to. But I wouldn't, and I don't understand Mrs Detmar's doing it."

"We did not mix with Christians at all in Birmingham," said Mrs Jacobs, anxious as a newcomer to be on the right side. "None of the respectable Jews did, only those who couldn't get anyone else. The money lenders and that sort of people."

"Well, never mind! Are we going on playing or are you too unwell after that 'abundance,' Mrs Levy?"

said Mrs Lucas with a sneer, recommencing to shuffle the cards.

The sarcasm passed unheeded and the four continued their game.

Two or three young girls were clustered by the fireside, its twilight making of them a sort of decorative background and bringing into relief their curious race likeness.

They settled their light dresses, they smoothed their curly hair, they clasped and unclasped their bracelets, and played with their rings. Mrs Collings's daughters were considered to be well brought up girls. The elder was stout and dark. She wore glasses and her manner was dictatorial.

Her sister was her exact antithesis. She had hair of an auburn shade and blue eyes. Her curls were untidy and dishevelled, and the colour in her cheeks was vivid and glowing. Her lips were carmine and her figure had none of the angularities of girlhood; it was ample, almost redundant. She looked like a French china doll, but was more disorderly in her make up and more irregular in her colouring.

The third of the group, Sophia Jeddington, was slender and aquiline. She wore her clothes awkwardly, as the room wore its furniture. Her father, whose original name had been Moses, had made his enormous fortune by selling ready made and second hand clothing to the colonies. Now they were socially ambitious: they belonged to that class of Jews who see in every Christian a probable "swell," in every Jew a direct descendant of an old clothesman or a hawker.

The expected guest of the evening aroused mingled feelings in Soph's bosom; she yearned for her friendship and intimacy, but dreaded the effect the card party would have on her.

"I don't believe they will come at all now," said Mrs Detmar dejectedly, after about the eighth disappointment. "Mrs Phillips was at Marshall's sale this morning

4

and I daresay she knocked herself up. We had better begin, John," she said, addressing the footman who was bringing in little glasses of lemon squash. "Get out some more card tables."

There were murmurs of dissent and murmurs of approval, the girls, especially Sophia, were not pleased at the order.

"Awfully bad form, I think, don't you, Ray? Fancy her coming in and seeing them all playing cards as if they could not wait a moment."

"You know her, Soph, don't you? Tell us what she is like," asked Ray, the elder of the Collings girls.

"Yes, I know her. I met her at the Phillips's one afternoon last week. She is one of the most beautiful women you ever saw, and dressed—well, I never saw anything fit better than her bodice did. I do hope she will come—at least, I did hope it; I wanted to get her to tell me who her dressmaker was; but now I don't much care. I should hate her to see mother and all these people playing cards as if their lives depended on it. I must say I like Christians; they are ever so much better style than our people."

"Yes, but mamma says there is not any good in them," rejoined Ray with decision. "Papa generally asks two or three from the stock exchange to our dances, but he always says we had better not dance much with them ourselves, especially after supper."

At that moment the conversation was interrupted, the card players stopped short in the act of commencing, the door was flung open, and the footman announced, as if he too shared in the general excitement: "Dr and Mrs Phillips and Mrs Cameron."

All eyes were immediately turned towards the door. It was as if the curtain had drawn up on a new piece. The actors were revealed and the audience waited for the first words of the story that was to be, scene by scene, unfolded to them.

The first thing the black eyes saw was the tall,

familiar figure of their dear doctor, his stooping shoulders, and the black beard, whiskers, and moustache that hid all his features; then, passing over Mrs Phillips's loose and unwieldy bulk, they concentrated their glance upon a really beautiful woman. Her white profile was crowned with corn coloured hair, her dark blue eyes had starry centres. Her black velvet gown fell about her beautiful figure in statuesque folds, and she moved among the dark skinned women like the moon in a cloudy sky.

She responded to them with a charming and graceful warmth. She recognised Soph Jeddington, and spoke a few soft words to the girls. They followed her and clustered round her. Dr Phillips watched her for a moment and, seeing she had made a favourable impression, went downstairs to join the men. Mrs Phillips, in her lethargic ill health, sank heavily into a chair and detailed her latest ailments to an imprisoned listener.

Mrs Cameron was already the centre of a circle. At first she spoke very little, but listened, while they looked at her and admired. Then Soph reminded her that she had promised she would sing next time they met.

At the first suggestion there was a movement and looks were exchanged, half of wonder, half of doubt. Music at a card party! This was a decided innovation.

Paying no attention to the dark looks of their elders, the girls led Mrs Cameron in triumph to the piano. But she had not been singing long before two or three young men, lured by the unwonted sound, came upstairs to inquire the meaning of it. Thus encouraged, she sang again, but only Florrie listened, all the card players commenting loudly and angrily on the noise.

"I can scarcely see my cards, and my head is aching so that I don't know what to call," snapped out Mrs Levy at the end of a song. "I can't understand how people can be so inconsiderate."

Not being in the least degree deaf, Mrs Cameron heard this observation and rose from the piano at once.

"I fear I have interrupted your game by my noisy singing," she said, standing by the table and looking quite grieved. "What are you playing?"

"Solo," was the curt response. Mrs Montague Levy was never very famous for her suavity, and tonight she had been losing. "It's your turn, Mrs Lucas; how I hate a slow game! What do you call?"

But Mrs Cameron was not to be baffled when she had set her mind on anything, and just now she had set her mind on charming all these people.

"Don't you think five is a better game than four?" she asked insinuatingly.

"Yes, of course it is. Why, will you play?" and Mrs Lucas became quite animated.

"With pleasure. I am so fond of cards."

This was an "open sesame" to the hearts of the four Jewesses. Mrs Lucas was warm and the others were quite gracious. They had a chair fetched for her, offered her a footstool, informed her what points and what rules they were playing, and took her into their midst almost with enthusiasm.

And her joining their ranks gave an impetus to the others; all resumed their normal occupations. The men went downstairs to their forsaken whist; the women, including Mrs Detmar, sat down to loo, to bluff, to solo whist; the girls resumed their old places by the fireside and continued their conversation.

"I wish she had gone on singing," said Florrie. "What a nice voice she has! You ought to get her to sing duets with you, Soph."

"But just fancy her playing cards! I don't think it at all nice of her," said Ray, ignoring her sister as usual.

"Oh, I don't think anything of it. You see, I know so many more of them than you do. A great many of them play, though not so often as we do, nor so high," replied Soph importantly, anxious to prove her social knowl-

7

edge and establish her supremacy. "Besides, she heard what that underbred Mrs Levy said and could not do less than leave off singing. As I said before, I'm very sorry she came; I hate to see Christians coming among Jews like these; they carry away quite a false impression and it strengthens the prejudice we already find so hard to overcome."

"Oh, that's rubbish!" said matter of fact Ray. "She knew she was coming among Jews and if she had any prejudices she could have stayed away. Besides they must know we are better than they are. Mozart was a Jew, and Heine and Beaconsfield."

"You can't argue from three people, of whom two denied their Judaism and the third refused to admit it. I tell you, I am awfully sorry Mrs Cameron came here this evening. She is a splendid woman and a perfect lady, and I shouldn't wonder if she belonged to a first class family. What can she think of all these people, who hate her, to begin with because she is better bred than they? I liked meeting her at Dr Phillips's. Dr Phillips is a gentleman. He is in a profession. He went to a university and he doesn't give card parties. I can't imagine why they brought her here."

"Dr Phillips would not have liked to miss his whist, and Mrs Detmar would have been awfully offended if he hadn't come," answered Ray, who heard but only half comprehended her companion's ideas. To her, her people were everything; and her narrow horizon was bounded on all sides by old fashioned Judaism. She was not a particularly intelligent girl and the social incapacities and disabilities of her people, dimly struggling through the synagogue mists into Soph's mind, had not yet disturbed her placid self complacency.

Florrie, dominated and overpowered by her sister's density, as usual, said nothing. Yet had it begun to dawn upon her that there was a city outside Jerusalem and had the choice been given her, and a certain pair of brown Christian eyes been by to assist her in her choice, she might have foregone the grand privilege of being one of "God's chosen people" to have dwelt in that city in spiritual freedom.

The girls continued to talk and the women to play. The temporary brightness Mary Cameron had brought into the room had vanished. The red light still played on the money, on the cards, on the diamonds, on eager faces and grasping fingers. The play went on almost in silence; no light jest or merry quip, no sacrilegious sound of laughter disturbed the devotion of Judaism to its living God. Such mystic words as "Solo," "Misère," "You're loo again" alone broke the silence.

Many religions have had their day upon this earth, have been born and exalted, whether in the stable or on the Mount, but the great Single Deity, the "I am the Lord thy God, and thou shalt have no other" that binds Judaism together, is as invincible now as it was when Moses had to destroy the Golden Calf on Mount Horeb. And that Deity is Gain.

At last the clock struck twelve. John announced supper.

The card parties broke up, not suddenly or all at once, but as each pool was cleared or round completed so each little party rose and commenced to discuss the affairs of the evening. The men came up by ones and twos and threes and joined in the general discussion.

"A d——d good looking woman", were the first words that startled Dr Phillips as he came into the room with his host.

"Who is the lady under discussion?" he asked his neighbour smilingly.

"Mrs Cameron, and I don't think there are two opinions about her," answered Mrs Detmar. Try and get them to leave the subject and to go in to supper, will you, David?" she added to her husband. "The soup will be cold, and Mrs Cameron will hear what they are all saying."

9

"Well my dear, she'll only be flattered: women like to be talked about." And David Detmar had a good look at her himself.

In the course of Dr Phillips's journey to the farther corner of the room he heard many opinions freely expressed about his wife's friend. Ladies unhesitatingly stopped his progress and held on to his sleeve or the lapels of his coat to compel his attention. It was easy to see the estimation in which he was held. The other men were treated merely as husbands, were shaken hands with and listened to, were even talked to, inattentively. But Dr Phillips's was a royal progress. Everyone had something to ask him or to tell him. You could see at a glance he was essentially the lady's doctor. So easy, so tactful, replying to all and satisfying all. At the same time a close observer might have seen an added interest and a keener glance in the eyes behind the glasses when Mrs Cameron's name fell upon his ear.

He went from group to group and heard how she had sung and how she had played cards; how some condemned her for the one thing; and some, a very few, for the other. Broken phrases of conversation buzzed round him and through them Dr Phillips, always observing, listening, weighing remarks, and saying little, made his way from the door to the corner by the piano where Mrs Cameron was still sitting, wedged in between Mrs Lucas and Mrs Levy, fighting over again the battles of the evening.

"Oh, here you are, Doctor!" exclaimed Mrs Levy, a constant and remunerative patient of his. "I've just been telling Mrs Cameron not to play trump through the solo. What do you say? You know the game thoroughly."

Mrs Lucas did not give him time to reply.

"Dr Phillips always plays trump, don't you, Doctor?"

"Well, I don't call it the game," said Mrs Levy.

10

"The doctor plays as if it were whist, and the rules are quite different."

Nether the fact that they had not given him time to reply, nor that Mrs Levy condemned him unheard, disturbed the doctor's equanimity. He stood quietly waiting until the ladies had finished their little discussion.

"Will you come down with me?" he then said to Mrs Cameron, offering her his arm. "Mr Detmar is taking my wife." Then, more softly, he added, "Has it bored you terribly, dear?"

"Bored me? Not at all! I have been immensely amused. I never saw anything so funny as some of the dresses. And the masses of diamonds! They would have been perfectly exquisite if they had only been clean. And what magnificent ornaments and pictures!"

"The ornaments are nothing. Detmar sells that kind of thing. And when he is overstocked he brings them here and puts them about the place. You will see quite a different set, I dare say, next time you come. By the way, you will have to sit next to Detmar; I can't spare you that."

"John, take that fried salmon to Mrs Collings, tell her I recommend it. Mary, Mrs Lucas's glass is empty, what the devil are you doing standing there idle? Mrs Collings, cucumber is very good with that smoked beef, take my tip—Jane, hand Mrs Collings the cucumber."

Mr Detmar, at the top of the table, was in the full swing of his hospitality.

"Well, is the doctor looking after you? What are you going to begin on? What do you think of our fried fish?" he asked Mrs Cameron almost before she had time to take her seat.

"Very nice indeed," she responded, having been supplied with the luxury, and vainly endeavouring to ignore its oily flavour. "I shall ask Mrs Detmar to give me the recipe."

11

"She'll be delighted, I'm sure. Hullo, Doctor, not stopped already I hope! Known the doctor a long time, eh, Mrs C.? Great man with the ladies!"

Mary's eyes went down and a sad expression stole over her beautiful face.

"Ever since my dear husband died Dr Phillips, and lately his kind wife, have been almost my only friends," she said softly.

"Humph! Died of *dt*, I suppose. Must find out," thought Mr Detmar to himself. But aloud he replied in his hearty way. "Well, well! you must cheer up now. You've made a lot of new friends tonight. With our people, the motto is 'Once one of us, always one of us!' Stick to them and they'll stick to you. What do you say, Phillips? We're not a bad lot, take us altogether, are we?"

"My wife and I have already told Mrs Cameron to try and forget her troubles a little in society, and her appearance here tonight is the result of my prescription. She wanted to go home directly after dinner when she found we were going out; but Mrs Phillips persuaded her to come, and I don't think she will require so much persuasion next time."

"No," interrupted the lady, who by this time had got over her difficulty with the fish and was playing with some grapes. "My reception has been too kind." And she smiled again at Mr Detmar and won his heart by talking to him intimately and telling him of her dear and only little daughter.

In the hall, whilst wraps were being put on, Dr Phillips was overwhelmed with questions and requests for appointments. He was promising in one breath to see a Bennie, a Harry, and a Sam, who were all causing anxiety to their respective mothers.

Mrs Cameron looked at them and him half wonderingly. The thoughtfulness was still upon her when she was in the brougham with Mrs Phillips.

12

Both the women were quiet, but there was not much resemblance in their quietude.

Mrs Phillips's asthma made her breathe loudly, and she half closed her eyes. Presently she asked if Mrs Cameron had had a pleasant evening and if she had won or lost at the card table; and, having said a few eulogistic words about Jews, she relapsed into a wheezy silence which she did not break until the carriage drew up at No – Portsdown Road.

"You'll see Mrs Cameron home, won't you Ben? I'll go to bed. Good night!" she said, when her husband had helped her out with some difficulty.

"Oh, certainly not!" expostulated Mrs Cameron from the cosy depths of the carriage. "I couldn't think of troubling the doctor. I shall be quite safe: my maid is sitting up."

"It is really no trouble at all," interposed the doctor courteously. "Clothilde is quite right. I couldn't think of leaving you to go home by yourself. Good night, my dear." And he went into the hall and kissed his wife's plethoric cheek. "Mind you don't take cold standing there!"

Ten minutes later they were at Brunswick Place. The coachman seemed to know the house very well and stopped full at the little door.

Dr Phillips assisted his companion to alight. Then he put his hand in his trouser pocket and drew out a large bunch of keys. It took him no time to select one from the number. On his inserting it into the keyhole the door yielded at once, as to an accustomed touch.

There was no sound in the house; if the maid were sitting up she had evidently fallen asleep in the occupation. The street lamp opposite threw its light into the hall, and discovered one candle and a box of matches on the table.

"Are you coming in, Benito?" she said when he had lighted the candle for her; and her voice had a weary timbre.

13

"No, it is late—and I can see you are tired. Good night!"

Had the coachman been gazing at them instead of discreetly looking the other way he would have seen a quiet kiss. Then the door banged, the carriage drove off, and the quiet little street was at rest.

Book I · Chapter II

At four o'clock next day Mrs Phillips was sitting in the
drawing room, feeling as usual rather out of sorts, and
embroidering in cross stitch a cover for the sideboard.
Mrs Cameron's appearance with her little girl broke the
dullness and Mrs Phillips, making an effort, rose to
welcome them.

"This is good of you. I didn't think anybody would
be coming in so I just took up my work. Is this your
little girl? Will you let me kiss you, dear. What is your
name?"

"Baby Nita," the little one responded gravely, fixing
her dark eyes on her interlocutor.

Mrs Cameron's only child was a very fragile little
creature. A transparent skinned baby with blue veins,
and black eyes that seemed too large for the tiny
features. Mrs Phillips looked at her and sighed, and a
sentimental sadness filled this fat German woman's
soul. She was not a mother; she was only a very stupid
woman who had been sent over from Frankfurt to
marry Dr Phillips; but she had a tender heart, and tears
filled her eyes as she took the babe on her knee, and pity
was in her voice as she talked to her guest and
overflowed with kindness for her.

"Now then, since you are come, you must make
yourself comfortable and take your things off. Tea will
be up in a moment. Will Baby Nita have some tea with
me—milk and cakie, Nita? Come, let me take your
bonnet and pretty coat off. There, now warm your little
hands and sit down on the foot stool," she said cordially
with an indescribable foreign accent.

"But I'm afraid you will be fidgeted by her, dear Mrs
Phillips; you know you are not strong. Nurse is

15

downstairs to take Baby home; I brought her on purpose. You were kind enough to say you wanted to see the child but I did not think of inflicting her on you for the afternoon."

"Oh! no, she won't fidget me, please let her stay; I dearly love children." And her voice faltered. Her childlessness had been a great trouble to this woman, who in her husband had not found a sufficient outlet for all the tendernesses of her large heart.

"It is sad for you," said her sympathetic companion. "Heaven knows what my life would be without Nita. Nita, darling, come and kiss your mother. But then you have your husband, while I ... "

"Yes, yes, dear, we all have our compensations. There, there, let's talk of something more lively. Here's tea coming, that will liven us up a bit. Put it here, Jane," indicating a table by her, "and give the child a chair. She will have some milk, won't you poppet?"

A very silent child was little Nita Cameron. She ate and drank slowly what was given to her. She was unchildlike and wistful looking, a plain baby for the daughter of so handsome a mother.

The women were in earnest converse when the doctor came upstairs. It was only a week ago that he had told his wife of the lonely widow who had sent for him to see her ailing child and who seemed so desolate in her trouble. Mrs Phillips's kind heart had warmed to her at once, and the two were already growing into intimacy. Today she had been telling her guest about some of her domestic troubles and also about her weak state of health, and Mrs Cameron had proved a most sympathetic and patient listener.

"What with my nights being so bad with my back aching constantly, and the doctor being called out so often, if it wasn't for the chloral I should never get a wink of sleep, and even that he can't bear me to take; he says it will destroy my constitution. My dear, I haven't had a constitution, at least not one to speak of, since I got married. I was too young, that's the truth of it. But it was such a good chance and papa and mamma didn't like to throw it away."

Her reminiscences would have extended to much greater length if Dr Phillips's entry hadn't caused a diversion.

He came into the dim twilight of the crude ugly room, patted and smiled at the baby, kissed his wife, greeted his guest and set himself to the enjoyment of a quiet hour.

Dr Phillips was tall, slender, and stooping. He was a very ugly man, or would have been but for the redeeming dark eyes with their long lashes. His nose was large, and the rest of his features were hidden beneath wiry black hair, but he had a very soft voice and small sensitive smooth palmed hands. An hour such as the present suited him to perfection. The presence of these two women, and the peculiarity of the real relations between them, tickled his fancy. His imagination was stimulated by the situation. He found Mrs Cameron's sympathetic attention to Mrs Phillips's ailments very amusing. It delighted him to see Nita on her little stool by his wife, and his eyes wandered from the woman to the child in most perfect content. Then he admired the manner in which Mrs Cameron's small bonnet, with its black velvet strings, brought into relief the exquisite contour of her ear, and felt happy as he listened to Mrs Phillips, fat and placid, talking in her monotonous way for their entertainment while she poured out the tea. When he joined in the conversation it became livelier; and when he took the child on his knee Mrs Phillips subsided into silence and enjoyed her husband's unaccustomed society. He was at once so amiable and so entertaining that she almost forgot that it was Friday evening and that the dusk was fast approaching. The servant's abrupt entry with the candles reminded her of the religious duty of the day.

"Why, how the afternoon has slipped away! It must

17

be almost time to make Sabbath in. Get the prayer books, Jane. If you'll excuse me, Mrs Cameron, I'll just go and wash my hands."

"Oh, pray don't let me keep you! I was just on the point of going, only the doctor's charming conversation detained me. It is really too late for baby to be out; the evenings are still so cold. Come, Nita, let me put your things on. Don't trouble Mrs Phillips."

Over the doctor's face spread a frown not quite pleasant to look at. He drew out his watch.

"Surely you make a mistake, Clothilde, it is not yet six."

"But Sabbath comes in at a quarter to." She either would not or could not see his meaning; but if she had it would have been too late. Already Mrs Cameron had drawn on Nita's coat and hat and was bidding her hostess farewell.

"Let me see you again soon," said Mrs Phillips. "You see, I'm such an invalid I can't do much visiting myself, but if you come over of an afternoon and chat with me I should take it as a kindness; and the doctor won't come in and interrupt us every time; it isn't often you can get home so soon, is it Ben?"

"No, not often. Perhaps it would be oftener if Mrs Cameron were always to be found here."

His suavity and good humour notwithstanding, it pleased him to make a speech that might penetrate through his wife's dullness and hurt her. Just then Mrs Cameron shook hands with him and he went to the door with her. He lifted up the child and carried her into the brougham, kissing her.

"Mind you keep the glass up; it's really too cold for the child." The servant was standing at the door, but the doctor managed to lean forward and say, "I'll see you tomorrow, some time in the afternoon. Goodbye!"

"Goodbye! Don't scold your wife for telling me it was time to make Sabbath in. Perhaps it would not have come in at all if I had stayed—a Christian, you know."

18

And she smiled up at him with a humorous twinkle in her eye.

But this did not restore Dr Phillips's placidity, and he returned to the drawing room to give his wife the benefit of his opinions.

The sight of the open prayer books and the lighted candles only annoyed him further.

"Still at this mummery! I wish to heaven you would learn to treat your friends with civility instead of devoting your very limited intellect to keeping up all the exploded traditions invented by fools for fools."

"I'm sure Mrs Cameron wasn't a bit offended, Ben, so you needn't be so put out on her account; and even if she were she would know it wasn't your fault, so it would make no difference to you."

There was in the Phillips's household a convenient fiction originated by the doctor, and thoroughly credited by his good wife, that it was necessary, to keep the doctor's practice together, that he should be on friendly, not to say affectionate, terms with many women. During the six years of his married life this theory had been the means of procuring him many a licence that might have been wanting under other circumstances.

Dr Phillips had married when, and because, his fortunes were at a very low ebb. His wife had interposed between him and ruin; and with the dowry she had brought him he had purchased a practice in Portsdown Road, Maida Vale, and commenced his career of popularity.

Marriages under such circumstances have been known to result favourably, love following esteem in a natural sequence. And on Mrs Phillips's side that is what actually occurred. When not irritated by untoward incidents Dr Phillips was kind and gentle in behaviour; he speedily won his young wife's heart and his occasional outbreaks of temper were powerless to alienate it. She saw him everywhere making friends and

19

was constantly congratulated on her charming husband, whom many envied her.

In the exercise of his profession he found plenty of scope for his intellect; in the constant society of women of all ranks, stations, and classes, he had room for his sympathies.

But his character retrograded. He fell into the half indolent ways of a man whose slippers are always warmed and whose meals are always ready. And the domestic qualities of his German wife helped to drag him down to a dead level of ease. It was no trouble to him to extend his practice and his income. Women liked him naturally and his adaptable nature enabled him to secure and utilise that liking. He made money, bought a carriage for his wife, and Mrs Cameron for himself. The man of whom his colleagues at the hospital had predicted such great things, the man who had so easily taken prize after prize contended for by hundreds of his contemporaries, the man who according to his tutors and his lecturers was to be the greatest surgeon of his time, the man whose delicate touch at the operating table had been the admiration of the whole theatre, had degenerated into the pet of Maida Vale drawing rooms.

His powers of intellect failed. As the mistletoe twines round the oak and sucks the great heart out of the forest tree, so all these women, his wife, his patients, and others, clung around him and were gradually killing his heart and mind and conscience. He had too much to struggle against and the physical comforts of his home, added to his indolence and Jewish love of comfort, dragged him helplessly down in the octopus arms of many tempters.

He liked ease, so it was very seldom he quarrelled with his wife. Often and often he lied to her, often and often he deceived her; but generally he lived his own life and let her live hers, in good natured and lazy indifference.

When, as today, she had irritated him into speech it

was tolerably certain she would either fail to understand him or would put his ill temper down to some foreign cause.

"Since you are home, dear," she said, "won't you sit down and read prayers with me?"

She made the request rather hopelessly, more as a duty than anything else. Somehow or other he had drifted away from many of the forms that bound him to his race; and he found he managed just as well without them.

"No, put it off a few minutes. What do you think of Mrs Cameron's little girl?" The doctor had flung himself into a chair and prepared for conversation. He seldom quarrelled with his wife, but he as seldom made his convenience subservient to hers. That was chiefly her own fault; from the first day of their wedded life she had allowed him to act the master, grateful at being allowed to become his slave. Now that he knew she wanted to read her prayers he determined to stay and talk.

She kept the prayer book open before her as she answered: "Yes, dear little thing, she was so good too, but dreadfully delicate looking. I don't think she has very long to live."

She had amply avenged herself for any want of consideration he had shown her. A pang went to his heart as if a heavy hammer had fallen on the quivering flesh. He was struck dumb and remained silent so long that his wife's eyes stole back to her book, and she began again to repeat to herself "Shemang Yeshroile."

"And what the devil do you know about children?" he burst out at length, choked by an emotion that almost rendered him unconscious of his words.

"Why, what's the matter, Ben? What is it to you if Mrs Cameron's little girl is delicate? You look quite put out."

"Put out!" he sneered bitterly. "Mrs Cameron's child, so you think that is what annoys me?" He had

21

collected himself by this time but not sufficiently to be civil. "I am only annoyed at having such a fool for a wife that she cannot amuse herself in a more rational fashion than by lighting candles and condemning people to death whenever they have colds in their heads. I wish to God you wouldn't speak at all! Then you couldn't talk such utter trash."

The servant here announced: "A gentleman to see you, sir, in the consulting room."

Dr Phillips got up and strode towards the door, and in the silence that followed its closing Mrs Phillips said to herself, with her hankerchief to her eyes:

"He was annoyed because I said the child was delicate."

Book I · Chapter III

When Dr Phillips reached his study he found awaiting
him, with his back towards the fire, a robust and
healthy looking young man. A young man nearly six
feet high, with broad shoulders and big brown hands
and an appearance of never having either taken a dose
of medicine or paid a visit to a surgery in his life.

"How do you do, Mr...?" He nearsightedness forced
him to come quite under the gas before he could see the
name Doveton on the card.

In the interval from the time the doctor left the
dining room until now he had collected himself and had
put on his usual charming, interested, professional
manner.

The visitor shook hands with him nervously, hesitated, and finally, in response to an invitation, took a
seat, and plunged recklessly into the weather.

"Awfully cold, isn't it, for April too! Why, it might
be the depth of winter."

"It is cold, but you look quite able to keep yourself
warm," returned the doctor smiling. He had had to do
with nervous patients before and was quite prepared to
allow this young man to recover his composure at his
leisure.

"Well, I find it very cold here. When I left Devonshire
all the trees were budding and the buds were bursting
into leaf; the country was just beginning to look
beautiful."

"You must have found it quite hard to leave."

"No, oh no! I came up to play in the annual
tournament, Lillie Bridge, you know." Confidentially,
"It's next week and I believe I've got as good a chance
as anybody." He was talking quite eagerly now and

seemed to be throwing off his shyness. "I played Ross in the Surrey handicap and he only gave me fifteen. I beat him; so that makes my chance a pretty good one at evens, doesn't it? And I'm not afraid of any of the others. Taylor is too cocky, and Groves isn't as strong as I am. Besides, he can't last."

"And you have come to me because...?" He paused for the hiatus to be filled up.

Strange to say, the young man's embarrassment and confusion at once returned. He hesitated, and half rose; then said suddenly, as if a thought had just struck him, "Well, you see, you've heard of lawn tennis elbow, haven't you? Well"—speaking more slowly, but abruptly—"mine feels awfully stiff, and it wouldn't do to break down, and so I came, and I thought...I thought you'd give me some stuff to rub in, or something...Elliman's embrocation or something like that...to make me as strong as a horse...no fear of breaking down or anything of that sort."

"Will you take your coat off?"

He did so; turned up his shirt sleeves and offered for inspection a brawny, muscular arm.

The doctor examined it closely, employing himself in the meantime in keenly watching Mr Doveton's changing countenance. He saw no trace of disease in the arm but much embarrassment and uneasiness in the face. He thought of his overcoats, of his books and instruments; set himself to detain his patient while he sounded him as to motives; and determined not to let him go until he had been into the hall and seen for himself if his umbrella with the silver top and ferule, and his favourite gold mounted stick—both presents from grateful clients—were still in their places. But Mr Doveton looked at once too young and too ingenuous for a swell mobsman and the doctor felt himself at fault.

"You can put your coat on, sir. I don't think there is much the matter with the arm. A little weakness perhaps. I will write you a strengthening lotion, and you shall come and see me again. When did you say you were going back?"

"Oh, I don't know when I shall go back. I've never been to London before, and now I am here I mean to enjoy myself and have a bit of a spree. At least," correcting himself hurriedly, "not any harm, but just to do the theatres and see the sights." Then he got confidential again: "I'm my own master, Doctor. I have got my own little place, my mother's, you know, and though I'm my uncle's heir he has no sort of authority over me, only, poor old chap, he's not as young as he used to be and he feels pretty lonely without me to go over the place with him of a day and see-to things a bit."

"And when did you first begin to grow nervous about your arm," asked the doctor in his gravest professional manner, looking up from the paper on which he was writing his prescription.

A rosy flush mounted to Charlie Doveton's cheek as he replied: "Oh, just now ... I mean, a long time ago ... I don't know! I say, Doctor!" and a pleading look came into his bright eyes, "I want to ask you something but I'm awfully afraid you'll be riled."

The doctor rose. At last the young man seemed coming to the point. He placed his hand encouragingly on his shoulder and said, "My dear young sir, you can tell me confidentially anything you choose. We men of medicine are quite accustomed to be the recipients of secrets and are not at all likely to betray them."

"Well, it isn't exactly a secret. I mean, I wasn't going to tell you anything, only just to ask you ..."

Dr Phillips had his most encouraging and softest manner on. His dark eyes were fixed inquiringly on his visitor, questioning him and helping him at the same time. A sort of half smile lingered about his lips and he showed no trace of the bewilderment he could not help feeling.

But a red flush on the fair, country face of the lad and

25

a half furtive glance of the honest eyes betrayed a real embarrassment—an embarrassment the doctor could not apparently relieve. So he waited. There was a moment's pause.

"Who was that lady? Would you mind telling me who that lady was who left the house about five minutes before I came in?"

To say the doctor was astounded is a mild way of putting it. He felt very much as if he had received a slap in the face from an unknown adversary. His guilty conscience saw an object and a meaning in the question; and in the first shock of the moment he was unprepared with a reply or a defence. Had Charlie Doveton really known how matters stood and waited for a reply, he would very probably have received a different one from that given him. But no: having broken the ice he plunged boldly on.

He had caught a glimpse of Mary Cameron in her plain dark dress as she was leaving the house; had recognised her as she had stood on the curb while her little girl was being lifted into the carriage; had, in point of fact, actually run after the carriage for a moment or two; then had returned, dejectedly enough. But seeing a doctor's name upon the door he had boldly entered, trusting to providence to help him discover what he wanted to know. His boldness had deserted him when it came to the pinch and he had hurriedly invented the first ailment he could think of as an excuse for his intrusion.

Charlie Doveton had only been in London five weeks; but he had wasted the greater portion of that time in a vain pursuit of a beautiful face.

He had seen Mrs Cameron in Regent Street; he had followed her into Charbonnel's; he had stood next to her at the Grosvenor Gallery. His dreams had been full of her fairness, his waking hours tortured by the impossibility of getting any nearer to his idol. It was simply a young man's first passion, with nothing to feed

26

upon but itself. Pouring out his soul to the doctor, he went on: "I saw her on the doorstep as I was passing, the most lovely vision that ever appeared to a man only to vanish. I saw her get into the brougham and I tried to follow, but I couldn't see a hansom. It was no go, so I came here. Help me, sir"—here he grew quite impressive in his boyish and ingenuous ardour—"I've heard of love at first sight; I only saw her for a moment but by God, sir, I love her to distraction."

A weight had been removed from the doctor's mind by this speech. He gazed on the young man with an expression of stern disapproval and rang the bell.

"You are going to tell me, doctor?"

"Sir, I have rung the bell for you to be shown the door. Your insolence in wishing me to assist you in prosecuting your amours is on a par with your impertinence in endeavouring to persecute an unprotected lady. Neither ought to remain unchastised, but I will let you go. That lady is a widowed friend of my wife's and, therefore, of mine. Follow her, molest her in the smallest degree, and by virtue of that friendship I shall give you in custody to the nearest policeman. Go sir, and beware how in your country ignorance you again offend the canons of civilised life."

Shamefaced and abashed by the doctor's tone and manner, Doveton went.

Left to himself, Benjamin Phillips leaned back wearily in his chair and gave himself up to melancholy reflection.

Twice today he had nearly betrayed himself; twice today he had been attacked and come off victor. He felt sad but with a sadness that had no meaning or depth in it, with only the indefinable melancholy of a mental weariness.

He had had a long day of tedious work—measles and bronchitis; nothing to stimulate his brain or do ought but produce physical fatigue. Then a faint smile stole over his countenance. He was thinking of the little figure he had carried downstairs, of the soft feel of the little face that he had kissed and that had smiled up at him with the dark eyes brightening. He could feel again the thrill of pleasure it had given him when he had asked, "Will you kiss me, Baby Nita?" and Baby had answered, "Nita loves Doc-doc."

This man—this clever, intelligent, thinking man—loved little children, and this child especially was sunshine to him in the shady places of his life. The shock his wife's careless words had given him had been too great to resist. But now, softened by his recollections and strengthened by the medical knowledge which told him that, father and mother being healthy and free from disease, the child, however delicate looking to an ignorant eye must have inherited a sound constitution, he went back in thought to the wife he had left with words so angry that he could not even recall them without shame.

"I must go to her, poor thing!" he said to himself, "or I shall spoil her prayers, and her Sabbath, and all the rest of it. How could I have been such a fool as to lose my temper?"

"Clothilde!" he said when he reached the drawing room, and finding her prayers ended and herself luxuriously before the fire with a paper in her hand, kissed her gently on the forehead. "Was I very cross just now? I came in so tired, and finding that woman and her child here bored me so that it made me worse."

"No, dear, you weren't very cross," she replied with a putty-like resistlessness. "You know I never mind what you say when you're out of temper; I know you don't mean it. I'm not very clever, but I know you love me. When a man is worried in business his wife must expect him to be a little irritable. Lie down here, darling, and rest your poor head on my lap."

Her German sentimentality could have carried her triumphantly through many a scene like the last; and Dr Phillips had never need to restrain passion of any sort for fear of disturbing her. Her placidity was too deep seated; it had its root in weakness of intellect and unbounded indolence. And, despise her as he did, poisonous as was the influence she undoubtedly had over him, a certain sensuous pleasure that woman's society had for him linked her to him in a bond that, if not one of affection, was curiously like it.

He had taught her to be silent; a loquacious fool he could not have borne with. And now, thoroughly wearied, he lay on the hearthrug, his head on her knees and her fat hands gently rubbing his hair up and down in a manner that he found soothing and pleasant. It calmed him and titillated his fancy. While she, holding her *Jewish Chronicle* in one hand, gently played with his hair with the other, his thoughts wandered off to another woman and another scene and imagining that it was Mary Cameron's blue eyes that were over him and Mary Cameron's tenderness that was enfolding him he fell calmly off to sleep and slept until the noisy entry of the servant woke him for tea.

Then he partook of his cold fried fish with an easy mind.

29

Book I · Chapter IV

Mrs Cameron's house in Brunswick Place was very small but very pretty and tasteful. The entrance hall and staircase were decorated in white. A dado of Lincrusta-Walton, painted white and relieved with gold, was surmounted by an enamelled wall. Bluish grey druggeting blended into the green of the ferns that filled the conservatory on the landing.

On the left of the hall was the dining room, long and narrow, got up in the purest eighteenth century style, with dog stoves and dados, panelled walls and inlaid furniture. Above this was the drawing room, irregularly running the whole length of the house. Here Liberty had been allowed to use his own discretion, and a confused medley of crude gold screenwork, faded colouring, and careless drapery was the happy result. There was not a straight backed chair in the room, nor one that matched another, but everything was cosy and comfortable. There was nothing to fatigue the eyes or the limbs. It was essentially a place to lounge, to lie, to dawdle, but not to work in.

Of a female presence there were few traces. No half finished work, no full basket, lay on the Moorish table. There, Mudie was represented, and books of all descriptions lay about in reckless confusion. Poetry and fiction predominated, but Quain's *Dictionary of Medicine* and Huxley's *Physiology* were not alone in their class. A large draped easel, on which was the rough portrait of a girl, took up the whole of one corner. The brow, eyes, nose and bust had been finished; but the mouth remained blurred and uncertain, to testify to the inadequacy of the painter. The whole thing was amateurish, and as the doctor stood before it, waiting

30

till Mrs Cameron should come down, he criticised it severely.

"Now, what is it it lacks?" he pondered. "The colouring is excellent, anybody can see that. The likeness, at least of the upper half of the face, is striking; yet the thing would never find a place in the humblest exhibition ever opened by an enterprising speculator. Yet while I was doing it I thought I had suddenly discovered a new talent in myself, a new power. Only three years ago too. How one's opinions expand! I wonder why she got it out and where it has been lying all this time." His meditations were interrupted by the original of the picture, who, in a dull green plush tea gown, came into the room looking like a grown up cherub—not the usual costume of a cherub, still that is what Mary Cameron insensibly reminded one of, with her fairness, and sweet curves, and dimples.

There was very little pretence about their greeting. She came in with a soft smile of pleasant expectation and he took her in his long arms and kissed, gently but familiarly, the red lips.

"Well, child"—and he held her a minute at arm's length—"that is a very becoming gown. You remind one of harvest time instead of spring. Your hair is corn, your eyes bluettes, your lips the poppies, and your gown the green background of the sunlit picture. There! Isn't that a pretty speech?"

"Yes, but like a great many other things it won't bear the rude touch of the analyst. My eyes are much darker than bluettes, and this"—she touched her gown—"is not grass green. It is an idealised tilleul. You should have likened it to the sea in the distance. I suppose you've been thinking of pictures because I got out this old thing again. Do you think it like me now? Of course I look centuries older and uglier, but I wanted something to stand on my new easel and I haven't got anything else."

"I've seen something that will do for you. You must

throw that away; I have just discovered it is out of drawing. I will get you instead a small study I saw at Carl Schloesser's studio. It is only a scrap of a thing—a bare-footed ragged little lad playing the violin under the blue of an Italian sky; but the artist has caught an expression of rapt devotion underlying a certain boyish fun and twinkle that makes it a gem. I thought of you immediately but I did not know where you would put it"—as he gazed at the well filled walls—"or I should have made an offer for it then and there. His work is always good."

"You have not many pictures in Portsdown Road, Benito," she said, half humorously, half reproachfully.

The doctor frowned.

"Let me forget Portsdown Road when I am here. Maida Vale and its friends are all at synagogue, preparing to eat biscuits for a week. Well, what do you think of our Jewish society?"

"Was that Jewish society?"

"Yes, the party at Mrs Detmar's, where you made such an excellent impression, is a very fair specimen of a large section of Jewish society."

"Well then, please let us talk of something else."

"Why? Are you afraid of hurting my feelings?" And he smiled.

"Oh no, but it's dull enough to be there, without discussing it afterwards. Good heaven!"—and she shuddered—"Do those people really all meet each other, and only each other, over and over again?"

"Yes, and enjoy it. But let us have the baby down. I fancied she had a cold coming on yesterday.

"Oh, she has always got a cold or something! I'm sure I am strong enough."

Nita was muffled up to the throat in a light cream cashmere dress with a large pink sash. In fact, she looked all sash as the nurse brought her to the doctor.

He took her on his knee and gave her his watch to play with as he questioned the nurse about the child's sleep, her breathing, her cough, and her symptoms generally. His interrogatories received very satisfactory replies. The nurse, a respectable looking middle aged woman, who had been with Nita since her birth, was able to assure the doctor that a slight cold, or perhaps a new double tooth on its way, was sufficient to account for the pallor and general appearance. And the child was bright enough; she shut the case of the watch and opened it again at least fifty times calling "Again, again" with obvious enjoyment.

"Have you heard her count, sir?" asked the nurse, who knew where she could go for sympathy with the progress her little charge was making. Mrs Cameron did not care for children and was bored by their exhibitions. But Dr Phillips listened with interest while Nita went through her performances; while Nurse said "One" and she said "Two, four"; while Nurse said "Jack and Jill fell down a..." and she said "hill" and chuckled with baby delight at her own cleverness. While Nurse said "Dance" and she contorted her little body into undulatory movements.

He was amused, interested, charmed. But Mrs Cameron was bored and failed to share his emotion.

"This room is so much colder than her nursery," she said at length. She did not wish to betray her utter want of interest in the exhibition, it being her constant and most successful endeavour to hide her faults. But the attention paid to the child irritated her. She wanted the doctor's exclusive attention, and considered she had a right to it: it was the sole excitement in her monotonous existence.

"Nurse, you had better take her upstairs again."

The doctor looked at her earnestly; he felt hurt at her tone.

"Mary," he said when they were again alone, "you're not like yourself today. What troubles you?"—seating himself by her on the sofa and taking her hand caressingly in his.

33

She laid her head on his shoulder as she answered in an open, engaging way.

"Shall I tell you candidly, Benito mio?"

"Don't you always talk to me candidly?"

"Well, the fact is, I can't bear going among all these people and letting them think I am a widow. I love you, Nito. I am proud of you. You have taught me there is nothing wrong in our life together; but surely there is wrong in this deception." Then she went on more rapidly: "I am better looking than they are; I am better educated than they are. Why then should I go among them under a false name and false colours? Nito, dearest"—and she drew closer to him in bewitching abandonment—"why do you want me to do all this?"

"I have gone over it all with you a hundred times," he said in a tone half impatient, half tender. "You are as pure and perfect, you are as modest and as innocent, as any woman you can meet in this or other society. We culminated our intellectual union after mature deliberation. I respect you, knowing you and knowing that you are a woman to be respected. But if the world—not only this little one but the world at large—knew that the meaningless buffoonery of a priest in a church or of a layman in the registrar's office had not been performed over us it would never argue the case on its merits but would condemn us unheard. Therefore purely out of regard for ourselves we must keep it in ignorance." Then he kissed her. "Don't be silly. Your life is too dull, with nothing to break the monotony but my visits and Nita. Go out and about among these people, amuse yourself with them, play cards with them."

"But dear, if they *don't* amuse me?"

"Then go to oblige me. I like to see you there when I come in from whist; it seems to clear the atmosphere."

Many were the arguments he used, all interspersed with caresses and endearments, with tender words and looks. In Dr Phillips's tenderness there was an infinite depth, and the magnetic touch of his smooth palmed

34

hands had a remarkable power of nerve soothing. He had the faculty of at once exciting and gratifying the imagination. He was conscious of this gift and fond of exercising it; to it he owed his successes among women. But the circumstances of his intercourse with Mary had left her impervious to these interludes of mock passion. And his arguments she scarcely listened to; for in truth her morality as not so much shocked by the situation in which she found herself, only she fancied her modest remonstrances would enhance her value in his eyes; so she made them periodically and received assurances of his unaltered esteem.

Mary Cameron had been a governess in one of the few Christian families Dr Phillips attended. He had been struck first by her beauty, then by her intellect. Clever and intelligent, she could meet him at his own level and evade or reply to his advances equally brightly. They met of an evening in the beautiful summer time, when everybody, Mrs Phillips included, was out of town. Through the gates of Regent's Park, over the little wooden bridge of the canal, they strolled together, while the balmy air of the warm evening touched their faces like baby fingers and excited them to happiness and love. On every subject, from religion to philosophy, they spoke with openness and freedom. She told him of her life, of her lonely girlhood with a widowed mother, who herself had been a governess and who married a drunken penniless artist's model, captivated by the beauty of his person and sick of the intellect by which she was forced to earn her bread. Repentance had followed long ere the husband died. Then the mother, teaching other people's children for money and her own from necessity, and the daughter, gradually promoted from the drudgery of learning to the drudgery of teaching, passed dreary lives in endeavouring each day to provide for the next day's wants.

In the struggle the mother grew hard and cold and weary, till she died of the strife that had never held out hope of victory; and the girl, still teaching, went on her way in bitter and callous defiance of the world, until she met her fate.

Her fate! Yes, it was her fate that this man, with his love and his reason, should come to her, should arrange meetings with her, should explain to her with cogent logic that an intellectual union between them—a union such that they could meet daily and gratify in each other's society their need of companionship—could neither harm the wife of the one nor the conscience of the other.

He told her that with a dull invalid wife he could never taste the joy of mental mating. He had not a very obstinate antagonist to argue with. She admitted the justice of the plea; and, as for herself, she had no ties—no tie to her employer who underpaid her, no tie to the mother whose mortal remains (immortality, Dr Phillips taught her, was a myth) lay in a neglected and rotting grave. She never dreamed of danger, for she knew herself to be heartless. What she did not know was that there are feelings which will sway even a woman whose heart has been killed by years of semistarvation and cold. And in the fullness of time she descended without a struggle the velvet covered steps which lead from hungry virtue to well fed vice.

An intellectual union he called it; and so it remained for many golden weeks. He was but a surface cynic, a cynic by reason. Her cynicism had its root in experience and lay deep. He told her, by implication, that the only happy hours in his life were those spent with her. She confessed unreservedly that their daily walks were her only pleasure. They talked endlessly. Benjamin Phillips revelled in these evenings; for him their secrecy added to their charm. For her the secrecy was no attraction; but she felt her nature expand in the sunlight of his interest. Even the hansom in which he took her home was to her, for whom an omnibus was an extravagance, a real joy. She found in him a shelter and an infinite solace, and still they walked and talked until one fine August evening, standing together beneath the shadow of the trees while the sluggish canal gleamed in the rainbow hues of the setting sun he turned to her and said, "You have never kissed me, Mary." But he did not move nearer to her, only stood looking at her with softening eyes.

The heart of the woman was stirred with a mighty tenderness. The season, the hour, the mystic feeling that might have been love and was but passion, wrought within her and thrilled her as a mother when her first child stirs with life within the womb. Air, earth, and sky sank from her. Passion agitated her; custom held her back. The blood burned in her cheeks, her pulse, her brain; she could neither speak nor look him in the face.

"Mary," he said again, and put his arms about her. The farce of their intellectual union was over and the tragedy began.

There were few preliminary difficulties to get over. Dr Phillips met with little resistance when he explained that, formed as they evidently were by natural affinity for each other, it was challenging providence to endeavour to live apart.

He offered her, instead of tramping to and fro in all weathers—through rain, mud, and frost—to keep body and soul together by teaching the rudiments of language to unmannered children, a home and a companionship and comfort for both body and mind. He took every precaution against discovery and jealously guarded her reputation at her old lodgings and with her employer. She left, it was understood, to be married. After an interval of seclusion she reappeared in a new personality as the widow of a friend of the doctor, who found in all these arrangements, as in his anticipations of future diplomatic devices, vistas of infinite delight. There was nothing to prevent her acceding to his demands, no ties of relationship and no qualms of conscience. Of real love, the love that is self sacrificing and holy, she was ignorant. Novelty and passion were sufficient to carry her through the many lonelinesses and drawbacks of the first few months of their life together. But her wild and evanescent love burnt itself out and now it was only self interest that made the dull ashes glow.

He took a house for her in Alfred Place, WC, and there a child was born to her in pain and anguish. With the birth of the child died the love for the father. But she had no inclination to go back to her life in lodgings and the struggle for bread. So she supplied in caresses what she lacked in feeling, and in blissful ignorance Benjamin Phillips continued to satisfy her daily wants with liberal hand.

She at last complained of the dullness and monotony of her life, which she attributed to the comparatively little she was able to see of him. He set to work to remedy what he could not but consider a just complaint. And the result was the removal from Alfred Place to Brunswick Place and the introduction of the widowed Mrs Cameron to the exclusive interior of Jewish society.

Now she grumbled that it did not amuse her. He was quite able to criticise his coreligionists with biting humour, but at the bottom of his heart he had the genuine *esprit de corps* of "the people." He loved them. They were his people and he could not help feeling that it was a privilege to be received among them intimately. These people are bound to each other by so many ties of interest, association, and feeling that they can never become effectually estranged. They may try to live as Christians, they cannot but die Jews. When she complained they did not amuse her he scarcely understood the complaint, rather attributing her weariness to the fact that she was unaccustomed to society of any kind. But he could not leave her today without impressing his will upon her.

"You must call upon Mrs Detmar and tell her you had a pleasant evening; tomorrow is her 'at home' day. No. Tuesday. Go on Tuesday. Charm them, delight them, as you alone can. Do this, Mary, not only for your own sake but for mine. Society of any sort will do you good, and one thing leads to another. Play cards; I will come in some time tomorrow and give you a lesson in bluff. I shall not be content until I see you at every house I go to of an evening."

As he was talking he walked up and down the room, his hands clasped behind him, the bend in his shoulders detracting a little from his height. She was lounging on the sofa, and looked at him with thoughtful eyes.

She knew perfectly well she would yield. In small things his will was much stronger than hers. Nor was she at all really averse to the proposition. Anything was better than sitting alone evening after evening waiting for him until the servants had gone to bed, hearing his key turn in the door, and then having to endure and return his caresses for the rest of her entertainment.

He had at first attracted her towards him by his clever conversation, by his treatment of her as a mental equal, and his choice of interesting topics. But now his caresses—caresses nauseating and, under one aspect, a source of fear—were the only offerings he brought to the woman who was so much lonelier in her wealth than she had been in her poverty.

Every trace of intellectuality was banished from a union in which he sought her love, and she shelter from want.

She was a most beautiful woman and a consummate actress, and Benjamin Phillips, with all his knowledge of the world, of men and of women was as plastic in her hands as the merest clay. His love for women in general was objective. His love for this particular woman was trustful self abandonment and his love for his child, the only child born to him in all his thirty seven years, that love had so broadened and deepened that it coloured his whole life and actions.

Today, when he left her, she sat silent and sleepily thoughtful on the sofa.

"I will go among his people," she thought. "Anything must be better than the dullness of life by myself, and I dare say I shall get very fond of playing cards. Heigho! I wish I were as much in love as I used to be. Life was doubly worth living when I counted the hours till I could see him again and spent half my time with my nose pressed against the dirty window pane in Alfred Place. I wonder it did not spoil its shape." And she rubbed it reflectively with her white hand and, roused from her reverie by the act took up a novel from the table and listlessly read herself to sleep.

Book I · Chapter V

In broad daylight Northwick Place is not an attractive
thoroughfare. The high houses on one side, the bare wall
on the other, the stables at the end, are then seen in all
their blank and formless ugliness. With reference to its
tasteless grandeur Dr Phillips had once called Mrs
Detmar's house "a mausoleum in a mews."

This afternoon the exterior was peculiarly uninviting,
and the large staircase with the light walls struck cold
to Mrs Cameron as she followed the footman to the
drawing room.

There were bonnets and cloaks on every chair, and
through the warm, tea scented atmosphere came the
shrill voices of children and the rustling of sumptuous
silk gowns.

"These are some of my small fry," said Mrs Detmar
after the usual greetings. "Come here, Davie. Come
here, Dan! You must excuse them if they are a little
spoilt; and I am afraid they're rather shy as well."

"It is very difficult not to spoil children; it hurts us
more than them if we have to punish or speak severely"
was the reply as Mrs Cameron drew one shock headed
little creature towards her and endeavoured to kiss it.

"Now kiss the pretty lady, there's a good girl! Really
I shall have to send you upstairs if you don't."

"Oh, don't compel her, please! We shall become very
good friends when we know each other better. How
many have you, Mrs Detmar?"

"Don't ask me; I am quite ashamed to tell you, I am
sure I don't know where it will end. This is the
ninth"—as the nurse entered carrying a long white
bundle.

Mrs Detmar being still quite a young woman, there

really was no saying where, or when, it would end; but so many of her friends had similarly contributed to the population and consequent prosperity of the State that in her circle of society nothing under the dozen was considered exceptional.

It seemed to Mrs Cameron, who found herself among exactly the same people she had met the previous night, that none of them had since left the room.

Mrs Collings and Mrs Lucas were admiring the baby, and Mrs Levy was drinking tea and eating muffins greedily.

"Did you win the other night?" she asked Mrs Cameron with her mouth full. "We couldn't make the money right."

"I forget. May I look at the baby? Dear little thing, it seems to know its nurse, doesn't it?" as the featureless red thing squirmed over to one side and made a pitiful grimace.

"It's a fine baby," said Mrs Collings dogmatically, "but it's not as big as my Evy was at three months. You remember what a fine baby she was, don't you, Flora?" Mrs Collings was addressing Mrs Detmar.

"Yes. That was the one that had something the matter with its eyes, wasn't it?"

"Oh no! nothing at all. You used to fancy she squinted a little, but there is no trace of such a thing now, is there?"—to her sister.

"I think Eva had a decided squint!" was the uncompromising reply. "Do you often play cards, Mrs Cameron?"

"Take off your cloak, Mrs Cameron, do! Here's a nice hot cup of tea and a muffin."

"Thank you very much; it is quite cold enough for tea to be acceptable. I have not played cards since my widowhood, but my husband was a constant player and taught me nearly every game."

"Well, if you play bluff, and you've nothing better to

do, I wish you'd come over to me tomorrow night. We want one to make up," said Mrs Lucas, abruptly.

There was a slight pause in the conversation. This was rather daring of Mrs Lucas. After all, they knew nothing of Mrs Cameron. True, the Phillipses had introduced her; but then she was a Christian and it was decidedly unusual to invite any but Jews to these informal meetings.

"I shall be very pleased," replied Mrs Cameron simply. "Mr Cameron used to say poker—bluff, you call it—was the best game on the cards."

"Was Mr Cameron on the stock exchange? Stock exchange men generally like those gambling games," said Mrs Detmar with interest.

"Well, not exactly on the stock exchange," she answered as she put down the cup and commenced to draw on her gloves.

This was a pure evasion but was taken by them as a declaration that Mr Cameron was an outside broker. Then curiosity was satisfied for the present, Mrs Detmar making up her mind that she would ask Mr Collings to find out all about him. She didn't think that would be difficult, and the anticipation of knowledge to come made her more cordial still to her guest.

"Don't go yet; it is quite early. Or does your little girl expect you? You must bring her with you next time, to play with my young ones. There, run away now, children; that's the nursery tea bell."

The children, as they filed out, looked more like a school than a family. The freer space their absence made seemed to improve the atmosphere. Mrs Cameron stayed on conversing about children and cooks and cards. Somehow the fact that Mrs Lucas had asked her for the morrow seemed to have broken the ice; and then they knew, or rather thought they knew, that her husband had been connected with the stock exchange. This made her seem more like one of them. They

43

warmed to her, and talked to her, as Ray Collings said afterwards, "almost as if she were on an equality with them."

Mrs Collings, however, held herself somewhat aloof, maintaining a manner which was rather like that of an offended cock on a disputed dung heap. And when at last Mrs Cameron did go, with many a promise to call again soon, to be early at Mrs Lucas' on the following evening, she gave vent to her dissatisfaction.

"What did you want with that woman, Adelaide?" she asked her sister. "We were four without her."

"I asked her because I like her and Alphonse admires her. I suppose I may ask whom I like to my own house. Ain't I right, Mrs Detmar?"

"If you take to asking everybody Alphonse admires you'll soon have a pretty lot of people at your house!"

Alphonse was Mrs Lucas' husband and, in virtue of his occasionally talking to the ladies when he might have been playing whist, was considered fast.

"Well now, really, Tilly, what fault do you find with Mrs Cameron?" Mrs Detmar interposed. "I am sure she is quiet enough, and quite a lady, and I should think she has been left very well off, as far as one can judge from the way she dresses. I am going to call on her this week and shall see what her house is like."

"I've nothing to say against Mrs Cameron but I don't approve of Christian society for our young people; you never know what ideas may be put into their heads. I don't even approve of their father bringing home strange young men, although that's business; but there is no excuse for our asking strange women. I am surprised at Adelaide's being a party to it. Goodbye. Come along, Ray; your aunt doesn't seem to have finished her gossip. Goodbye, Mrs Levy. You agree with me, I know!"

"Oh, I like Mrs Cameron," said Mrs Levy, feebly and disloyally. "She's quite like one of us. I think it very narrow minded to distrust her merely because she's a

Christian. I think her a useful acquisition: she can play anything!"

"Very well! You go your way, I go mine. But, mark my words, no good will come of this sudden rushing into intimacy with a woman you know nothing about!" And in offended dignity Mrs Reuben Collings sailed from the room.

There is always a great temptation to discuss the absent, and despite the presence of her sister, Mrs Collings's narrow minded views about Christians were adverted to with much heat.

Mrs Levy suggested that, her girls having money, she was afraid that Christian fortune hunters would make love to them. But then, as Mrs Lucas said, "Ray was so plain, poor girl, that she wasn't likely to attract anybody; and as for Florrie, with her dreamy and untidy ways, she might be looked upon as little better than a natural."

Mrs Jeddington and Sophia, who were also present, wouldn't allow this remark to pass unchallenged. Mrs Jeddington, conscious of deficiencies in her H's, generally spoke little and left it to her daughter Soph to act as her mouthpiece. But she was bold in defence of her favourite, and gave it as her opinion that Florrie might be untidy but that she was no fool.

The argument began to grow heated. The ladies were glad not to have to commit themselves too positively just yet on the subject of Mrs Cameron and were glad to have Florrie Collings to rend instead.

They said she was plain, they said she was stupid. And Mrs Detmar considered it a remarkable confirmation of the latter opinion that she had either refused, or failed to encourage, the addresses of a certain Mr Israels, whose father was a cousin of Mrs Detmar's husband and who was a distinctly wealthy young man.

Mrs Detmar's mind was constructed on a peculiar basis. She saw herself as the centre about which all things ought to revolve. If people persisted in forsaking this orbit of revolution she bore them little malice; but she considered them eccentric, not to say mad. As a girl she had desired to make a wealthy marriage, and had succeeded. As a woman she desired to have a circle sufficiently large to enable her to play cards at a different house every night of the week, to be richer than anyone she played with, and in a position to give better suppers. She had succeeded in all these, and in a good natured way wished to help others on to similar fortune.

Two months ago Mr Israels had met Florrie at a dance. Her white neck and face had fixed his wandering attention and he had immediately asked to be introduced. He got the introduction he wanted but found the young lady abstracted and cool. His vanity was piqued; he redoubled his attentions and had even gone so far as to hint at a carriage. To be married and keep a carriage was the highest ambition of all who moved in his set; he was therefore considerably surprised when his hint fell upon heedless ears. It was treatment that confirmed his purpose. The serene consciousness of being a good match, which had given him assurance of easy conquest, had received a shock. In his dilemma he consulted his cousin in law, who in great delight sent for Florrie and, with whispering and mystery, told her of the golden chance that was awaiting her.

Florrie said she hated Mr Israels. He couldn't dance a bit; he bit his nails, dropped his H's, and talked about his business. She thought he was awfully common; his nose was on one side and he had a hideous stoop.

Mr and Mrs Collings, when they heard of her folly, were disappointed; but Florrie was only eighteen. Her elder sister was as yet unmarried: if Mr Israels would take her instead he could have ten thousand pounds with her.

He wouldn't, and there the matter ended. But Mrs Detmar washed her hands of Florrie Collings's future and predicted a bad end for her. And, in the opinion of her friends, Mrs Detmar's prophecy was likely to be verified in the coming years.

All the afternoon, in the full drawing room, gradually getting hotter and hotter under the combined influence of fire, gas, and the warm, eager breath of the women, Queen Gossip reigned supreme.

About Mrs Cameron they were all rather shy. By a species of mutual consent the subject was not thoroughly threshed out. In a sort of jealous exclusiveness these Jews lived by and among themselves. They fancied they did so from choice. It was not so: it was a remnant of the time when the yellow cap and curiously shaped gaberdine marked them out as lepers in the crowd. The garb had been discarded but the shrinking feeling of generations was still lingering. There is a certain pride in these people; they are at once the creatures and the outcasts of civilisation. The difference between Jew and Gentile was once one of religion. Now it is a difference that it will take as many centuries of extermarriage to overcome as it has taken centuries of intermarriage to bring about. The Jews feel this acutely. They remember the leper mark that has been taken from them, and they shrink from accentuating the remembrance by association with the people whose ancestors affixed it.

Put two strange Jews, one from London and one from the Antipodes, amid a hundred people of other nationalities and in a quarter of an hour they will have recognised their kinship and have gravitated towards each other in unconscious Ishmaelitism against the rest of the company.

Sections of them are trying very hard to struggle against this race barrier, and with a modicum of success. But they have much to contend against.

Mrs Collings was one of the old school. She felt it would be abjuring the creed of her life to allow a heretic to enter into intimacy. Public opinion, expediency, and

47

a certain sheep-like habit of following had led her to admit a few Christian men to her dances. Three times she had allowed Florrie and Ray to attend dances at the Kensington Town Hall under the chaperonage of Mrs Jeddington. But when it came to women she felt it her bounden duty to protest.

She actually believed all women except those of her own race to be unchaste. She had drawn her conclusions from her experience of servants—most of whom had nieces or cousins dependent on them, and calling them "Mother" when no one was within hearing; from observation of dressmakers and milliners' girls; and from perusal of police reports.

"I can't think what your aunt meant by asking that woman to her house," she said to Ray in the evening, rather drowsily.

Reuben Collings was asleep in one easy chair; his wife lay back in the other. One large foot, decorated with a ragged Irish-looking slipper, was on the fender; the other, in a black worsted stocking with a hole in it, had gone a little further over and rested on the tongs. She wore an old dressing gown, looked very greasy and after dinnerish, and was in fact taking her vulgar ease in the bosom of her family.

The young ones had been in to dessert, had said goodnight to papa, and had gone to bed. Ray and Florrie were still up; Ray doing fancy work, Florrie reading.

"She wanted a fourth," answered Ray. "And Aunt is never very particular."

"I don't think I shall take you girls with me tomorrow night or you'll be getting intimate with her, and I don't want her here."

"She sings beautifully," said Florrie dreamily, looking up from her book. "Her voice would go beautifully with Ray's."

"Or we could have trios with Soph," put in Ray.

"I won't have her here," went on Mrs Collings, her head nodding a little and her cap on one side.

In two or three minutes she began to snore.

When Mr and Mrs Collings did not go out of an evening this was their usual way of enjoying the charms of domesticity. They ate their heavy dinner, the two elder girls dining with them, and Mr Collings talked about money. The children came in to dessert and were petted and caressed. Often their father gave them pennies for their money boxes and questioned them in arithmetic. Then they were sent to bed, and the father and mother took each an easy chair. The father read the closing quotations in the special edition of the *Evening Standard*; the half finished cigar dropped from his fingers; and he slept. Mrs Collings had a little talk with her girls, chiefly with Ray, whose mind ran on the same lines as her own, then she slept too.

Seeing her asleep, the girls talked a little in whispers about Mrs Cameron.

"I like her," said Florrie reflectively.

"So do I," said Ray, with assertion. "And I mean to visit her; but we must do it gradually or there'll be a fuss. There's one thing: Pa and Ma are too lazy to oppose us if we really mean anything. Look how we went to Kensington Town Hall—by simply worrying until we got leave.

"I wish we'd never gone!" said Florrie in a whisper, and her voice trembled.

"What nonsense! I mean to go to the one next month. Alec Murphy asked me if I was going and made me promise him two waltzes. He's the best waltzer I know. I shall make Ma ask him to our dance."

A loud snore startled them into silence.

Poor Florrie's thoughts went out to Kensington. She had promised Alec Murphy four waltzes and supper. She half hoped and wholly dreaded that they would not be allowed to go.

49

"What's the good of meeting him again?" she thought. "I wish I had never seen him." He was always coming across her thoughts and sending her into reveries. He was very attentive to Ray, too; and Ray liked him very much. Girls all liked him very much. He always danced the whole evening, even if there were ever so many more men than girls. He was the tallest man in the room and the best dressed and had constantly worn two little tube roses in his coat since she had said it was her favourite flower. He used to offer them to her at the beginning of the evening. Her sister had sharp eyes, so she hid them among her other flowers and nobody had ever noticed them. She believed Ray thought he was fond of her. How funny! Perhaps he said the same things to Ray—one never knew with Christians.

Florrie sighed.

"What are you sighing for? How stupid!"

"I'm tired," said Florrie. "After all, I think I should like to go to the next dance."

"Well! Our blue dresses are quite clean enough. What are you sighing for?"

"They hate us to go among Christians."

"Yes! But they like us to go with the Jeddingtons. That's where you're such a fool. Pa makes half his money through Mr Jeddington, and we can easily manage by saying he'd be offended if we weren't allowed to go where he thought good enough for Soph. You don't understand how to do things! If it weren't for me you'd never have any fun."

"Why is mother so hard on Mrs Cameron? What do you mean to do?"

"Oh, I shall work it through the Phillips's. Ma would do anything Dr Phillips told her, on account of Teddy."

Teddy was very delicate. He was the baby. His little funny ways had twined round his mother's heart, and he was her Benjamin.

50

"Dr Phillips did him more good than West or Jenner or any of them."

"He's ever so much cleverer. He's the nicest man I ever met. I wish I were Mrs Phillips!"

"Oh, Ray!"

"So I do! There's no harm in saying that. I think her a very lucky woman. And she didn't have much more money than we have."

"Dr Phillips must have been in love with her; he is not the sort of man to marry for money."

"Who could have been in love with Mrs Phillips? What rubbish! Dr Phillips married her because he knew a professional man must have a wife and she was the first one that offered. Ma told me, and she ought to know. They visit everybody. Dr Phillips must be awfully rich with all he makes, and his wife's money, and everything."

"They don't seem rich."

"Oh, she's mean! He isn't. I know he subscribes to everything. His name is in every list in the *Chronicle*."

So they continued talking; and the parents slept. Ray dogmatised and Florrie acquiesced. She always gave way to Ray and was quite unaware how much the cleverer, prettier, and brighter she was. But it certainly was beginning to dawn upon her that Mr Murphy thought her nicer than Ray.

She contrasted him in her own mind with Mr Israels, and shuddered. She sighed too and was rather uncomfortable; but still she slept quite soundly that night, and her appetite was unimpaired.

51

Book I · Chapter VI

Mrs Cameron went to Mrs Lucas's, played bluff, and lost money. This deepened the good impression she had made; and after much discussion her conduct was pronounced irreproachable.

She did not encourage the attentions of any of the men, and she was especially distant towards the bachelors. She devoted herself chiefly to Mr and Mrs Detmar: confided in them a great many fictitious details of her former life; and when she rose to leave Mrs Lucas followed her downstairs, pressing upon her many invitations. As time wore on she became a recognised feature of these heretofore exclusive card parties. She was always ready to make up a table; did not seem to mind for what points or at what game she played; and, in a word, gave Mrs Lucas no cause to regret her experiment in Christianity.

The Detmars greatly contributed to her popularity, and when necessary they fought her battles with vigour. Mrs Detmar prided herself very much on her liberal mindedness in this matter. She didn't like Christian society, but she had made a very special exception in Mrs Cameron's favour.

Nita was a constant visitor in the Detmar nursery; poor little thing, she was timid and miserable among those big rough boys and girls and clung to her Nannie. The ruling powers in the nursery did not get on well with Nannie; she was reticent and declined to gossip about her mistress's affairs; but then Mrs Cameron always gave the head nurse something whenever she came upstairs, so on the whole she did not object to the intruders.

Dr Phillips found them there one day when he had been summoned in a hurry because one little Detmar wretch, fighting with another, had got its arm pulled out of joint.

The children shrieked in chorus while Dr Phillips manipulated the bone into its place, but Nita crept to his side and stood there watching.

When it was over he took her up and kissed her tenderly, holding her a moment against his face. She returned his caresses with evident affection; and Mrs Detmar felt a little offended.

"He never kisses our children," she said afterwards to her husband, "but he took that ugly little black child up and kissed it as if it were his own."

"Perhaps it is, my dear" answered David Detmar lightly.

"How can you say such things, David! Considering, too, that Dr Phillips never even knew the Camerons until a few months before Mr Cameron died."

"Oh, all right! I thought you said so, I didn't. I suppose the child is delicate, and Phillips has seen it oftener. Thank God our's are all strong enough."

"Nita isn't delicate. Mrs Cameron pampers her too much, and I should advise her to get rid of that Nannie of hers. Nurse thinks she spoils the child and makes her shy and strange."

Mrs Detmar didn't believe in delicate children. Her's were quite strong, which she flattered herself was because she knew how to manage her nursery. She spoke to Mrs Cameron very seriously on the subject of Nannie and Mrs Cameron replied by saying that Nannie had been with them in her husband's life time and his dying wish had been that she should remain always with his wife and child.

In reality Mrs Cameron hated Nannie with a bitter hatred. She was a Jamaican woman whom Dr Phillips had known from his boyhood; and one of the few points he was firm upon was her retention. He could trust the child with her; he could not trust it, in thorough confidence, with its mother.

The society into which Mrs Cameron had insinuated herself with such skill became gradually more and more used to her. Mrs Collings doubted her, but with a general and a passive doubt. For the rest, they pitied her loneliness, spent hours gossipping with her in Brunswick Place, invited her child to their houses, and felt they had known her from girlhood.

She went to all their card parties and all their "at homes." But Mrs Phillips and Mrs Detmar remained her closest and most intimate friends. This went on for a month or six weeks.

Dr Benjamin Phillips revelled in the situation. Mystery and diplomacy were meat and drink to him: the salt of life. He loved to meet and greet this woman of an afternoon or evening as an ordinary and uninteresting acquaintance, to lead her with cool courtesy to the door, and afterwards spend hours of rapture with her in the delightful solitude of Brunswick Place.

And his love for her grew. He ignored her position; he half believed in the dead Mr Cameron at times. His was an intellectual sensuality: loving and revelling in the possession of what he scarcely desired to possess. Actual possession was at this time the least of his pleasures.

He saw her, fair and slim and beautiful, among his people, and his heart throbbed at the sight like a boy with his first love. He would sit with her alone at midnight, his pulses calm and his senses filled with the sight of her yellow hair against the blue plush of the pillow, the soft white dressing gown showing dark against the softer white of the creamy neck. When he took her slender hand and held it and touched her gently, stroking her and carressing her tenderly, he tasted supreme delight.

54

"Dear, you look beautiful," he would say. "Don't let us talk, let me sit and feast on you."

Poor woman, wearied to death after sitting three or four hours in an overheated room with the cards swimming before her tired eyes, she had to remain an hour or perhaps two hours more enduring this travesty of domesticity and yearning, half asleep, for her hour of deliverance.

He thought very tenderly of her as he gazed on her fairness, thought of her future, and provided for it in fancy; forgot the worries of his life, though they were sometimes pressing; forgot his fat wife. The dark eyes of his babe were with him too. He had here all the happy sensations of a husband and father. Passion had become sanctified to domestic love.

Poor bored Mrs Cameron!

Sometimes in the midst of his gazing and caressings and loving murmurs she would fall asleep. Then on tip toe, for fear of waking her, he would steal upstairs to the nursery.

Here Nannie, in a cap made grotesque by the shadows of the dim night light, lay snoring with her mouth half open—a black blot on her tumbled bed. The little cot was in one corner and Dr Phillips stole to it with professional lightness of tread. He bent over the baby. The little fists were clenched and the beautiful long lashes lay on the pale cheeks. He put the heavy hair away from the face and kissed, oh, so softly, the little cheek.

Soft as it was, the kiss woke her. One little fist went up and rubbed open an eye; the other eye tried to open itself. Then the other little fist went up, and Nita was awake.

She was quite used to her nocturnal visitor. She put her thin nightgowned arms round the shaggy bending head.

"Doc-doc, tell Nita a pretty story."

55

He lifted her out of bed, put the quilt round her, and told her stories about good little girls and naughty little girls, and oceans of toys and rivers of sweeties until Nita, her imagination glutted, fell off to sleep again. Then he replaced her in her bed, covered her up as warmly as a mother would have done and went out into the cold and quickly to his legitimate home.

Sometimes Nannie woke; but it made no difference. There were no secrets from Nannie. She had been "Master Benjamin's" nurse. She adored him. Her notions of morality were on a level with his. She may not have admired his taste, but she served Mrs Cameron as faithfully as she would have served Mrs Phillips or Mrs Anybody-he-pleased, and she was a second mother to his child.

Thus these two people led their double lives.

In Portsdown Road Dr Phillips led a quiet and domestic life, not quite free, notwithstanding the opinion of the world, from money cares. Mrs Cameron's was an expensive establishment. She had her own brougham now, and he grudged her nothing. Dr Phillips was a gambler, and lately had not been a lucky one. The stock exchange, and a hankering after high interest for his savings, ran away with a considerable portion of his large income. But nobody knew anything of this. In fact, notwithstanding the respect, the confidence, even the affection he inspired, nobody knew the real Benjamin Phillips.

His virtues and his vices were secret. Only his talents were public property. His professional brethren liked to meet him and consult with him, notwithstanding the low position he had taken up. He had the gift of diagnosis. He gave the lie to the saying that "a rapid diagnosis is a wrong diagnosis." He could read life or death on a patient's face with unerring instinct. And when it was death he grieved, for he had a tender heart.

Tender and sympathetic, grave and courteous. As undercurrents a love of mystery and excitement; a curiously complex character, and misunderstood. A fascinating individuality that anyone but Mary Cameron must have loved. He loved her with devotion; she was everything to him. If ever he awoke to the situation it would go hard with his pride and his passions.

Up to now he was happy: happy in meeting her, in seeing her, in knowing her to be the mother of his child.

He could not but see that she did not adore the child as most mothers adore an only child; but he read no lesson therefrom. He escaped present trouble by ignoring facts, and silenced the voice of his knowledge as he had already silenced that of his conscience.

Book I · Chapter VII

Short's Hotel is in Panton Street. It is a dissipated out-all-night and red-eyed-in-the-morning sort of hotel. Families do not patronise it, nor any ladies whose reputations equal or exceed their charms.

It was nearly one o'clock in the morning when Alec Murphy and Charles Doveton came home, but the sturdy night porter, with his friendly manner and air of being able to settle with a refractory cabman or carry a drunken nobleman to bed with equal alacrity, was still patrolling the hall and they were soon provided with some cigars and brandies and sodas.

"I can't turn in yet," said Charles Doveton, yawning. "I'm too dead beat; I know I couldn't sleep."

"I'll have a cigar before I go. Cheer up, old chappie! I am sure I don't know what's come to you. You're not half the fellow you used to be."

"I can't cheer up. I believe I hate London. If it weren't for you I'd pack up and go off tonight."

"This morning you mean, but never mind. I don't mind telling you, I have no idea why you didn't go back last week. You came up to enjoy yourself and win the Cup. You haven't enjoyed yourself and—well, you didn't quite win the Cup. I know I'm a very fascinating companion, but...what is detaining you?"

"I don't know," said Charlie, shortly. Then he sat gazing into the fire with a most woebegone expression.

He had altered very much since the day six weeks ago that he was at Doctor Phillips's; the sunburn had gone off and so had the appearance of exuberant health and spirits. He looked older and somewhat worn. Town life had not proved all his fancy painted it. In his harmless country conceit, fostered by bucolic surroundings, he had come to show these Londoners what he could do. But he had not had the success he expected. He had not only not beaten the champion at Lillie Bridge but had been overthrown by such second and third rate men as Taylor and Aspinall. Then, at cricket, the fact that he was captain of his county eleven had not saved him from getting a duck's egg.

Beaten at his natural pleasures he had endeavoured to participate in new ones. Fruitlessly. He didn't care for drinking and ballet girls bored him. Yet he did not attribute his rapidly growing depression wholly to these matters. Alec Murphy had no notion what it was all about. He thought he had behaved exceedingly well to his country cousin; and had certainly done his best to repay the hospitality he had always received at Bourne Hall. Athletics were more in his line than dissipation, but he had tried Charlie with both.

In virtue of his superior age and experience, he began to question him now. As they sat over their cigars and drinks he asked him if he were in debt, and many other deep and equally probing questions. But Charlie answered monosyllabically.

"Now look here, old fellow!" he said, at length. "I don't want to offend you but I seriously think you'd better go back to the pigs. You're homesick my friend; that's your malady. A pretty girl like Violet de Vere asks you to supper and you tell her you're not hungry!... after all you've been taught, too! I was quite ashamed of you."

"Damn Violet!" was the uncivil response. And Charlie gazed moodily into the fire.

"Tell us all about it, old man!" went on Alec kindly. "There must be something wrong. Perhaps I can give you a helping hand."

A gleam of hope came into Doveton's dull eyes.

"Oh, Alec!"

And then he entered into a long explanation, rambling, incoherent, and excited, in which frequent

59

allusion was made to flaxen hair and starry eyes and sloping shoulders. He told in laborious detail how he had seen a lovely woman getting into a brougham and what livery her manservant wore. How he had once sat in the same row of stalls with her at the theatre and once followed her into Charbonnel's and eaten heaven knows how many of their sticky cream cakes in order to have an excuse for remaining near her. All this and a great deal more of the same character he poured forth.

His friend listened to him, as young men will to anything resembling an adventure; at times interested, but when the description became very prolix undisguisedly yawning.

Telling the story did Charlie good. He looked to Alec for help, although he could make no guess in what form it would be forthcoming. He was anxious not to bore him; yet his eagerness and his desire to show both himself and the lady in the most advantageous light made him long winded. He rather slurred over his encounter with the doctor; his feelings had been too deeply wounded on that occasion for him to desire to dwell upon it.

To tell the truth Murphy hadn't an idea what advice to offer. But he looked wise and waited for a pause in the narrative.

"Doctor Phillips said she was a widow," wound up Charlie rather wistfully.

Murphy sprang to life again.

"Phillips. Do you mean Benjamin Phillips of Portsdown Road? What's he got to do with it?"

"Haven't you been listening?" said Charlie indignantly.

"Not to the whole thing. You couldn't have expected me to. Just tell me again what Benjamin Phillips has to do with it, tell it as shortly as you can by the way, and then I'll fire away with my advice." So Charlie went over his unsavoury interview with the doctor again; and when he had finished Alec went deliberately over to him, pausing to relight his cigar on the way, and shook hands.

"Keep up your spirits, my boy. Is it Benjamin Phillips, the Jew doctor, a thin black chap with a long nose? That's all I want to know."

Charlie confessed he had not entered into religious discussion with him; but the personal description was certainly applicable.

"Well, never mind! We'll take it for granted. Now listen, while I my plans unfold, as they say at the play. What you want is an introduction, all cut and dried and proper, to Mrs Incognita. You rush pell mell into the doctor's study and demand one. Naturally he refuses it, and in return you call him by all the names you can lay your tongue to. Don't interrupt! You know you do! And quite right too if it eases your mind; only it doesn't bring you any nearer your object. That proud office is reserved for me; and I'll tell you how I'm going to do it. You are listening, I believe you said?"

"Go on."

"I will. Phillips is a Jew; Jew men are cads. That's nothing to do with what I am going to tell you but I thought I'd better warn you before I go any further. I don't know anything against Phillips; on the contrary, I know a fellow he pulled through an attack of typhoid when he was close upon corpsed, but that doesn't alter what I've said. Jew men are cads; and they can't do anything. They may have brains. What's the good of brains? They haven't got muscles, they haven't got pluck, and they haven't got breeding. They've got one thing, however, and that is clannishness. They stick together, and ..."

"For Heaven's sake, Alec, don't give me a dissertation on Jews: get to the point."

"All right, don't be impatient. You talked for an hour and a half, and I've only just begun. Well! there is a certain little girl. Oh, you needn't be frightened, I'm not going to tell you all about her eyebrows and the set

61

of her shoulders. Her people have a dance, and for that dance I've got an invite. Phillips and his wife will be there, I know; probably their friend will be there also. This of course is only a guess, but anyway I can take you with me and if you don't succeed in meeting her you will be able to learn something of her, of her friendships and her movements generally. What do you think of that?"

"Oh, Alec!" The young fellow's eyes were limpid with gratitude and hope. "When is the dance?"

"Tomorrow night, tonight rather; and very handsome you'll look if you don't go to bed! You can dream of Mrs Incognita's blue eyes."

But the young men did not separate just then. They drifted into a conversation about love. They were both good hearted, clean living young fellows with more muscle than brain, but perhaps little the worse for that.

Alec told Charlie all about Florrie Collings. She was a dear sweet little girl; not one of those girls that ride and play cricket, but a simple little thing with soft blue eyes. The sister was rather of the she dragon type, but she was a capital waltzer and was always very civil to him. He was getting on for six and twenty and he didn't think it a bad idea to settle down. Then Charlie discussed eagerly the advantages of early marriages. Each young man was thinking of himself while he let the other talk, and Alec talked most. He confessed he hadn't said anything about marriage yet. In fact he had hardly thought about it. He knew a young fellow who married on £800 a year and was awfully jolly. Not carriages and horses or anything of that sort, but a pretty little place in Kensington and a bit of ground large enough for tennis.

He owned he'd never seen the parents of his little girl: they went about generally with the Jeddingtons. Awful cads, these Jeddingtons. Father an old clothesman or something of that sort, but piles of money and an immense house in Portland Place. "And a rum lot you meet if you go there to dinner," he added, "but Soph Jeddington is rather a jolly girl, if she didn't talk so much about good form and social position."

Altogether Alec was exceedingly confidential, and a little outstepped history in relating his love affair. He had merely danced with her a dozen times or so and talked a little in the interval. Perhaps Florrie had been complaisant in the matter of dances, but then the knowledge of an insuperable obstacle to any nearer tie gave her the confidence with him that a young girl feels with a married man. She deceived herself into the belief that the obstacle that would prevent marriage would avert love; but of this obstacle, and consequently of its effect, Alec Murphy was totally ignorant.

There had been a long discussion and a great deal of argument over this ball of the Collingses. Mrs Collings wanted no Christians invited; she reminded her husband of the young stockbroker who had got drunk last year. Besides, what was the good?

But there were two or three who always came and had been proved harmless, so these were included. Then in going over the lists they found they were short of dancing young men. Mrs Collings didn't think that mattered as they had collected together some very good matches; but Ray was of a different opinion, and with a great deal of pressing gained her point. Thus she got permission to ask the Jeddingtons to bring some of their friends, and this meant a card for Alec.

Then there was a great deal of conversation over Mrs Cameron. Often as Mrs Collings had met her she had never invited her. She had been friendly with her and civil to her, but she had not got over her unreasoning instinctive distrust.

Ray had to bring Mrs Detmar to bear upon the matter before she got her own way; and a word from the doctor, who was just then in frequent attendance upon Teddy, helped her a great deal. So at length and, as it were under protest, Mrs Cameron's card was sent; and

63

thus, the last door being opened to her, found herself in the arms of "the people."

Benjamin Phillips was highly gratified. He didn't dance himself but he thought it well Mary should have that amusement, so he bought her a magnificent white dress for the occasion, determining to go early and observe the effect she produced.

Book I · Chapter VIII

The ball was in full swing when Murphy and Doveton arrived at Mrs Collings's. A long room, with a white drugget, on which two florid chandeliers showered down light and heat. Immediately on entering you were impressed with the predominance of women. Fat women blazing with diamonds sat upon the benches; tall girls, stout girls, loud laughing and loud talking girls were scattered about in groups all over the room. Yet numerically considered they were by no means in an overwhelming majority. There were plenty of men but they were so short, so plain, so insignificant generally that they passed unnoticed in the brilliant confusion of shoulders and skirts.

There was much animation and gesticulation. The girls were very richly dressed and many of them wore jewels.

Murphy quickly singled out Florrie and took her programme from her.

She entered a feeble protest and said she was not going to dance that evening.

"Quite right," he replied, coolly, inscribing his name right across, and then putting it in his waistcoat pocket. "I'll take care of this for you, and if any fellow bothers you send him to me. Come, we'll finish this waltz together. By the way is Dr Phillips coming?"

"Yes. Why?"

"Is Mrs Cameron coming?"

"Yes." Florrie did not ask why this time, but she looked it.

"Take my arm and come along. I'll tell you all about it. First I must see Doveton." A succession of energetic and heedless waltzers dancing every variety of nondescript step bumped up against them and impeded their progress. Judæa, when it dances, is an ungainly spectacle, and Murphy could barely refrain from uncomplimentary comment as he was buffetted and trodden upon and generally incommoded.

"Why on earth don't they all go one way? Then we could have waltzed round to him. Charlie, this is Miss Collings. She tells me they expect Mrs Cameron here tonight."

Florrie was relieved to find that Murphy's interest was not a purely personal one.

As they stood conversing together the dance came to an end; the music suddenly stopped and the couples commenced walking about and fanning themselves, trying to dissipate the heat of the oppressive atmosphere.

At this moment of comparative repose Mrs Cameron made her entry, coming into the room with Mrs Phillips. It was the first time she had been seen without the conventional mourning she had worn for her deceased husband, and many of those present felt they never had seen her before.

Her dress was of the purest white, falling in long and graceful lines. It was cut low and finished merely by a shoulder strap. The curves of the rounded bosom were half hinted at, half displayed, beneath the cobweb lace of the rising tucker. A dimple in the shoulder was plainly visible. The pale yellow of her hair was reflected, so to speak, in her costume. Her dress was looped up with yellow feathers, she carried a large fan of the same in her hand, and looked as if she had just stepped from one of Millais' canvasses. The garish surroundings threw her quiet beauty into full relief. In the chaste charm of her aspect there was no one present but looked crude and unsatisfactory.

Florrie looked uneasily at Murphy. He smiled at her reassuringly.

Poor Charlie felt the blood rush into his face and his

heart began to throb. He watched her; he noted her gracious smiles and manner; he saw Florrie introduce Alec. He grew excited; he felt his hour was near. When Alec came to him some four minutes later he was cold and trembling.

"Pull yourself together; don't look like a fool! I've ascertained she can dance and you will be one of the first to get hold of her programme. Put your name down for at least three and then go in and win. I wish you luck!"

Charlie did not feel like winning, and he could not help feeling he did look like a fool. But he put his name down for three, and blushed very much as he was doing so. He felt glad the first one would not be until number 8, for he thought the respite would enable him to become master of his feelings.

Mary fully intended to amuse herself. She knew she looked beautiful and was glad to see that other people knew it. Dr Phillips had not been able to come with his wife, so Mrs Cameron had called for her. Perhaps the absence of the doctor added a little to the feeling of exhilaration that possessed Mary; she felt for the moment young and free.

Mrs Phillips took her seat among the dowagers on the benches. Mary joined the ranks of the gay and giddy dancers. Very speedily she discovered that Doveton and Murphy were the most accomplished of her partners and gradually permitted them to monopolize her attention.

As the evening wore on the hilarity grew more pronounced, the laughter and talk louder, the complexions redder and greasier, the fringes a little out of curl, and the warmth more oppressive.

Dr Phillips came in late. He stood in the doorway watching. In a few seconds, to his eyes, one figure had disentangled itself from the throng. Neither the heat nor the exercise had disarranged her hair, or flushed her face. She was gliding gracefully round in harmonious

67

motion with an expression of happiness on her face. She was not speaking. It was a sensation of youth and freedom, to which she had ever been a stranger, that was making her eyes sparkle. For the first time in her life she felt like a girl, with possibilities widening her horizon.

The doctor looked at her with changing feelings. He had a power of intuitive sympathy that made him feel her newly found youth. His thoughts went back to the old days, the days of the Regent's Park walks. But in vain he strove to recall her present expression, for she had never before had it; youth had not dawned in her then. Care for the future, care for the present, had held her in its icy grasp.

"I have given her her lost youth," he thought. "It is to the love and happiness I have given her that she owes her rejuvenescence ... And there are women—ay, and men too—who would call it wicked." A glow of philanthropic satisfaction warmed his heart.

He did not know Mary's partner, who was, as it happened, Alec Murphy. But he was conscious of an instant's dissatisfaction that it was not one of his own people. He would have felt safer.

Then as she passed him he noted the curves of her neck, and admired how she had done up her hair away from it and wore no necklace lest it should break the line. He admired the harmony of yellow and white, the absolute match of feather and hair. He experienced the pride of possession. He pictured himself going home with her afterwards. In fancy he assisted at her toilette, unclasped her bracelets, and felt the warm flesh between in his hands. He saw her letting down her hair; he stroked it and smoothed it from her forehead. The increasing heat of the room affected his imagination, which began to run riot among the anticipated pleasures of the night.

He forced himself from the contemplation. He looked at his wife. She was dressed in violet satin, with a confused medley of lace and artificial flowers scrambling down the front of the bodice, a mass of ungraceful creases. She was nodding in time to the music. Her imagination had also been affected by the heat and the light dresses that fanned her as they passed. She fancied herself in bed, her eyes were closed, her loose bosom heaved, and every now and then a sound issued from her nostrils that provoked a smile on the placid faces of her bench companions. It did not amuse her husband.

When Dr Phillips looked again at Mary she had changed her partner.

"Surely...Good God!" The doctor looked again, but there was no mistake. He recognised the gentleman whom he had turned so ignominiously from his door. Charlie Doveton's broad shoulders were thrown back; he scarcely touched her waist with one hand, with the other he held hers lightly. He was taller than she and was looking down on her with an expression of rapt adoration. The lad was in heaven, and his ingenuous countenance was unable to conceal his feeling.

The doctor's first feeling was one of blind unreasoning rage. "He!...Curse him!...That brainless, impertinent boy! What right had he here? What did he mean, after the warning he had had, by taking the liberty, by having the impertinence to follow her here?"

Phillips would have liked to seize him by the throat and fling him out there and then. He looked at his throat savagely, and the high masher collar was a fresh offence. How dare he put his hand on her waist! How dare he look at her! How dare...

The doctor's rage nearly overmastered him. He had always suffered from these violent fits of temper. He clenched his hands until the nails dug into the flesh; the lights and the heat, the people and the music, got mixed together in his brain. It is an awful feeling for an intelligent man: he was losing his self control. He made a step forward—

The music suddenly ceased, and that saved him. The promenading began.

The raging fury died away and in its place came an

equally unreasoning fear. First a terror lest anyone should have noticed him; then an agony of doubt.

Had he told her? Would he tell her? How had he come there? Whose doing was it? Was Mary...? Supposition refused to go further. Dr Phillips felt sick with the unnamed thought. He banished it. No! Mary was not to blame. Who was to blame? And how should he act?

As he stood thinking, Mary and Charlie came towards him. He saw a mocking smile on Charlie's lips. The mock was but a fancy but a fancy that teemed with danger.

He clenched his fist; he thought he would strike the fellow down. Once more his feelings were at boiling point.

"Thank you, I will only take an ice. How do you do, doctor? How late you have come!"

Mary's voice broke the spell that was on him. He took her offered hand. His beard hid the workings of his features; he was uncertain of his next movement. Should he recognise or ignore Charlie Doveton? And how would Charlie Doveton behave?

Mr Charles Doveton was as concerned as the doctor. He showed it by his blushes and his awkwardness.

"Dr Phillips; Mr Doveton" said Mary, easily. "Are you coming down to supper, Doctor? We are."

The doctor acknowledged the introduction with a slight bow. Charlie grew a shade redder. It was an awkward encounter, and one the probability of which had not occurred to him. He felt that if his pure idol should know of his course intrusiveness, if Phillips should betray him, all would be over of his slender chances of improving her acquaintance.

They remained together in the doorway as the stream of people filed gradually past into the supper room. That Mary's hand should remain on Doveton's arm angered the doctor, but he said nothing. He was beginning to appreciate the movement, and a false

70

move might bring him to irremediable disaster. But he
could have thought more clearly if Mary had removed
her hand.

He looked at Charlie Doveton's face and the expression he saw there arrested his attention. His
pleading eyes plainly said, "Don't betray me, sir."

So Mary didn't know; and it was a chance encounter.
His heart felt lighter. He returned Charlie's look by one
of grave disapproval and said steadily to Mary, "This
gentleman and I have met before. How is your arm, Mr

Doveton? Allow me." And he offered his own to Mary. "You cannot, I presume, submit it to any pressure yet?" It was a chance, and the doctor tried it.

Charlie quickly put his other hand lightly on Mrs Cameron's, as if to retain it in its place. His embarrassment, vexation, and fear made him appear more awkward than ever.

"My arm? Oh it's better; it's all right. Come along, Mrs Cameron, or we shan't find a place."

And Mrs Cameron, bowing to the doctor, and ignoring an enigma to which she possessed no key, went downstairs.

The doctor was left alone. He had failed. His intention had been to frighten Doveton away. He had gone away, but he had taken Mary with him. And Phillips wanted Mary very much just then, to soothe his ruffled feelings and calm him down generally. Unfortunately he was not even left time to collect himself, for Mrs Collings, Mrs Detmar, and Mrs Lucas surrounded him and he had at once to assume his most amiable society manners. It was very bitter and very difficult for him to abstract his thoughts from the trouble that was oppressing him and throw himself into the uninteresting chatter of these narrow minded women. But his habit of dissimulation aided him, and they noticed nothing.

Finally he was permitted to escort Mrs Detmar to the supper room, and chance arranged that the only vacant seat should be one adjacent to the small table at which sat Mrs Cameron.

The room was full of little tables and a long sideboard laden with provisions took up the whole of one side. The popping of champagne corks, the clinking of glasses, were heard through the din of a hundred conversations.

Doveton, Murphy, Mrs Cameron, and Florrie were together, and the doctor could hear the gay tones in which *she* was talking, though he could not so entirely ignore his companion as to follow what she was saying.

Florrie was very silent. There had been things hinted at and things spoken by Alec that evening that had thrilled her into quietude. Things were going too seriously with her to allow her lightly to laugh and jest. Doveton was silent also. The beauty of his companion, a feeling of unsubstantiality to see his fondest hopes realised after months of weary waiting, the danger from the doctor, overwhelmed him.

But the other two were flushed and excited with triumph. Murphy had forbidden Florrie to dance with anyone else, and she had braved the probable wrath of her parents and obeyed him. He had assumed a masterful and proprietory air and she had submitted.

He had made love to her; there was no doubt in her mind about that. But she allowed her thoughts to go no further. He had even asked her to kiss him, and although she had not done so there was something deliciously alarming in the suggestion. She had asked him if he did not admire Mrs Cameron and he had told her "she was not his style, he didn't like fine women." He had explained about Mr Doveton's wish to meet her, and Florrie, feeling herself taken into confidence, was very happy, albeit she had to keep her thoughts in subjection. She might think of the past, of the present, of looks and hand pressures. Into the future she dared not go.

So Alec Murphy talked to Mary all through that short supper hour that the doctor found so endless. And when it was ended, and they all flocked upstairs in their light garments like glutted pigeons, the latter followed moodily and led Mrs Detmar to her bench without any of his usual pleasant speeches.

He looked for Mary, but the music had burst forth again and she was still in Doveton's arms. More and more bitter grew the doctor's feelings and more and more moody was his brow. It was more than jealousy he experienced, it was jealousy complicated by alarm. He began to reap the reward of his burrowings in the dark. He dared not come forward as the lover, the protector, of this woman; he had perforce to stand by and listen to her laughter and see her smiles, and the black arm round her waist that filled him with such a hell fire of raging impotence.

He watched and watched as couple after couple went past him fanning with their light skirts the warm air into his face. The contortions and grimacing, the airs of conquest of the fringed and loudly dressed girls, the vinous look about the blustering little men, no longer struck him as being comical. He was longing for the mad carnival to end. The music set his teeth on edge and jarred in his brain. It seemed to him hours that he stood there watching while Doveton danced round and round; till his head and his heart ached with giddiness.

When it was over, when girls were beginning to appear on the top of the stairs and in the hall, with opera cloaks on, when anxious mammas were bestirring themselves to persuade their still jigging daughters to accompany them to their yearned for couches, Benjamin Phillips roused himself and sought again for Mary.

He found her standing for the moment alone with her white fur cloak draping her shoulders. They were surrounded with people, there was danger on every side. Doveton was approaching to tell her her carriage waited. The doctor resolved to offer her his arm in his character of old friend and guardian and seize the opportunity for a few words. But even as he offered it, even as Charlie drew back in disappointment and despair, Mrs Phillips clutched heavily at the outstretched member, and exclaimed: "Here you are, Ben, at last! I've been looking for you everywhere; the brougham is up. Good night, Mrs Collings, I'm sure we've had a very pleasant evening." And she yawned visibly.

There was no help for it. Before all these people he

could do nothing but bow to his hostess, refuse the cigar Mr Collings was pressing on him, and conduct his wife to her carriage.

As he passed, his eye met Mary's...and she laughed. She had thought the incident amusing.

Book I · Chapter IX

Fortunately, after remarking that "she could sit up all night for she always slept so badly that it made no difference whether she was in bed or not" Mrs Phillips closed her eyes and remained in suspicious quietude until they reached home.

In the doctor's study the lamp that stood upon the table threw its shadow on the shelves full of books, on the closed cabinets that held his instruments. The outstretched wooden arms of the writing chair invited him to work and rest. But Mary's laugh was still ringing in his ears. The ebb and flow of his tempestuous passions still bereft him of the power of calm reasoning. He felt like a man just escaped from a railway accident, jarred and bruised and shattered in nerve.

He walked restlessly up and down the quiet room, unable at first even to put his thoughts into shape. The fire was out; his depression increased as he noted it.

Mary's laugh!

That was all he heard. It had thrown Charlie Doveton in the shade; it had obliterated all the other sensations of the evening. At one moment he was for rushing off to Brunswick Place, at another he had almost vowed never to go there again. His mind went maddeningly back to the dreams of the earlier part of the evening, stayed there an instant and then was suddenly summoned back by the sound of laughter. He ground the carpet with his heel.

Dr Phillips was jealous! Nothing else could have affected him in this way; but he refused to recognise the truth. Mary had been so much to him these last four years. She had belonged to him body and soul; he had bought and paid for her, and proved the value of his purchase. There had been no break in their relations, no lovers' quarrels, nothing but peace, and—for Phillips—happiness. It was love, and love was a feeling the doctor had never before experienced; it had never entered into his many liaisons, it had never occurred to him as a danger for his future.

He loved the girl who was so utterly dependent upon him; perhaps the dependence deepened his love. He loved the woman who had given him the only child of his manhood. It was the first time he awoke to the knowledge that feeling was obscuring intellect, that he loved instead of reasoned, and the moment of discovery was bitter to him. A dim knowledge came to him of the wrong he was doing himself by the life he was leading. He was conscious of a feeling of dismay when he reflected how much room in his thoughts this woman and his child had taken up, how he had drifted away from the ambition of his youth.

Once Brain has been his God and his passions trivial incidents. He had started in his profession with ardour, he had studied with avidity the secrets of life and death and had held them sacred. But the luxurious prostitution of his marriage had developed in him an Eastern virility that brooked nò denial.

His nature craved excitement. He had never found it with his wife; he no longer found it in a struggle with his competitors. He commenced to play with his knowledge. He experimentalised, half idly, half maliciously; the lives that were at that time in his keeping had trembled in the balance and had been sacrificed or almost sacrificed to a curiosity which was not a thirst for knowledge.

So he sported with the King of Terrors and gambled with humanity.

From this his intercourse with Mary Cameron had saved him. She became his centre of interest, and with this sole outlet for all the energies of his intricate mind he drifted into the easy life of the satisfied sensualist.

And now came the question: How would this lifting of the veil affect him? When he calmed down, when he ceased to walk up and down the room wrestling with his vain ebullitions of rage, astonishment at himself was the first feeling that possessed him. He had loved women, in the flesh; he had never dreamed of making one part of himself. He had always had a theory, and until the last few years his practice had corresponded with his theory, that for certain purposes women were necessary. He had dallied with them and pleased himself for the time by so doing, but he thought one as good as another. So long as the skin was soft and the hair fine and the figure yielding, what matter if it were called Annie or Susan or Mary?

He had never analysed his sensations about Mary; he had accepted the situations as they succeeded each other, but the child, the piece of feminality that was wholly his, had always been to him a wonder and a delight.

Now, as he thought it all over, as he remembered that all these years his wife had been nothing to him but in name, all women had been nothing to him save only Mary, he stood aghast. He had been faithful to her and was full of disgust at his own fidelity. He thought, and the thoughts came quite clearly now.

"I have been a fool! I have been like other men and have drifted into jealousy because I have only her to be jealous of. I, who always despised others for their dependence! I have had my turn and it has been a long one; let that young idiot or any other have his now. I have had all the best of it. There lives no woman who would be faithful to her husband for more than five years of married life if she were properly tempted. Curiosity, if nothing else, would lead her astray. How could I expect more of Mary?"

But while he reasoned he knew it was all false; knew that he loved her and more than half believed in her. He was miserably indignant with himself for his weakness.

He no longer heard her laugh now, but he saw the black arm round her waist. It was horrible for a man of his capacity to be suffering like this; he could not endure it. His state of restless excitability was terrible and to know the cause of it to be but a woman made him despise himself.

He sat down, took up the current number of the *British Medical Journal*, and tried to concentrate his mind upon Hughlings Jackson on neurology. Right across an elaborate paragraph about the degenerative changes of atheroma glided Mary's white hand, with its pink nails and no ornament but the thick wedding ring. He flung the paper from him in disgust.

Then there came over him, suddenly, an irresistible longing for woman's society; a desire to be cooed over and petted and soothed; a feeling that only in some cosy boudoir warm with the presence and scent of woman could he find balm for his present pain.

He made up his mind suddenly. He snatched his great coat and hat and went rapidly out, forgetting himself so much as to slam the door abruptly behind him.

He went out and did not return till an early hour the next morning. But he had not been to Mary Cameron's.

Book I · Chapter X

For days after this Dr Phillips avoided meeting Mrs Cameron, neither going to Brunswick Place nor meeting her in the evenings. He was very irritable, very depressed, abrupt with his patients, brutally rude to his wife, and uncertain in his actions.

Everyone forgave him. They all ascribed his altered manners to a very bad case he had just then. Ever since the night of the dance little Teddie Collings had grown rapidly worse, and Phillips at this time did such things as one scarcely expects from a thriving and popular surgeon. He stayed with the child for hours. He sat up one whole night with him when the lad was struggling for breath in one of his croup seizures, sharing the watch with the mother and comforting them all by his presence and hopefulness.

If Florrie crept about with a pale face during this anxious time there was no one to wonder at it; if she went out sometimes by herself and spent an afternoon with Mrs Cameron there was no one to rebuke her for doing so. The eyes of the household were concentrated on Teddie's sick room.

Dr Phillips pulled him through, and when all danger was over felt the force of reaction.

He had exerted all his energies and used all his genius to save Teddie, and all the time he had watched by his sick couch he had thought of Baby Nita and yearned for her.

He had been unable to replace Mary's image by another, and Nita's wondering eyes had lately haunted him night and day. As Teddie lay tossing and struggling on his fevered bed the doctor had pictured Nita in her tiny crib, with her little clenched fists and straggling dark locks. He longed and yearned for his home. He had left off reasoning with himself; he worked hard—harder than he had ever worked—in his laboratory, at his desk, but work as he might he could not forget. The elaborate paper he was preparing on the ætiology of thrombosis hung fire; he was unable to get on with it.

He sat at it one dull afternoon until his temples throbbed and his hand trembled, and he could neither write nor think.

It was one of those April days that borrow their tints from November. Already, at four o'clock, a fog resembling and anticipating twilight was settling down over the park and aiding a light drizzle in obscuring the streets.

The brougham was at the door; he had many visits to pay. And as he went from house to house the cold and the rain affected his spirits and he felt inconceivably low and wretched.

The window was down and he had been too inert to shut it. He looked out; he was in that roughly paved district that lies between the West End and the City, near the wilds of Tottenham Court Road. The grating of the wheels over the stones of the newly mended roads irritated him to distraction. A sudden unaccountable impulse seized him.

He put his head out of the window and called to the coachman, "Brunswick Place."

Then he leaned back and wondered why he had stayed away so long, and could scarcely account for it. He no longer felt the cold or the rain or the stones; he left off thinking and there was a pleasant smile of anticipation on his lips as he rolled along.

Mary was in the drawing room, not reading but wondering. The day had affected her spirits also; she was commencing to feel very uneasy, and for the first time the precariousness of the position that gave her ease and luxury appalled her.

"Good God!" she thought. "What should I do if he

81

tired of it ? " How could she go back to the cold and the bareness and the toil of her former life. She shuddered in horror. It was too terrible. Face to face with such an idea, the tedium of his affection, the boredom of his embraces, seemed visions of celestial joy. Should she send to him ? Should she go to him ?

For the first few days that had passed she had rejoiced in her comparative freedom. She had lounged about and done nothing. Yes, she had done something : she had entertained as visitors Charles Doveton and Mr Murphy. Florrie Collings had been with her when they came and the four had passed a cosy afternoon together ; something had been said about a day on the river and an appointment had been almost made. It was to this afternoon Mary's thoughts flew when she commenced to feel alarmed at her solitude. He might have heard of her reception from Collings. All this uneasiness had been accentuated by a dream.

Only the night before she had dreamed of her old life. She had dreamed she was on her hard, insufficiently covered bed and had heard the grimy little maid-of-all-work rattle at the door to tell her it was already seven o'clock. She was tired ; her limbs were aching with the cold ; but she had to get up, to stand her already chilled feet on the cold boards of the uncarpeted room, wash in half frozen water, go out into the fog, and be at the other end of London by half past eight, breakfastless and shivering.

She had awoken from this realistic dream to the delights of her feather couch, and had lazily put out her hand and rung the bell to have the fire lighted. With a warm fleecy shawl over her shoulders, she had sat up to drink her hot cup of chocolate. Then she lay back again nestling luxuriously beneath the eiderdown in her soft lawn nightdress with its Valenciennes frillings, and stretched her limbs out with voluptuous enjoyment of her physical comforts.

But by the afternoon the dream had reasserted itself, and it was to this Dr Phillips owed the warmth of his reception.

She flung herself into his arms and wept upon his breast. She kissed him and clung to him and reproached him all in a breath. It was a very happy moment for him and the haunting shadow of her indifference, the mocking ghost of her laugh, passed away.

Although it was so nearly summer there was a fire burning; the plush and silk of the furniture melted in its shadows into the softest colourings. The chairs looked inviting and easy, with dim outlines and red glows of warmth.

Mary was in a tea gown of a peculiar blue, her hair was loose and half unbound. She exhaled beauty and happiness. He embraced her, feeling for once ashamed of his infidelity, not as a question of morality but as one of taste. Against his first lesson in love he had attempted rebellion by resuming old habits. But Mary had been too strong for him. Passion may be stimulated by a change—love is disgusted. Benjamin Phillips had been disgusted. Now he banished all uneasiness, put the incident from his mind, and with utter abandonment once more enjoyed the society of the only woman his nature had ever let him really love.

They sat together on the sofa hand in hand like two young lovers, his arm around her waist and her fair head against his shoulder. He let his lips glide over her forehead, then lingering dwell from place to place until they reached her mouth and rested there awhile. The gold of her fairness mingled with the black of his coarse beard.

And she, as she lay there, felt that protection and safety had come back to her. Her past faded again, yet not so utterly but that she could remember the first days of her changed life. She recalled her installation at Alfred Place; she recalled how her heart used to beat

83

when she heard his knock at the front door and a thrill which was half pain reminded her of the pleasures his visit would bring.

In that hour he almost regained his ascendancy over her. She at least felt he was capable of arousing in her some emotion, by whatever name it might be called.

They sat together and renewed the youth of their intimacy. He confessed he had strayed; but he en-wrapped the confession in verbiage. At the time she scarcely noted or commented upon it. She felt she had perchance exceeded her privileges in permitting Dove-ton to call. So, by mutual consent, they spoke little of the time during which they had not met.

By and by Nita came down and played quietly in the corner by herself after being kissed and fondled by her dear Doc-doc. The shades of the evening enwrapped them in calm, the virtuous peace of the twilight descended on their hearts. The charm of the domestic picture was complete.

Tired of play, the little one crept up to the doctor and put her tiny hand into his. Those smooth palmed hands of the doctor's that had done kind things cruelly and cruel things kindly lifted her up and laid her on the sofa beside her mother.

The baby slept, and the father and mother, bound to each other by no holier tie than the one she was testimony to, talked in low murmurings of love and faith.

Lured on by the quietness and content, Dr Phillips grew confidential.

During his few days of disquietude and uneasiness he had heard that the *Lancet* required someone to go out to Egypt, partly to report on the sanitary condition of the troops, partly to gather material for a series of articles on the comparative morality in the hospitals and ambulance tents. In his anxiety about himself and his mental condition he had hurriedly applied for the post and been accepted; he was still willing to go, for something told him of the danger of his present position, but he had to explain all this to Mary, and make suitable arrangements for her in his absence, and his heart failed him when he thought of leaving her.

But another thing that decided him was that he had been somewhat troubled in money matters lately. His speculations had not turned out successfully and Mrs Cameron's establishment was an expensive one. He had to bear the expense of Portsdown Road as well, because although Mrs Phillips had an income she hoarded it. Economy was one of her chief amusements; she did not lavish her husband's money, but she simply declined to touch her own. Dr Phillips was an essentially liberal man; he knew Brunswick Place was a luxury, Portsdown Road a necessity, and he was willing to pay for them both. But he was always and above all things a Jew, and he could not see the balance at his banker's running low without anxiety.

The sum he would receive over and above his expenses for this Egyptian journey was not very important to him. But it would be ready money, and he saw his way to making more of it. His profession brought him into contact with men who had knowledge and he very often picked up information that he had been able to turn to account. This was the case just now.

He was not required to start until June. He explained to Mary that she ought to go to the seaside during August and July, for Nita's sake. As for his wife, she would be going to Ischl for a course of waters. He would not accompany his wife; he could not accompany his mistress; and most of his patients would be scattered over the coast of Great Britain. Under the circumstances he thought the best thing he could do was to utilise the time for his professional or pecuniary advantage.

85

"I hate leaving you, my darling," he said as he looked down on her fondly, "but I think it best to go, if you can spare me."

"I can't spare you, Benito," she replied softly. "If you must go, go—I must bear it, but you can't call it sparing you when I shall be so miserable! But we need not talk of it yet, surely—it is only April now." Then she caressed him, and they talked of something else. Perhaps a vague vision of Charlie Doveton cheered the prospective loneliness of her lover's absence as she contemplated it.

Be this as it may, Dr Phillips went home light hearted and refreshed that night, and even his obtuse wife noted the new liveliness of his expression when he came down to breakfast the next morning.

The dining room at Portsdown Road was not nearly so cosy as the drawing room at Brunswick Place. A mahogany legged, wooden topped table, now covered with a white cloth, a hissing urn, and other breakfast paraphernalia; a dozen mahogany chairs upholstered in green leather, a dumb waiter now covered with old *Punches*, *Chambers's Journals*, and other literature destined for the delectation of his patients, for it was here they waited; a Turkey carpet somewhat worn and two appalling photographs of Mrs Phillips's parents, complete the inventory. A strip of grey drugget reached from the door to the fireplace; Mrs Phillips was an excellent housekeeper and found that the carpet wore out more there than elsewhere.

Dr Phillips certainly came down looking very fresh. His glasses dangled unused from their string and his eyes looked bright and soft; his spotless linen and small hands, his air of morning lighted up by the sun against whose rays the coarse hairs of his beard looked blacker than ever, all became him. He looked young, wiry, and masterful.

He flung open the window and inhaled the morning air with relish. There was a great change since

86

yesterday. The weather was soft and warm and spring-like, and the doctor, who was very susceptible to climatic influences, felt exhilarated.

"Aren't you coming to breakfast, Ben? The eggs will be cold," broke in his wife's monotonous voice, interrupting his communion with the morning breezes.

Doctor Phillips was thinking, and she had to speak twice. When he did sit down he did not eat a good breakfast; the country had begun to haunt him. It always did in the first days of spring. He wanted to take larger breaths; he felt hungry for air.

"I'm afraid I shall have to go to Bristol for a day," he said preparatively. "Johnson is laid up there and I don't like the idea of leaving him in the hands of a stranger." And he took a large gulp of tea and looked quite unconcerned.

"Oh, dear," replied his trusting helpmate, "I should think not! But how can you manage here? What will you do?"

"Well, I shall go Friday night and return either Sunday or the first thing Monday morning. Claxton will look after things here for me."

"And Teddie?"

"Teddie is out of the wood."

"What will you get for going, do you expect?"

Dr Phillips laughed: a genial pleasant laugh.

"Quite right, dear; always look to the main chance. It will pay me very well, you may be sure of that."

She was sure of that and was quite satisfied he should go, and he knew he was not only safe so far but that she would go all about the circle and explain how Johnson could not get on without him. Johnson being a mere myth, there was no danger of his appearing to complicate matters.

He went his rounds in the morning and received his patients in the afternoon. Then he went to Mary and broached his project. He wanted to take the child, but on her raising sundry objections he gave in. Then as to

87

where they should go? Here again Dr Phillips showed his eccentricity.

He decided on staying at Skinner's, at Maidenhead. Now whenever the Israelites assemble in any force on the river, Maidenhead is the point of their departure. At Oxford he might have been certain, or almost so, of escaping detection. At Maidenhead he would be running his neck right into the noose.

Mary pointed this out to him. He replied in the first place no one would be on the river so early in the year. Secondly, if there were anybody he could dodge them without danger.

He instructed her to leave word, in case of callers, that she was lying down, not well enough to see anybody. He advised her to give the servant instructions to go round to Portsdown Road on Saturday and say "Mrs Cameron was not well; would the doctor come round?"

Then when Friday came they prepared to enjoy their jaunt.

This was the form taken by that regret or repentance Benjamin Phillips felt for his infidelity or unfaith towards the woman he loved. A temperament such as his is subject to these sudden reactions. All he wished now was to wipe out the remembrance of his discomfort, but he rejoiced to find that a renewed freshness and vigour in his passion for Mary was the result of his endeavour to replace her.

And many times during that spring, which afterwards seemed to him to have been the happiest spring his life had ever known, he spent long days with Mary and the child, gliding down towards evening in a light oared skiff to a Lotus land, where was neither regret nor remembrance.

Once, it was on a Sunday, and it so happened it was the last of their jaunts. Chertsey was the scene of their holiday, and he had pulled the boat into a backwater, behind the weir, and moored it under a tree. Then he

took his place by her side and the child, worn out by the
heat, slept at their feet. The sky was grey, vast, and
vague, melting into azure overhead. The burning globe
of the sun, hidden from them by the trees, touched the
leaves with gold and illuminated Mary's profile.

Benjamin Phillips's sensitive nature drank in the
beauty of nature with thanksgiving, revelled in the
green and golden splendour, felt that to live was to be
happy. The lapping of the waters lulled him, the

nearness of his lady love thrilled him, the child at his feet completed his sense of perfect joy.

He had forgotten his journey and the complex motives that led him to undertake it. But, and this is curious, in the elation of his spirits, in the beauty of the hour, he found it in his heart to wish that Clothilde, his poor fat unattractive wife, could also share in the enjoyment.

This was the zenith of Benjamin's destiny. Much that was good in the man—and perhaps but for his race training and instincts all would have been good—was prominent at this time.

He was leading what purists would consider an immoral life; but he was leading it very purely. He was kind to his wife; he healed, as far as he could, the sick that came to him. If domesticity be a virtue, and certainly it is a corner stone of the Jewish character, could anything be more domestic than the ménage in Brunswick Place? He had rescued this beautiful girl from a life of unappreciated drudgery, and all his kindliness of heart redoubled at the thought of the happiness his personality shed upon his two homes.

The apprehensions which had come to him on the night of the ball, that his mind was retrograding, that if sensuality and intellectuality are to coexist the limits of each must be more clearly defined; these apprehensions which had led him to decide on his Egyptian journey had faded into the background again. And when at length the time came when according to his agreement he was bound to start he started with regrets and fears and misgivings. At the last moment he would have resigned, if resignation had then been possible.

It was not possible; he could find no substitute. So he departed, leaving behind him his wife, his mistress, his child; and though he knew it not the last clean page in the history of his life.

Book II · Chapter I

It was mid-August and Devonshire Park, Eastbourne, was thronged with exhausted Londoners. The band played on a raised platform in the open air; the electric light, like a playful and as yet untrained demon, sometimes threw into brilliant relief the faces of the players, sometimes went out with a sudden jerk and left them to struggle in darkness with their scores.

The distances in the tree encircled park grew vast and dim in the flickering light and the groups of people moving about threw grotesque shadows on the green sward and the gravel paths. There was a heavy enervating warmth in the air, and the young couples straying on the grass were influenced to thoughts of love. They whispered vows, they exchanged hand pressures. The music in the distance stirred them and the swaying movement it evoked was towards each other.

Florrie's heart was also moved mysteriously as she walked side by side with Alec; when by accident as they walked they gravitated together, and as his coat sleeve brushed against her jacket her heart began to beat and her pulses to throb in an unaccountable fashion. And yet they had spoken of naught but the approaching tennis tournament and like matters of no absorbing interest. They wandered where no vagaries of electric light could reach them into a pathway between the outer edge of the park boundary and a broad ivy grown path that separated it from the lawn.

There in the solitude a silence fell between them and involuntarily Florrie found her hand in Alec's; gloveless palm met palm and Florrie quivered again beneath the touch. It was the beautiful dawn of passion in a young maiden. A thrill towards knowledge and a shrinking from it. She could not put into words, she did not understand the feelings that possessed her. But she looked up and met his eyes, read in them what his lips had never uttered, and dropped her glance again with crimson cheek.

So they wandered hand in hand; then, still in mute communion, sat down together on a seat hidden amid the greenery. Out there in the darkness, remote from the world, they felt the solitude draw them closer to one another; all unchecked Alec's arm stole round Florrie's waist, and the fair head rested on his shoulder.

How wide a vista opened out in the mind of the little Jewish girl as she lay there in the arms of Christianity. How centuries of bigotry and generations of prejudice melted away in the flame of her passion. The spirit of separation that had rolled heavy between her love and herself seemed uplifted. She could see no Judaism and feel no Christianity. Formless visions of light and knowledge floated before her with their vanishing shadows flitting by the azure heavens beyond. It was love, love, nothing but love, and the whole world must be love now she was of that world of love. He clasped her ever closer, and she floated with him into azure skies and drifted with him into fathomless seas, and all of love.

It was half in a trance she lay. Her hands and feet cold with passion, scarcely drawing a breath lest she should dissolve the dream, her eyes half closed. And then the warm feel of lips meeting hers, the cling of those lips as if they should never part again.

And when the kiss was over, when at length they looked into each other's eyes again and close against each other sat there silent in their happiness, the song of the nightingale broke forth from beside them and Florrie's eyes filled with tears at the heavenly sadness of the melody, she turned to him for sympathy and again the mutual impulse moved them and their lips met.

92

The scent of the sweetbriar was about them and the softness of the summer night and the voices of the birds; and youth was in their veins; life could give no more than this.

"My darling," he said, and all was still again. What a word for a maiden the first time it breaks upon her. And to hear it for the first time beneath the dark sympathetic sky. She clung to him, she had no answer, her expectant ear listened for yet another glory to fall upon it.

"My darling, my own little wife" he said; but the glorious spell was broken. That word "wife!" It shattered the illusion and Florrie shuddered in her lover's arms. Her dream dispelled, she awoke to see—what? Misery and gloom and the heavy hand of fate. In one instant had risen up again in her mind the great barrier between Christian and Jewess—all the difficulties, all the impossibilities.

A chill air swept up from the ground. She disengaged herself from him, and while he, all surprised at the movement, stood quiescent she spoke, throwing up her first bulwark against the flood that was overwhelming her.

"We ought not to be here alone, take me back to Mamma," she said.

"What do you mean, Florrie?" asked Alec in natural astonishment. "Surely you can stay a little longer with your future husband." He advanced towards her, intending to renew his caresses, but she eluded him, standing up straight and solemn, her pale face set like a cameo in hard relief against the ever darkening sky.

"Take me back to Mamma," was all she said. It was the shibboleth of her generation.

But Alec was after all a man, and he had had a foretaste of victory. He insisted on an answer; he spoke roughly; he demanded her reasons.

"You are very cruel to me," he said.

Cruel! and to Alec. Florrie could no longer maintain

93

her stern attitude. She drifted back into his reach and in tears found an excuse for silence.

And thinking he had only the natural timidity of maidenhood to overcome, Alec petted and soothed her with words of love. But when they began to speak of the future and to call her again "his own little wife" she at length found courage to tell him it could never be; clinging to him all the while in a despairing way.

"You see you are a Christian: they would never let me marry a Christian," she sobbed out. "It is quite hopeless. Mamma would die of shame. We could not be married in a synagogue, or buried at Willesden, or anything."

As yet Alec did not understand at all. He lived in the world, but had no idea that there was a section of it that held to the views of the ancients on the intermarriage of nations. His mind, not too quick, only took in the words, not the spirit of her objection.

"I don't mind where I'm married," he said. "And as for being buried, I'm not in the slightest hurry."

"Don't, don't."—She could not bear him to treat lightly that which was to her so bitter and so inexorable.

So Alec, becoming aware that the girl was really in earnest and was impressing upon him the existence of an obstacle of which he had not dreamed, set himself to consider the matter in all seriousness. In broken words, and with many sighs, Florrie told him something of the draconic laws of the creed in which she had been educated.

He could not quite understand. It was almost an impossibility that he should. Knowing himself to be fairly well off, fairly well educated, fairly—well, he flattered himself quite fairly—good looking, he had conceived no idea that any difficulty could attach to his wooing and winning the girl of his choice.

A season's waltzing, a few days together on the river, an evening or two like the present, had proved to him conclusively that Florrie Collings was the girl in the world to make him happy. She was yielding; he was masterful. He knew or thought he knew she loved him, and a certain subtle flattery in that preference gratified his vanity, perhaps turned his liking into love.

And he had felt, perhaps, that in asking her to become his wife he was, if not stooping, at least condescending a little. He was no snob, but he knew that man to man his father stood on an infinitely higher social altitude than Florrie's. Collings was a stockbroker. A gentleman might have become a stockbroker, true! But Collings was not a gentleman. Alec's father had been of a county family; his mother was Lady Doveton's only sister. He had imagined, although vaguely, that the Collings's would have perceived his superiority and welcomed him into their midst with more than satisfaction. If he had ever had any doubt it was as to his attitude towards them, as to how he could best limit his intimacy with his future wife's family and escape his friends' chaff anent his unattractive mother in law.

Seeing in her only a vulgar showily dressed middle aged woman, he thought it was from the ordinary type of nouveaux riches he was taking a wife; and he pictured with amusement the snobbish deference that she would pay to his uncle the Baronet.

He had a little exulted in his radicalism and would not be exactly averse to arguing the matter and explaining the merits of democracy and the physical advantages of the marriages between classes; but it seemed all this was not for him. The open arms and the enthusiasm would not be there to greet him—at least so Florrie was trying to impress upon him.

But Florrie might be wrong! In fact he could not but think she overrated the objections that might be raised. He might have to promise to let his wife follow her own religion; but there could be nothing more serious than that, and he endeavoured to impress his hopeful views upon his companion.

95

But Florrie was not to be convinced. Deep down in her heart she felt it was hopeless and the knowledge how far she had drifted from her kindred, and whither her feelings were leading her, shocked her with a sense of disloyalty. She felt desperately wicked and abandoned.

Meanwhile as the lovers were talking the weather was changing. The rapid clouds had massed themselves into gloomy mountains; the sultriness was dissipated by a cold damp wind that seemed to rise from the ground, and then almost without warning a pattering on the leaves was heard and the great raindrops fell heavily.

Startled, the lovers rose. Florrie feared she would be missed. She had wandered away from her parents and Ray with Mrs Cameron. They had met Mr Doveton and Mr Murphy and somehow or other had separated into pairs. Now Florrie yearned for the shelter of a woman's companionship. The first glow of the passion that is the crown and glory of girlhood was damped and chilled; a reaction had set in, a vague sentiment that she had been in danger and had escaped was all that remained behind. To live the pleasure over again in imagination would not come till later.

To return with Alec alone would be to admit that she had been with him all this long time, all this age—for she had lived an age since she had left her companions. She peered vainly into the darkness for the welcome form of Mary. She walked about, regardless of the rain, looking for her. In her state of nervous excitement Alec could give her no comfort.

"Oh, where is Mrs Cameron? I do wish I could find her! Can't you see her?"

"Stop a minute, Florrie! I'll soon see if they're about and if not I'll take you home quite safe; don't be frightened."

"How can you see? It's getting too dark."

Florrie was crying with the terror of a lost child.

"Coo-ey, coo-ey" sounded from her side; an answering "coo-ey" came from a little distance. Charlie and Alec had too often bird nested in Doveton woods, had hidden too often, after some boyish transgression, in the thickets around the Hall, not to have devised a means of communication. And now Alec bethought himself of the old double whistle of his boyhood.

Mrs Cameron had been almost as anxious to find Florrie as Florrie had been to find her, for she did not wish to rejoin Mrs Collings alone after the girl had been entrusted to her care.

Florrie clung to her arm availing herself in silence of the shelter of her umbrella.

"We must hurry," said Mary in her clear tones. "They are playing 'God save the Queen' now. If we go this way we shall be at the gate by the time your people come out. We will bid you gentlemen good night now," she went on. "We can manage quite well by ourselves," and she extended her hand.

It was a very rapid parting, but Alec just found time to whisper Florrie an appointment for the morrow. Then Mary hurried them away diplomatically, and rejoined their party at the park gate.

It was a loud and noticeable party. The Collingses, the Detmars, and their friends were all gesticulating and talking at the top of their voices without any regard for the fact that they were in a place of public resort. The advent of Mary and Florrie passed quite unheeded, for a terrible event had happened and they were all engrossed in commentary and discussion.

One of Mrs Detmar's little ones was missing. He had been with them all the evening—at least they thought he had although now they remembered they had not seen him for the last quarter of an hour. In the midst of their vain search the inspector informed them he must close the park: it was half past ten. It was dreadful to think of poor little Isaac being shut up by himself in that great dark place all night. Mrs Detmar threatened hysterics. It took Mrs Collings and Mrs Lucas and the

97

whole party all their time to keep up her spirits. What wonder under such circumstances that no one noticed the tear stained cheeks and general agitation of the girl?

Isaac was found at last; by the tea stall, with his pocket full of buns. He had been bargaining for a seventh for his sixpence, pointing out that as they would not keep fresh until tomorrow they might just as well let him have them on his own terms. This argument had finally prevailed.

David Detmar was so delighted with his child's sharpness that he would not allow him to be scolded for his truancy; so his weeping mother folded him to her heart, and all was forgiven.

As Mrs Cameron was staying at the Queen's Hotel and Mrs Collings and her sister had a large house in the Seaside Road they all walked home together. Florrie quite silent but Mary taking her part in the general conversation.

But when she was alone in the solitude of her room at the Queen's she allowed herself to think and her thoughts took dangerous shape.

She thought of Florrie and pitied her that she could have no solitude but would be compelled to put up with Ray's companionship and her constant self satisfied conversation.

Why did she take interest in Florrie, and in Florrie's love affair? She knew herself too well to take credit for philanthropy. Charlie Doveton and Alec Murphy were cousins; but what was that to her who was bound by every possible tie to Dr Benjamin Phillips.

Well, Charlie amused her; and she had lately been very conscious how little amusement life had offered her. Yet she was a very beautiful woman. The buzz of admiration with which she had been greeted at the Collings's party and Charlie's adoration had opened her eyes to this fact. And since she had been in Eastbourne she had noticed admiration on many a countenance.

There was nothing retiring about her loveliness: it flashed upon the passer by and compelled him to look again. Yet, excepting Benjamin Phillips, she had never had a lover, or as she put it to herself, she had never had a chance. She began to reproach herself for having taken the first thing that offered, and even to blame Benjamin for taking advantage of her youth, forgetting for the moment how very ready she had been to be taken advantage of.

She thought if she had waited she might have married—perhaps have made a rich marriage. She almost felt herself blush in the darkness. Charlie's adoration was so humble, he treated her as a goddess unto whom he dared not aspire; and the thought how far removed she was from his ideal almost made her feel ashamed.

But she had always kept him at a distance, was very circumspect in her behaviour to him; by nature a cold woman, she had not found that difficult. But his respect, his fair smooth face beaming with smiles when he saw her, his bashful compliments, all this pleased her; and the fact that his uncle was a Baronet did not lessen her pleasure in his devotion.

If she had been really a widow now instead of being so absolutely dependent upon one man that if she failed to please him he could leave her at any moment utterly penniless; had she been a widow with a large jointure she might have thought seriously about Charlie. She could not help these ideas coming to her.

She would have liked to have known something of his estates, whether he was dependent on his uncle, what sort of a place Bourne Hall was. Not that it was anything to her, but the inquiry was interesting. Alec Murphy would know. He was much older than Charlie and had great influence over him; and there was no doubt Charlie thought a great deal of his opinion.

That brought her back to the starting point of her reverie: her interest in Florrie Collings's love affair.

Certainly she would help her if she could; it must be awful to live constantly with Ray, poor little girl! and Mary knew quite enough of Judaism to be aware that the family would not regard a Christian alliance with favour. Alec was bound to be grateful to her for any little help she was able to give him.

All the time she was thinking she undressed slowly and luxuriously. Her room was one of the best in the house, and The Queen's is a good hotel. She was never stinted in money matters; Benjamin Phillips was a liberal, almost uncalculating paymaster.

The moon that shone forth after the rain showed her white shoulders and bare arms. The window was open, the distant breaking of the waves on the stony beach was pleasant to her, and she could see herself better in the moonlight than by the candle.

She gazed Narcissus-like, self fascinated, into her mirror. Whiter than the white satin stays and whiter than the lace that edged her chemise shone her shapely limbs and above all the aureole of pale gold hair. She took a hand glass and noted a dimple on the shoulder that Benjamin had often told her of. The curved lines from under her ear to her arm, from under the chin to the rounded bust were perfect.

Graceful and beautiful she saw herself. And the knowledge that all this beauty was but for him, the memory of his rough beard against her delicate skin, caused a revulsion of feeling. Abruptly she closed the window and drew the blinds, completed her disrobing and got into bed, the last idea she was conscious of as she sank to sleep being a sense of freedom because Benito was in Egypt and she in Eastbourne.

In the same hotel, in a small close room at the top of the house, lay the little child who called her mother. Nita was broad awake. The summer storm had frightened her, but she did not like to wake Nannie so she sobbed as quietly as she could, her dark untidy locks grown damp and her bed tumbled and hot. As she thought of the doctor, who used to come and tell her pretty stories and take her in his arms and let her sleep there, her sobs grew heavier and her baby grief deeper, for she felt that now her dear doctor was away there was no one to love her.

Book II · Chapter II

The beach at Eastbourne is stony and unsatisfactory, but the sea walk that runs above it is very pleasant. The morning after Murphy had asked Florrie the fateful question dawned bright and clear. The air was warm, even before the sun had risen; the sea was calm but flecked with foam.

Alec was at the trysting place first, but he had not even had time to get uneasy before Florrie, in her fresh print dress, with her untidy locks curling beneath her sailor hat, came round the corner. She met him timidly and blushingly, and they walked side by side in the pleasant air for a few moments, talking of the weather.

Lovers are so strange.

Alec had on a suit of flannels, striped like a Neapolitan ice; a linen shirt and collar preserved in him that appearance of being well dressed, which was one of his characteristics, a brown pot hat went well with this attire. Florrie was undeniably proud of her lover's appearance. She felt awfully wicked meeting him like this; and she had told Ray she was going for a swim with Mrs Cameron. However, she made up her mind she would never meet him surreptitiously again. Only just this once it was necessary, so that she might tell him how impossible it would be in the future.

"Well, Florrie, have you been thinking over our last night's conversation?"

Had she been thinking it over? Why, she had never once closed her eyes all night! She had kept awake on purpose, just to go over it again and again, so as not to forget a word or a look. She did not tell him this. Still he was satisfied.

Then they talked of each other and found endless

interest in the topic. She confessed she had been almost jealous of Ray; and they laughed together over one of Ray's dictatorial little speeches. But that reminded Florrie of her allegiance, and her conscience smote her. It had been very delightful; but she must go home, now; and never meet him again, and...and "Goodbye!" She held out her hand, but averted her eyes lest he should see the ready tears in them.

He began to reason with her, but it is very difficult to reason with a woman. She repeated again and again that if she married him she would not be allowed to be buried among her people, or to "go to synagogue or anything"; and yet he somehow failed to appreciate the terrors of the punishment.

He said he should speak to her father, and that prospect roused her into fresh expostulations. She begged and implored him not to.

"I shall never be allowed to talk to you again, or to go out without Ray, or to go to Kensington or anywhere. They will think it is all my fault—that I've encouraged you, Papa will be so dreadfully angry with me. Oh, Alec, don't!"

It is not very difficult to persuade a young man to avoid a dreaded interview with Papa, so Alec consented to wait.

"As long as you meet me when I ask you, and write to me and do as I tell you, and are not frightened, I'll wait a little while. But, look here, Florrie! There must be no humbugging or shilly-shallying. I'll be civil to your people and let them see as much of me as possible. Then, when they are used to me and know that though I have the misfortune to be born a Christian I am a very harmless person, I shall tell your father exactly what I want and if there's a row we must brave it out together. You must not tell me any more that we can't marry. I mean to marry you and it's not a bit of use discussing the subject any more."

This sounded very reassuring; anyway Florrie was respited from the "speaking to Papa," which had terrified her so. She made a sort of compromise with her conscience and decided to "break it off" gradually. Very weak and troubled was Florrie. Perhaps her weakness appealed to her strong, tall lover. Certainly her prettiness did. The rising sun made her look very

104

fair, the ringlets of hair on her forehead were tinged with gold, and the soft down on her cheek showed seductively in the strong sunlight.

It came across Alec's mind that although it was daylight and they were on the public promenade, still it was too early for anyone to be about and he might just as well have a kiss, if only to remind her that she belonged to him.

He put his project into immediate execution.

They were on that rounded portion of the sea walk that leads to the public promenade. Florrie had no time to protest, and even Alec felt a little ashamed of himself, as Mrs Cameron came full round the corner and greeted them with a smile. It was quite useless for them to try to look unconscious; she could not have missed seeing them. Florrie's shame was painful to witness. Mrs Cameron drew Florrie's arm into hers and walked on a moment with them.

"I'm very sorry," she commenced.

"You needn't be," said Alec, taking his course quickly. "I am sure you will help me. I have been trying to persuade this little girl to marry me. She puts me off with some excuse about differences of religion; and I have promised to wait a little while before I go to her father."

Mrs Cameron was somewhat taken aback by this sudden confidence. The thought just crossed her mind, not without bitterness, that if this outspoken young man knew rightly who she was he would not have been so ready to enter into particulars anent his promised wife.

But she threw off the feeling and entered readily into the situation, promising her help, and soothing Florrie by the mere fact of her womanhood. She walked up and down with them, listening while Alec gave her the brief outline of his design. To get them accustomed to him before he spoke out; that was his idea; and it sounded to Mary a very feasible one.

105

She promised her help, and was rather surprised at herself for doing so.

She was very intimate with the Collings's now. Mrs Collings, having once given way, had seemingly forgotten her distrust; and as for Mr Collings, he admired Mrs Cameron very much, and occasionally told her so. She had received this confidence with such modesty and tact that the gentleman now thought very highly of her and occasionally trusted his daughters to her chaperonage.

She asked Florrie to dine with her at the Queen's and talk it over. As Ray was already rather jealous of Mrs Cameron's friendship Florrie did not think she would be able to go. It was no uncommon thing for Ray on hearing of such an invitation to coolly substitute herself.

"I am the eldest; she must have meant me, only you were there. Besides, I mean to go. Mamma says I am to."

Arguing thus, Ray had more than once unexpectedly inflicted her company on Mrs Cameron. But now the latter promised Florrie to make diplomatic provision against such a difficulty.

Then she advised Florrie to go home. The town was beginning to stir; and if she was supposed to be bathing she would do well to wet her hair before letting herself be seen. Dreadfully ashamed, Florrie went down on to the beach and followed out the suggestion.

Mrs Cameron advised Murphy not to see the girl home.

The sun was getting hot now, so Mary put up her red parasol, which tinted her pale features and enhanced her beauty.

But Murphy looked at her unadmiringly. She was too statuesque; not his style; his mind was filled by a different picture. He thanked her, however, for her promised help; and she gave him the invitation for the evening that he so evidently expected. Then he left her to go to his hotel and she walked on alone.

She had a letter from Dr Phillips in her pocket unopened, and she had come out to read it.

He was still in Egypt, fulfilling a position of trust and, to a certain extent, honour. Six or seven years ago the work he was doing would have filled him with enthusiasm and intellectual pleasure. Now—well, even now he was still competent, his reports clear, his style concise; his colleagues liked and trusted him and his editor was satisfied.

He himself was not satisfied. The close atmosphere of the dirty hospitals—an atmosphere by the way in which his whole manhood had developed—weighed upon him and affected his health and spirits. His iron constitution suffered under the horrors of an Egyptian summer. He worked painfully and with an effort; and, true to his instincts, he redoubled that effort so that those with whom he was working should see in him no loss of vigour. He was rewarded when he heard them remark on his extraordinary vitality.

Mrs Phillips was in Ischl, surrounded by a throng of German relatives. She took baths, and wrote regularly and complacently to her husband on their effect. He replied to her letters with difficulty, and even found little pleasure in writing to Mary.

He could hardly bring himself to write to her unreservedly. He never had written to her until this separation; their intercourse had been uninterrupted. Very early in his life circumstances had impressed upon him the principle *litera scripta manet*; and, notwithstanding his apparent security, a reticence was still observable in his letters.

But, little as he wrote, and meagre as were his letters, Mary and her child were constantly in his mind. He slept badly; a sort of low, intermittent fever hung about him and prevented his resting. In the silent watches of those close and wretched nights two forms were ever as a mirage before his eyes. When he fell into a short doze he fancied he was with them—always tantalisingly near

107

and not near enough. And his mind dwelt persistently upon Nita's fragility and Mary's inexperience.

Of this subject his present letter was full. Mary read it on one of the seats on the sea walk, her red parasol shielding her from the hot sun and marking her out a conspicuous object in the midst of the wearisome glare.

In the letter he always alluded to the child as "Nita," or as "your little daughter."

"Don't let her go out after five or six o'clock," he wrote, "nor in the heat of the day. I should let her play on the beach until about eleven or eleven thirty and then sleep. From four to five thirty or six will be a good time for a country walk." And more in the same strain.

Mary tore up the letter when she had read it through, but still sat thinking of it.

Nannie looked after Nita. She herself had not bothered about making these or any other arrangements; but now she came to think of it she did remember how Nita had been looking a little pale and fragile the last day or two. The thought was an annoyance to her. The child was her only duty, but she hated duty. One of the strangest and most unnatural things about this beautiful woman was the absence of maternal feeling.

She was conscious of this, and it irritated her—against Nita. She knew that as a rule women in her position found their greatest happiness in their offspring. That it was not so with her she attributed to the child's ugliness. Knowing she failed in her duty toward it, she disliked the thought, the memory, and above all the presence of the babe.

Perhaps circumstances had been against her. She had been unable to nurse her child, and her only remembrance of the first few months of its existence, beyond the physical weakness left after its birth, was the sound of its feeble but constant crying which the thin walls and limited architectural arrangements of Alfred Place had been unable to shut out.

The first instinct of maternal love follows from the feeling that another life is utterly dependent on one's own. That feeling Mary had never had; the child had always looked to Nannie for its bottle, for its clean linen, for its powder, and all the other little necessities of baby life.

She had felt it her duty to see it once or twice a day, but it always cried when she took it, which Nannie attributed to incompetence in handling and Mary to a reciprocated want of affection on the part of the child.

Perhaps there is nothing loveable in an ailing, crying, dark skinned baby, and excuse might be made for Mary if the child had failed to arouse enthusiasm in her during its first year or two of life. But even when an awakening soul, an awakening mind, began to look out of the baby's black eyes the mother, who should have been ready with response and guidance, still felt and saw nothing.

Nannie's soul was a limited one, but the doctor had recognised its existence. Nita's eyes had found answer only in her unacknowledged father's and her little breast was filled with adoration for him. Between the two there was today a link that would have brought joy to a student of the occult science. Benjamin Phillips was pining in Egypt and Nita was pining in Eastbourne. Mary was well and happy.

Only yesterday Nannie had drawn her attention to Nita's languid looks, of which Phillips's letter had reminded her. She made up her mind she would see to it, but was bored at the thought.

She got up to walk homeward; she met Doveton and they strolled along the still empty promenade together. She rather lost her sense of boredom; it was so amusing to watch his eagerness to agree with her in everything and his struggles to express and at the same time restrain his feelings.

She was not even herself quite conscious how interested she was in his endeavours to please her. She played with his hopes, encouraging him by a glance and cooling him down by the turn of a phrase. Her newly discovered powers pleased her. She had never coquetted with Benito—at least not in the same way.

Altogether it was a very pleasant walk, and she forgot her resolutions about Nita. Nita was already out for the morning when she finally reached the Queen's, for in consequence of Doveton's entreaties they had sauntered twice up and down the esplanade. They lingered indeed until the advent of the flower women and the fruit sellers, of bun purveyors and other itinerant gentry warned her that the fashionable hour for promenading was at hand.

The walk gave Mary much food for thought. She became contemplative and introspective. She questioned herself on a subject to which till now she had never given a thought. That subject was love.

She took her bonnet off slowly, looking in the glass the while. The blind was half down, the room cool. She sat on the chintz easy chair and wondered.

Love: such love as Alec and Florrie felt! Well, that was to her a sealed book; she had never loved Benito like that. Charlie Doveton...she smiled at the idea, and found it pleasant. He was certainly very much in love with her. The smile changed to a frown as her thoughts passed involuntarily to Dr Phillips. She remembered she had his letter to answer. She hated having anything to do; then it occurred to her that it was after all better to have to write than to have him with her. Her sensations were something like those of a schoolgirl in holiday time.

Dr Phillips had not done wisely in leaving Mary Cameron to herself just now; her mind was in too receptive a condition. He who had never trusted had been for once too trustful.

If he could only have known how Mary was leaning back in that comfortable chintz chair with a smile on her lips and Charlie Doveton's image in her mind he would have found Egypt even hotter and more intolerable than ever.

Not that she was in love with Charlie Doveton. She was right in her estimate of herself; love was impossible to her. But she was interested. The easy way in which she had yielded to Benjamin Phillips ought to have opened his eyes to her disposition. She was not of the stuff good women are made of; or even faithful mistresses.

She found herself thinking of Charlie; allowed her thoughts to drift that way very unrestrainedly. She speculated on his home and his uncle. Whether he was very proud, whether... There is no saying what she thought of, or what she did not think of!

Book II · Chapter III

After a somewhat heated discussion with Ray, Florrie was allowed to dine at the Queen's.

The woman who had tasted the Tree of Knowledge and the girl whose innermost spirit was yearning for the unplucked fruit sat face to face. Florrie made small pretence of eating, for her soul was large within her, and from the smell of the strong meat she turned away with loathing.

But when the silent meal was ended, and together the two women stood on the balcony in the moonlight, out of the fullness of her heart her mouth spake. Mary took the low garden seat, Florrie sank on a stool at her feet, nestling against her skirts, hiding her face from the light for very shame of her love. She spoke hopelessly, yet in the hopelessness might be detected hope. Mrs Cameron listened sympathetically and made light of the difficulties.

"My dear child," the elder woman said authoritatively, as if she knew all about it, "when they know you care for him very much and have quite made up your mind to marry him, you will find they will give way. It is quite out of date to make trouble about religious differences. Though," she added, reflectively, "your people *are* rather behind the times in these matters." And she smiled at the remembrance of some speeches on the subject that Dr Phillips had repeated to her.

Florrie tried vainly to comfort herself.

"They will never agree; I know they never will. I wouldn't have them know for the world. I am going to tell him so tonight. Oh, Mrs Cameron, help me to make him see it. It will kill me to ... to break it off; but it's no good, I know it isn't."

"Nonsense, child. He won't let you 'break it off,' as you call it. Besides, you don't want to. How can you be so silly?"

"What would Ray think if she knew?"

"She would probably be dreadfully jealous," replied Mrs Cameron, coolly, "and would consequently make herself as unpleasant as possible."

This was not quite a new idea to Florrie, and it was one that went further than any other in loosening the hold Ray had on her. Ray certainly liked Alec very much. As long as he had paid her attention she had never made any allusions to his Christianity; but lately—ever since their dance, in fact—she had talked a great deal about it and scolded Florrie very much, in her hard dictatorial manner, for having danced so frequently with him on that occasion.

Last evening, too, she had made some nasty remarks about his coming to Eastbourne.

"So intrusive!" she had said. But Florrie had thought Eastbourne was open to everybody.

"Do you think he would become a Jew?" at length, after a pause, during which Mary's thoughts had wandered far from her, she asked timidly.

"Good heavens! Do you think a white man would consent to go about with his face permanently blacked?" Mary was startled into replying.

This was a new view of her religion for Florrie, but she had no time to ask any further questions because just then Doveton and Murphy made their appearance.

It had struck Charlie as permissible to call on Mrs Cameron at her hotel that evening.

Casually at dinner he had said to his cousin that he should stroll down to the Queen's after dinner, and Alec had replied he was going there too. Charlie looked up nervously.

"Are *you* going then?" he asked with obvious surprise and annoyance in his tone.

Alec resented the annoyance, and revenged himself

113

by simply replying that he was and not explaining his motive for so doing.

Charlie was in that rabid state of love that admits of only one thought. He was quite ready to be wildly jealous of anyone, and he walked silently and sulkily from the Cavendish to the Queen's, harbouring all manner of unjust thoughts against his amused companion.

But after the pair of them had been about five minutes on the balcony he grew comforted. He remembered the confidences Alec had made him about "a little girl" and he recognised Florrie under that designation.

The moon was in full beauty; it silvered the sea and the reflected light warred with the lamps on the sitting room table. Mary sat still on the low chair, but Florrie had risen from the stool, and she and Alec soon went into the room and left the others to the solitude of the balcony.

Charlie had never felt so near to his divinity as now; the soft beams of the moon, the dreamy warmth of the atmosphere, with the calm sea and sense of isolation in the midst of it, entered into his veins and intoxicated him.

He stood by her side, leaning against the balcony. Mary was cool enough and calm enough, and felt particularly happy and comfortable after her good dinner, and the little glow of benevolence she experienced in having provided Alec with the opportunity of meeting his little love.

"Mrs Cameron," began Charlie in a low voice. Then he stopped short.

"Are you admiring the view, Mr Doveton?" asked Mary, banteringly.

He turned and looked at her.

"I don't admire anything but you," he blurted out.

Mrs Cameron laughed.

114

"Don't laugh; at least you needn't laugh at me," he said in a voice full of hurt feeling and pain.

"I must laugh if you are so tragic. It is very kind of you to admire me; but that need not interfere with your appreciation of nature."

"It interferes with everything. I can't think of anything else." He was still speaking very low, but any woman could hear the emotion in his voice. He was feeling too much to be eloquent. He waited for some encouragement.

"Tell me something about your chance in this tournament," said Mrs Cameron hurriedly. She could not allow him to become definite for obvious reasons.

"I don't care for the tournament."

"But I do. I should like to see you win."

"Would you, would you, really?" he asked excitedly. "Then I will win. You'll come and see us play, won't you?"

And she promised. Then she allowed the young man to take the stool at her feet. He sat there adoring. She fenced with him very cleverly, letting him compliment her, letting him imply his devotion; but by light laughter and all the armoury women have at their command keeping him to the indefiniteness of implication. He was happy and yet not happy. He was in the company of the woman he loved and she was kind to him; but yet it was not the kindness he wanted. Somehow or other she made him feel very young and boyish, and she would not let him tell her how he loved her.

Sitting there at her feet in the darkness, he kissed her gown. She saw the gesture and rose at once.

"Come," she said, but more coolly than she had spoken yet, "it is getting too cold here for me."

"Mrs Cameron, Mary, don't go yet." He rose too and put out a restraining arm.

"Mr Doveton"—this with dignity—"kindly allow

me to pass." She looked at him but the pleading in his eyes did not move her. He saw then she would not hear him, and together they went in.

In the meantime Florrie had had her opportunity of telling Alec all must be over between them. But she had apparently not made very stern use of it; for the tableau that presented itself to Mrs Cameron and Charlie was an embarrassing not to say embracing one, from which the young couple disengaged themselves as rapidly and unblushingly as possible.

Charlie made a sort of half apology to Alec as they walked home together; and Alec freely forgave him.

"But mind, old fellow, it was uncommonly stupid of you, and if you'd have asked me what I was going for I'd have told you in a minute. She is a dear little girl. How did you get on?"

"Oh, all right," answered Charlie in an offhand manner; and Alec questioned him no further. He was very well satisfied with the progress of his own affair. Happy in the possession of the whole heart of the young girl that loved him, he thought little or nothing of the objections she raised. They loved each other—that was enough for him just now—and secret meetings and stolen kisses were all the harvest he wanted.

Charlie did not feel so cheerful; but yet he was not altogether cast down. He believed she liked him. She seemed to like his society; only she wouldn't let him tell her all he felt for her. She put a sort of barrier between them, as if she were much older and wiser than he. And he didn't know how to break down this barrier, how to persuade her, how to ask her... The very thought of what he wanted to ask her made his cheek flush, and he quickened his step.

"Where are you off to?" asked Alec, surprised and endeavouring to keep up with him.

"I'm going for a walk; it's so hot. Don't be offended."

"Not a bit; in fact I'll come with you." But Charlie wanted to be by himself and he said so. He wanted to

116

think it over. He lay down on the beach near the incoming tide and let the monotonous breaking of the little wavelets on the stones accompany his thoughts.

He *would* ask her, to that he made up his mind; she must give him an opportunity sooner or later. If she refused him—he could not have felt very hopeful or that would not have been the first alternative to present itself—he would go abroad. He could never settle down again at the Hall and go through the dull round of his daily life. The very thought sickened him; he could not face it. He let his thoughts wander into groves of delight. He pictured her at the Hall. He saw his uncle emerging from his solitude to hand her in to dinner, to accompany her through the picture gallery, to do the honours of his ancient home to her.

Charlie's uncle was a scholarly recluse; it was to an agent he owed the prosperity of his estate. And this same agent, the keeper of his conscience, had assisted him in bringing up his heir. Charlie knew more about the estate than its owner could ever learn, and loved it better. When, at the age of eighteen, he had left Eton he had himself decided against going to college; and Mr Hailsham had helped him by so representing the matter to his uncle that there had been no obstacles placed in his path.

With Mr Hailsham and Mr Hailsham's sons he had hunted and shot and fished; played cricket and tennis and rackets. He had lived an open air life, honest and contented. His will had never clashed with his uncle's, or with anyone's for that matter. Everyone liked the cheery athletic young man and life had offered him nothing more desirable than that which he was contented to enjoy.

He had many neighbours and many friends, and until this visit to London he had not thought of any change in the country gentleman's life that he was leading so contentedly.

But now he felt he could never return to it. Then he

117

thought again of his uncle and wondered how he would take it. It was not from a material point of view that he cared; he knew the estate was entailed, and he had his mother's money as well. But he had a conscience; his uncle had been unvaryingly kind to him, and he knew he ought to go to him before he took such an important step as he contemplated.

Charlie was four and twenty and he had never been in love before. His fears were much stronger than his hopes, but hope was all there for all that. It was the feeling of her superiority that inspired his fears. He felt country bred and coarse beside her. She was a widow and she had a child; but he put away from his mind any misgivings he might have had on that score. Mary spoke so little of the child; the child was so little with her that it was easy to forget or ignore it. If only she could care for him; that was the burden of his thoughts. He had an idea his uncle did not think very highly of him: looked down rather upon his pursuits and ways of life. He felt that if he could secure for his own this clever and beautiful woman his uncle's respect would be augmented.

A long time he lay there on the stones within sound of the sea, and in the air of the warm summer night.

It was the love of a very young man for a woman who is older than himself—adoring and respectful. It was almost sacrilege to think of marriage, to picture her descending from her level to put herself on his. And yet he could not but think of it; and thinking he decided not to consult his uncle. Not to write to Mr Hailsham. If—and what a pregnant "if" that was—he succeeded in his suit, then they should all know her. He pictured his pride in introducing her to his friends. She could talk of books to his uncle and sport to his friends. His pride would be too much for him. It was a future almost too dazzling to look into. Poor Charlie!

The summer days went on, and to everyone was vouchsafed a measure of happiness. The Moseses and

Levys, the Jeddingtons and Collingses and Jacobses and all their German friends who had come to visit them and take the sea air in the summer met in the morning and discussed the relative dearness of Eastbourne and Maida Vale. Mr Simmons, the butcher, had his shop so full of them sometimes that he found it quite impossible to attend to any other customers. They liked meeting each other and they never seemed to have too much of each other's society.

After they had made their provision for the day they all went on the parade together to listen to the band. Some walked up and down; the girls in showy dresses and carrying tennis bats and shoes which they never used, while the mothers, fat and comfortable, sat down to commence the gossip that was to go on all day.

Mrs Detmar in a bath chair was the centre of a group, and frequently Mrs Cameron was with her. A bath chair did not mean that Mrs Detmar was ailing; it was merely the outward and visible sign of her superior wealth. She could not be on the parade in her carriage; to take a chair and pay a penny for it was to put herself on a level with her friends. So she came in a bath chair with a cushion at her back and a stool at her feet and explained to everyone who did not know that it was quite worth while to pay two shillings an hour for a comfortable seat.

These Jewesses, who fill Eastbourne from July to September and contribute much to the wellbeing of the town, are very gregarious. They separate at luncheon, certainly; and many of them take that meal with their children; but after luncheon they meet again in parties of threes and fours in each other's houses and play cards until half past four or five.

It was during this hour that Mrs Cameron and Charlie, Florrie and Alec enjoyed most of their walks and talks. Florrie's good resolutions were cast to the winds. She was not like a girl who had been brought up in an atmosphere of lovemaking and flirtation. Mrs

119

Collings had looked well after her girls until she saw, or thought she saw, that Ray was capable of taking her place. Florrie had not frittered away her affections; she was of a clinging and confiding nature, not very strong; and she came gradually to love and cling to Mrs Cameron and Alec. Alec was an ideal lover, not humble and fearful like Charlie but masterful and claiming as a right what Charlie would have sued for as an inestimable privilege. She succumbed utterly to his masterfulness, and gave up even thinking of the future. She trusted blindly in him and awaited events.

It is difficult to know what motive actuated Mary in helping these young people. But she did, and that effectually; and Alec, as well as Florrie, liked her for it. And Alec, when he spoke of her to Charlie, did so in high terms.

Charlie went through every phase of emotion in these days. Mary bantered him and laughed at him and played with him, and his humility and submission would have been oppressive to a woman of a different mind.

Perhaps she never had been so happy as she was just now. The only drawback to her lot was the necessity of writing twice a week to Dr Phillips to tell him she was miserable without him and to give him details as to Nita's health. The feeling of indifference towards Nita began to change at this time to active dislike. To be forced to inquire of Nurse about her and to give descriptions of her wearied and annoyed her. She was impatient of the smallest duty. Nita had an attack of bronchitis and they had had to send for a doctor.

When Dr Polegate came Nita had cried herself ill; she could do nothing but sob and cough. She had heard the doctor was coming and had looked forward to having her dear Doctor to love and comfort her weak little body and yearning little mind. The reaction at seeing a strange man was too much for her.

Mary was in the room preparing to pose as the anxious mother, but her plans were upset; she was powerless to comfort her child and did not even attempt to do so. She lost her temper with her and finally left the room. After that there was one man in Eastbourne who knew Mary Cameron as she was and was not led away by his external senses.

Mary was very angry with herself afterwards for her impatience, and for having exhibited it before Dr Polegate. Dr Polegate was a shining light in Eastbourne, a friend of Dr Phillips, and it was to him, as each autumn with its migration of Jews to Eastbourne came round, he was in the habit of handing over all his patients. Mary's anger with herself soon died away but left a new sense of resentment against unconscious little Nita.

Perhaps it was this incident which made Mary more gentle towards Charlie. Her kindness was such that the most sensitive of men could not have taken her nominal refusal to hear him as a dismissal.

She certainly liked his attentions, his flowers, his devotion, the fact that he neither had nor assumed any rights, and that she had no appearances to keep up. The two pairs of lovers met daily; but danger was ahead, in the shape of Ray. Ray had had her suspicions aroused by Florrie's going every afternoon to Mrs Cameron's. Twice she had insisted on accompanying her. Once Florrie had been able to warn Alec, but the second time Ray met him. In the evening she had cross questioned Florrie very severely as to how often the latter had met him; and the defendant had equivocated and answered evasively.

Ray scented mischief and determined to watch.

Book II · Chapter IV

Such was the position of affairs on the day of the final heat of the South of England Tennis Tournament. Florrie and Alec were engaged but had for the present dropped all talk of matrimony. Charlie, on the other hand, was not engaged, but he was passionately in love and only waited a hearing. Mary was happy and had merely let things drift. Her thoughts were not coherent, and she did not definitely meditate any infidelity to Dr Phillips, from whom, by the way, she had not heard for some days.

Devonshire Park was full. The rope that kept people from approaching too near the courts was constantly agitated by a struggling crowd. Front places were eagerly sought for. Prominent among those that had secured them were our friends the Collinges, the whole family of them; and they were as usual surrounded by their coreligionists.

Mrs Cameron had come in late; she had been unable to approach her friends and was seated on the other side of the court, at right angles to the side where they were.

The final heat was to be played, and by a curious complication of fate it had to be contended for by Alec and Charlie, who had outlasted all competitors.

Charlie had kept a seat for Mrs Cameron. She was in grey that day—white and grey. Her pure flesh tints came out well against this combination. She was slightly flushed with the heat, and her eyes were bright and clear. The pale yellow of her hair blended well with the faint colouring of her costume. Her beauty acted upon Charlie's excitement to an alarming extent. She felt his hand tremble as she placed hers in it.

"Well, do you feel like victory?" she asked him,

lightly, as she settled herself in her chair and prepared to enjoy the spectacle.

"There is only one victory I care for," he answered. He was unable to take his eyes off her. He was oblivious of his surroundings; they seemed to have melted away, and he was only conscious of the presence of one beautiful woman.

"Win this to begin with," she answered, smiling at him, as she unfurled her parasol and leaned back luxuriously.

"If I win this may I take it as an omen? May I ask you for the other?" He was eager to a degree in asking this question and Mary, who was by no means unaware that she was surrounded by people, was startled at his vehemence.

He felt certain of victory if he had this assurance to start with. The umpire was on his box; the line umpires in place. Alec was already on the ground. But Charlie did not stir.

"They are ready for you," she said, rather feebly.

"I shan't go till you've answered me, Mary!"

His ardent young face was close to hers, flushed with expectation and longing. Already many curious eyes were turned in the direction where the would-be champion was dallying with his lady love. And the publicity was not to Mary's taste.

"Very well," she said. Anything to get rid of him.

"If I win, you will let me?" he asked again with a certainty of triumph in his voice.

"And if you lose you won't worry me any more?" she asked lightly.

"Honour bright, I promise. Shake hands on it," he asked pleadingly.

She held out her hand.

"My darling," he said, clasping it closely. There were positive tears in his brown eyes and his emotion transfigured his face. He went forth to the combat like a young Hercules, with a certainty of a double victory.

124

Mary comforted herself for her imprudence by the recollection that Florrie had told her Alec was certain of victory.

Florrie was very nervous and anxious. She would have liked to be alone to watch her love's prowess and glory in his power and skill. The bystanders jarred on her and irritated her nerves. She was in a state of continual nervous excitement now, increased by Ray's questionings, suspicions, and espionage.

"Want a fiver on, Dave?" said Mr Collings to Dave Detmar, who was standing by him. "I'll back the young'un."

"You'll have to lay me odds," answered Dave, who like his companion found little interest in any amusement whereby no money changed hands.

"All right, five to four."

"Make it to three, and it's done."

"Then be it so. You like a bit the best of it, don't you Dave?"

"Nonsense! What's-his-name—Doveton isn't it?—is almost a certainty. I wouldn't bet at all, only to oblige you."

Mr Collings laughed, and David himself smiled at the idea of his disinterestedness. Mr Collings offered the same odds to any of the bystanders. Some of them frowned, some took no notice, one or two made audible observations about Jews.

The match was going too unevenly to be exciting. Certainly it was only the first set, but five games to one had been scored by Doveton and Alec's one had only been secured by the opponent's being "faulted" for having his foot within the line. Charlie was playing brilliantly. Nothing escaped him; he was all over the court at once. Some of his volleys were magnificent. With both hands he banged the ball down until it rose far above Alec's head, nearly at the end of the court.

"It's a walk-over," said a young man, one of the

defeated candidates, who was following the scoring with great interest.

"Walk over!" replied his companion contemptuously. "It will be a match, and a very fine one. Have you ever seen Murphy play? You don't understand his game, he always begins like this. Besides, Doveton can't stay—not in this form anyhow. Look at him now. Why it's only the first set and he's obliged to pull himself together with a lemon drink; and even then he's blowing like a grampus. Alec Murphy will simply sit upon him presently, you watch!"

But that was not the general opinion, which was very much in Doveton's favour. Both young men looked well in their athletic dress. Charlie was in white flannel, and a white flannel cricketing cap. His face was very much flushed, he looked handsome, and all the ladies hoped he would win.

Alex had a silk shirt and wore knickerbockers instead of trousers. He was a better made man than his opponent, although not so tall. His neat brown stockings showed a well turned calf. Through the light silk of his shirt you could see the shape of his fine shoulders and chest. His sun browned face was not flushed; he was rather paler than usual but looked quite calm, almost unconcerned. The two young men exchanged smiles and nods as they changed sides; they made it evident to the spectators that their rivalry, although new, was friendly.

Charlie spoke to no one, but Alec was sufficiently self possessed to exchange a few chaffing words with some of the young men about. They wanted to rally him into playing better.

"Try and hit a ball," said one.

"Why don't you give it him?" said another. "It's a waste of time playing it out."

"Remember the balls are to go over, not under, the net, Alec, old chappie!" said a third.

"Don't worry, you fellows," answered Alec good temperedly. "You shall have a good long drink out of the cup tonight. You know that's all you're anxious about."

"Not a bit of it, it's the honour of the club," said a member of the LAC. "You're chucking it away."

Alec only laughed and took his place again. But Florrie was very far from sharing his calmness. At every stroke her heart bounded against her side. At every score to Charlie she could have cried with disappointment. She wanted Alec to win. She knew he wanted to win, to gain the honour of the championship for his club, although he was sorry it was against Charlie he was pitted.

She could not hide her agitation from Ray's sharp eyes, as the second set went on and again Charlie was triumphant.

Then Alec came to them for an instant. Florrie could scarcely speak to him for her agitation, but she looked up at him with a face full of sympathy.

He smiled. "It's all right," he said. "Don't you worry, I mean winning; just watch, that's all." And he gave her a reassuring and familiar nod as he went off again.

"Well," said Ray, full of indignation, "I never saw anything so impertinent. Why, he's lost two sets already, and he doesn't play anything like as well as Mr Doveton."

"What did he mean by telling you not to worry, Florrie? What is it to you if he wins or not?" asked Mrs Collings with newly aroused suspicion.

Mrs Collings was not in her happiest mood this afternoon. She had missed her usual game of solo because Mrs Montague Levy, who was to have been the fourth, had been suddenly taken with a sick headache after luncheon and had gone home to bed. It was too late to procure a substitute, and Ray had asked her to go down to the park to see the tournament. Ray had asked her, too, in such a way that she imagined there was some motive for the request, and she had assented.

She had been sitting still for over an hour with the sun streaming just on to the back of her neck and unable to put a parasol up because the people behind her wanted to see what she could not help characterising as an "idiotic game."

Ray had given her a look when Alec spoke to Florrie, and she grasped its meaning and spoke to the girl sharply.

"Florrie has seen so much of him lately," answered Ray with meaning, "that perhaps he thinks he is something to her whether he wins or not."

"What do you mean by 'Florrie has seen so much of him lately'? When has she seen him?" Mrs Collings looked from one to another of her daughters for explanation.

Poor Florrie was overwhelmed with shame and terror, and her changing countenance revealed her emotion. Once the torrent of Ray's spite was let loose she went on without a pause.

"He's an awful flirt, and he must have spoken to her over and over again. He was just the same with me at first, but I soon showed him it was no good. Florrie did not dance with anyone else at our party; and then his coming down here after her! I think you ought to put a stop to it, Ma. That's why I made you come with me today to see what was going on. Just fancy his telling her not to worry about his losing—such impudence!"

"Oh, Ray!" said Florrie deprecatingly.

"Never mind about 'Oh Ray,'" interrupted Mrs Collings with decision, "just listen to me. I don't want my girls' names associated with those of any Christians, as if they were Soph Jeddingtons or some of that sort. You'll just not have anything more to do with him. You're not to speak to him again, do you hear? If you do I shall mention it to your father."

Mrs Collings did not trouble to moderate her voice, and Mr Collings heard, as indeed anyone could have done who had taken the trouble to listen.

"What's all that about?" he asked. "What are you going to mention to me?"

"That young Murphy has been paying Florrie attention. I've just been telling her she's not to have anything more to do with him."

"Murphy; of course not! certainly not! But then Florrie can't help his paying her attention. That's what it is to be a good looking girl—eh, Flo? Ray hasn't so much trouble, have you Ray?" asked her father jocularly. He was in high good humour at the prospect of winning his money, and Florrie was his favourite daughter. He generally saw through Ray's little artifices, and they understood each other too well to be very good friends. When he took the trouble to intervene even Ray was rather frightened at her father's penetration. But that happened very seldom. As a rule he left all domestic matters to his wife.

Mrs Collings would not let the matter drop so easily.

"Ray says she has encouraged him; you ought to forbid her to speak to him."

"There's no harm in speaking to him. Flo is a great deal too sensible to have anything else to do with him, aren't you, Flo?" asked her father, still unwilling to issue a harsh order.

"He's very—gentlemanly," at length brought out Florrie, feeling it her duty to say something for her lover, but too frightened to know what it ought to be.

Her father was astonished to be answered at all. When he did interfere in home affairs he did so as an autocrat. The fact of her defence, feeble as it was, made him regard the matter with more attention.

"Damn his gentlemanliness," he said sharply. "That don't bring him in anything; I tell you you're to have nothing more to do with him; and take care you don't! Isn't the game nearly over, I'm about sick of this."

But during this family colloquy the fortunes of war had somewhat altered, and when they again turned their attention to the score Alec had won one set against his opponent's two, and a desperate struggle was going on for the fourth. There are some people who cannot play a losing game. Others, on the contrary, can only be stirred to full exertion by approaching defeat. It was to the latter class that Alec belonged. The first two sets he had played in his ordinary manner; Charlie, on the other hand, as he never had played before. Then the latter began to feel too confident; he lost the third purely from carelessness.

In the fourth he was trying to regain his position, but he found no scope for the brilliant volleys on which he relied for certain victory. Alec knew this manoeuvre now, and knew that it was impossible for him to return a ball that was miles out of court before it came within reach of his arm. So he put it out of Charlie's power to volley by striking so low that the ball just escaped the net, or sometimes struck the top and then rolled over on to the ground. This change of tactics greatly irritated his already fatigued opponent; ball after ball was struck with such vehemence that it went outside the line. Charlie had too much at stake; he could not play with judgment and judgment is worth as much as activity at lawn tennis.

The fourth set was placed to Alec's score, and the young man who predicted his victory plumed himself upon his sagacity. There was a great deal of applause. The spectators had the pleasure of looking forward to a closely contested final.

Alec and Charlie changed sides for the last time, without a word.

Mr Collings began to feel uncomfortable about his fiver.

"I shan't stay and see it out," said Mr Detmar. "I shall go down to the club. Come along, Collings, we shall hear the result afterwards."

"The club" was the Park Club. Whist is played there for high stakes during three months of the year, when visitors are admitted as honorary members and elected by the hall porter. During the other nine it is used by the respectable inhabitants, and threepenny points are the highest average.

Collings agreed to go with him, but gave his parting injunction to Florrie.

"Mind you, Flo, I won't have it. Snub him at once. He'll soon understand you mean it."

In what frame of mind the little girl watched the final can be well understood. Her misery was too great for tears. She saw no outlet for herself nor any hope in the vast dark future. Without Alec, without seeing or speaking to him! It was a terribly desolate prospect. And yet she had no thought of rebellion. She sat there dully, hopelessly miserable. The fiat had gone forth; she was to be another of the miserable victims tortured to avenge the unforgotten Crucifixion. She had not even the questionable comfort of sympathy; nobody knew her feelings. Ray perhaps guessed them, and was the more satisfied with her work.

One thing Florrie made up her mind to: she would see him and speak to him once. She must say goodbye to him. She must have one last kiss. If they knew all they would not grudge her that. Then her love should go from her and she would bear her trouble quietly.

Meanwhile a torment of thoughts raged in Charlie's breast. All through the first two sets, buoyed up with his good fortune, his mind was occupied with the brightest anticipations. He made sure she would ask him to dinner. He would walk home with her. He felt she must love him, although she had been so cool to him sometimes. The cup, which it would once have been his highest ambition to win, he never thought of at all. He was playing for Mary. And those first two sets he had played demoniacally.

Then, when he felt victory and all that it meant to

him was within his grasp, he let himself dream. That lost him his third set. He never gained his advantage, though he played with the desperation of despair. Alec's was the calmness of certainty, and Mr Collings lost his fiver.

Charlie was broken hearted. He could not even go through the form of shaking hands with Alec. He put on his coat and left the park without a word to anyone, going out at the further entrance so as to avoid the people. And Alec, surrounded by his friends, thought it best to leave him alone for a while. As soon as he could extricate himself from the congratulations that poured in he sought out the Collingses, but they had already left.

He found Mrs Cameron, however, and she proffered him her congratulations very sweetly.

"I'm sorry for Charlie, that's all," answered this outspoken young man, "because he seemed to have set his heart on it. But I knew I could beat him; if you remember I told you so yesterday."

"Yes, I remember," answered Mary, who rejoiced at the turn events had taken. She was very nice and kind to Alec, and made him come in and have tea with her and rest in her cool pleasant room. They spoke a little of Florrie, and Mary half expected she would come in, but she did not make her appearance.

Although Mrs Cameron and Alec had never conversed much together, they were excellent friends and spent a pleasant hour.

Mary liked the young man. He was associated in her mind with Charlie, and Charlie she liked very much indeed, although she felt very relieved at his defeat this afternoon. Alec fought his battle all over again in the sitting room of the Queen's Hotel and pointed out to Mary that he could have won any time he liked. He knew his cousin's form thoroughly, and what were his weak points.

Mary led him on to talk about his cousin, and his

132

cousin's home life. She felt a curiosity on the subject and Alec was quite willing to gratify it.

He gave a vivid description of Sir Charles Doveton, his courtly old world manners, his pride and his exclusiveness. Perhaps he exaggerated somewhat the splendour of the old Hall and the dimensions of the fair estate, but on the whole his account was truthful and honest enough. It sounded very grand to Mary but in reality it was not grand at all.

Sir Charles Doveton was a baronet of moderate estate. Nature had intended him for a student, and he followed his instincts. He had married very young and had lost his wife. Since then he had shut himself up in his library and lived among his books.

Charlie was his heir, and early orphaned; and as a matter of course he had taken the boy under his care. Gradually he had learnt to love him, but it was an unobtrusive love. Charlie had matters all his own way; every wish was gratified, though it is only fair to say that up to now none of his wishes had been unreasonable. He had no idea of the wealth of affection lavished on him by the lonely man, or of the depths of loneliness to which he was condemning him by his long absence.

But Sir Charles was a proud man and sent no word of recall; and although Charlie wrote to him regularly he remained in absolute ignorance as to the cause of his delay.

Mrs Cameron was allured by the thought of the baronetcy. The calm country life spread itself out invitingly before her; she had it in her to wish she had never met Benjamin Phillips.

She was quite pleased, however, that Charlie had lost his match and did not come to her this afternoon; his society was not sufficiently attractive for her to desire it continuously. It is charming to be adored but it gets a little tedious unless the lover is clever; and Charlie was not clever.

Perhaps it was the reaction from the state of mental infidelity she had drifted into that made Mrs Cameron resolve to devote herself again to her Israelitish friends. She had rather neglected them for Charlie lately; and she knew them well enough to know her neglect would be commented upon, and this was undesirable.

Book II · Chapter V

So the evening saw her walking in the park with Mrs Detmar, and Mrs Detmar, who was by no means reticent, questioned her about young Doveton—his position, means—and prospects.

Mrs Cameron gave her the information she required.

"Now you can tell me," said Mrs Detmar confidentially, "you know people always confide in me, and though I can't say I approve of second marriages, still, there are occasions—and you only have one little girl. Tell me now, *do you think he means anything?*"

The brutal directness of this question somewhat startled Mary Cameron and for some minutes she was at a loss how to reply. Did he mean to ask her to marry him? That was Mrs Detmar's question, and Mrs Detmar was a friend of Dr Phillips! She felt the bitterness of her position one moment, and in that one moment hated Benjamin. If free she could have accepted Charlie. She was not free and her bonds were...but she did not pursue that train of reasoning. She repressed the bitterness of her thoughts and answered gravely: "I haven't given a thought to Mr Doveton's intentions. Dear Mrs Detmar, I would tell you in a moment if he had said or hinted anything. Perhaps I have been a little imprudent in seeing so much of him. But my own thoughts are so much with my poor husband; I forget that other people cannot know that."

"Oh, no!" said Mrs Detmar, pressing her arm affectionately, "I must say I didn't think myself there was anything in it; but Mrs Levy said something, and Mrs Collings said Ray told her she had met him with you of an afternoon, so I thought I had better ask you.

Nothing like straightforwardness; that's my idea, particularly between friends."

It was under this plea of straightforwardness that Mrs Detmar took such liberties with her friends; but they had become accustomed to her now and rather admired her courage.

Mrs Cameron did not admire it. It had pulled her up when she wanted to drift.

They joined one of the groups that were dotted about at the grass. Mrs Collings and Mrs Jeddington seemed to be having an argument in which Soph and Ray were vehemently joining. Florrie sat silent and depressed by her mother's side.

"What are you talking about? What is the point in dispute?" asked Mrs Detmar, as she unceremoniously joined them, and turned Florrie out of her seat, with: "Your legs are younger than mine, young lady, let me have your chair."

But they did not immediately answer her question. Mrs Collings looked meaningly at Mrs Cameron, and Mrs Detmar interpreted the look and knew the vexed questions of Jews *versus* Christians must have been the subject under discussion.

But Mrs Jeddington was more obtuse.

"We were talking of Christian young men. Here is Mrs Collings finding no end of fault with Mr Murphy—as nice a young man as ever lived, by the way—just because she thinks he admires Florrie. I only know one thing: I wish it were my daughter he admired."

"Well, you needn't say so, mother!" interrupted Soph with some asperity. Perhaps she also wished it.

"I think he is very impertinent," said Mrs Collings, forgetting it was not polite to talk so before Mary, "coming up like he did today."

"Florrie encouraged him," said Ray sharply. "He never did it to me."

"Perhaps he did not want you," Soph replied rather aggressively. The fact was that Alec Murphy was a most desirable young man in Soph's eyes, and he had been to a certain extent attentive to her until he met the Collingses. His defection was regrettable; but then Soph was rather fond of Florrie. Ray and she had been rivals before and she did not choose she should this time claim a victory that did not belong to her.

The two girls had a little quiet jangle upon it, while their elders went on talking.

Mrs Detmar, in no wise deterred by Florrie's presence, suggested keeping her at home until Alec Murphy left Eastbourne. Mrs Jeddington, on the other hand, tried to smooth matters by saying she didn't think he meant anything. "Christian men were often like that."

Mrs Detmar apologised to Mrs Cameron for talking the matter over before her, and Mrs Cameron replied that she found it very interesting.

She listened attentively and was astonished to see the open way in which Florrie's supposed suitor was dismissed without the girl being in the slightest way consulted or considered.

Unfortunately, while this conversation, so inimical to his interests, was progressing Alec came up to speak to them, as he had done hundreds of times before.

Mrs Collings, having made up her mind that he was paying attention to Florrie and must be repulsed, allowed no consideration for the laws of good society to stand in her way.

She professed not to see his outstretched hand, barely answered his polite inquiry after her husband, and pointedly showed him she did not require his company. Mrs Detmar seconded her with her tactics, commencing a conversation with her on alien topics even when the young man was in the midst of his greetings.

Alec of course could not but see the desire to offend. Even Mrs Jeddington, who had always been friendly to him, answered him coldly and nervously; and they all hemmed Florrie in so that he was unable to get near her at all.

137

She gave him one look, utterly miserable yet imploring. She wanted him to go away, but he misunderstood her, perhaps purposely.

It was throwing cold water on his suit with a vengeance, and came with an added shock after the congratulatory speeches he had been fed on since his victory. But he was not beaten yet; and as Mr Collings came up to them he turned to him and said quietly, "I was just going to ask your daughter to have a turn with me, Mr Collings. Have you any objection?"

Mr Collings was very much taken aback by the attack. He hummed and hawed, and finally said, "I don't approve of girls walking about without their mothers. Florrie is very well where she is."

Alec was very indignant; and the publicity of the treatment he was receiving made it harder to bear.

"Perhaps you will allow me a few words with you aside, sir," he said.

Mr Collings walked away with him.

Mrs Collings broke into fresh diatribes about his impudence. And then the subject of intermarriages between Jews and Christians was thoroughly threshed out before Mrs Cameron. Mrs Detmar even appealed to her to know if she did not agree with them, if she did not think it right that like should marry like, and Mary agreed with her, thoughtfully.

Mrs Collings said she would rather see one of her children dead than married to a Christian. Mrs Detmar would not go quite as far as that. Only she would, certainly, rather see hers married to the poorest Jew that ever walked, even to an absolute pauper. Mrs Jeddington said she did not think things were as bad as that; she would rather see Soph married to "one of their people," of course, but she did not think her father would mind either way.

Mrs Montague Levy said "Mixed marriages never come to any good," and instances were cited.

138

And Florrie and Mary, each with her own thoughts, sat and listened to this conversation.

Alec made his proposal in few words to Mr Collings, and stated briefly his position and prospects. Mr Collings scarcely listened to him. He refused him insultingly, accused him of taking advantage of Florrie's youth and inexperience, adding: "And if it's my money you're thinking of, young man, I tell you you're on the wrong tack. Not a stiver, not a cent. I'd see you starve rather, I'd sooner..."

Then Alec lost his temper.

"Did I ask you for money or think of your money? You can keep your dirty money bags—the only thing any of you seem to have any care for. I neither want you nor your money. I want your daughter..."

"And like your damned impudence it is to want my daughter," broke in the outraged parent.

"Well, sir," said Alec, recovering his dignity, "we need not converse any more about the matter. I have told you what I want, and I tell you, what is more, I mean to have it, with or without your permission, and when she is my wife I shall take care she holds no communication with a family who have insulted me."

Then before Mr Collings had sufficiently recovered to reply he had raised his hat and left him.

Mr Collings was so ill advised as to repeat this conversation, and somehow or other it cheered Florrie's drooping spirits.

The family, however, hardly took the words seriously, although Mr Collings found an opportunity to tell Florrie if she had anything more to do with him "he was damned if he'd leave her a farthing." But they had such faith in the religious barriers which they had brought up their family to consider insurmountable that they did not take any further steps to separate the lovers. Certainly Ray watched the girl very jealously for the next few days, but having accidentally discovered Mr Murphy had left Eastbourne her espionage was relaxed and the whole incident of the proposal fell into the background and the usual tenor of their existence was pursued.

Then followed a week of continual wet. Mary waited at home, attired in her most becoming tea gowns, but Charlie never came. He seemed to have taken her at her word and to have decided it would be "caddish" to break his promise "not to worry her any more."

They were dull and dreary days for Mary; Alec, too, had disappeared and she had no resource but the daily and nightly card parties of the Detmars and their circle.

The bad weather rather rejoiced them. When it was fine they felt, these stout and well to do wives of Jewish tradesmen, that unless they were a certain number of hours in the open air they were not getting their money's worth out of their annual holiday. But when it was wet, then they were happy because no qualms of conscience kept them from the amusement they delighted in. They played all day long; nothing interrupted them but meals.

It bored Mary intolerably; and often of an afternoon, in those small stuffy seaside rooms, seated at one of those worn out rickety old card tables that seem all legs when you are sitting at them, her thoughts would stray from the cards to Charlie.

It was strange to see this beautiful woman of loose morals accepted and moving among these heavy, coarse featured, narrow minded Jewesses.

Theirs is a society worth describing before, as must be in the natural order of things, it decays or amalgamates. It is a fact little understood that here, in the heart of a great and cosmopolitan city, sharing in and appropriating its riches, there is a whole nation dwelling apart in an inviolable seclusion, which they at once cultivate, boast of, and are ashamed at. There are houses upon houses in the West Central districts, in

Maida Vale, in the City, which are barred to Christians, to which the very name of Jew is an open sesame.

All the burning questions of the hour are to them a dead letter; art, literature and politics exist not for them. They have but one aim: the acquisition of wealth. Playing cards at each other's houses is their sole experience of the charms of social intercourse; their interests are bounded by their homes and those of their neighbouring brethren.

And it was amongst these people that Mary moved and thought of Charlie. Benjamin Phillips, who had almost escaped from them when he entered his profession, had not been able to resist the ties of brotherhood after he married. The influences of his boyhood, all the associations with which the nation binds her sons together, had combined to keep him amongst them. He was in them, not entirely of them. They were only weeds that had grown apace in the fostering warmth of commercial prosperity; he was the flower and fruit.

Mary, without Dr Phillips to spur her on, was now bored and wearied amongst them. She would have absented herself sometimes, but that Benjamin would soon be returning; and she knew he desired to find her among his people, as men desire for the object of their attachment all that they think best in life.

So she continued endlessly shuffling cards and paying out money, very weary, very bored, only finding time to notice Florrie's woebegone face and to tell her to keep up her spirits.

Somehow or other Mary felt that it was only through Alec she could get the opportunity to recall Charlie. Charlie was always present in her mind now. She missed his admiration; she missed the excitement she always had when with him, of wondering what her Benito would say if he knew.

Alec must be reached through Florrie, so she kept

141

herself in touch with Florrie and at the same time sympathised with Mr Collings when he confided in her his fears that Florrie cared for "that fellow."

She did not herself believe in Alec's sudden renunciation of Florrie. She did not agree with Mr Collings that it was only her money he was after and that when he found the father wouldn't hear of marriage he was quick enough to get away. It was this theory that made them lax in their watch over the girl, and it was this theory, insulting alike to her love and to his pride, that made Florrie's white face whiter and her aching heart more sorrowful.

Mrs Cameron was her only comfort. In her they all confided, any item omitted by the others being supplied by Mrs Detmar. Mrs Cameron lost her money steadily and good temperedly; Mrs Detmar won it just as steadily and was not above being pleased on that account. They all found Mary more charming than ever, and the slight pensiveness they perceived in her was set to her credit.

She thought so continually of her husband! That young man (what was his name?—Doveton) had proposed to her not knowing this, and it had been a shock to her, poor thing!"

They took to petting her amongst them, and she was so overwhelmed with hospitality that she need never have taken a meal in the hotel had she not desired.

But it was very dull; she missed her flowers, and she missed Charlie; she had no excitement at all now. She even took to missing Benjamin Phillips and wondering why it was so long since she had heard from him.

She could not understand what had become of the two young men. She watched Florrie narrowly, fully expecting she would receive a letter, but none came.

It was a waiting time; a break in the chain of events that was winding round Mary's life. She little knew how important a bearing Florrie's simple love affair would have upon her own fortunes. She only interested herself in it as an idle pastime. She only looked upon it as a stepping stone to renewed intercourse with the lad who had brought the first whiff of devotional incense into her life.

Book II · Chapter VI

The fourth morning after Alec's proposal, when the maid came into the room with her chocolate she was able to tell Mary the weather had changed. When the blinds were drawn the sweet morning sun streamed into her room. Nor was that all the morning brought her. There was a note, a little two lined note.

Dear Mrs Cameron,

    I must see you. Come out to me here.

        Yours, in great haste—ALEC MURPHY

She scribbled him a promise to be with him, and hastily dressed. She had a vague idea something had happened to Charlie, and he had sent for her; but she was not too agitated to don one of her prettiest morning dresses before she descended.

"This is good of you," said Alec, with outstretched hand and beaming face. "I knew I could rely upon you."

Mrs Cameron's notion that he had anything to tell her about Charlie vanished. She knew enough of the world to recognise that his repressed excitement and eagerness could only be about some matter that directly affected himself. But she greeted him warmly for all that.

"I must see Florrie, and you must manage it for me, if only for a few moments," Alec went on impetuously. "How soon can you manage it?" he asked anxiously.

Mrs Cameron smiled at him.

"Sooner than ever you could have expected," she answered him kindly, "for we have our usual morning swimming appointment for the first fine day, and I think this answers that description." And she looked up into the unflecked blue sky with its promise of heat.

"Do you mind giving us ten minutes—you're not offended?—by ourselves?"

"Offended! nonsense. I will leave you entirely. I have been young once myself." She said it lightly, but she thought that perhaps the presence of a third party in her interviews in Regent's Park with Benjamin Phillips might have had a great effect upon her life. Not that she repented what she had done; not that she would not have done it all over again under similar circumstances tomorrow; only she was beginning to have misgivings; to find it was difficult to be faithful to the absent; to allow curious thoughts of possible futures to dawn in her mind.

She watched Florrie go into the Queen's Hotel and let her wait two or three minutes in the sitting room, then she sent Alec in to her and herself sat down upon the parade to wait for them. It was not yet light; the air was fresh after the rain; the sun had not risen sufficiently long to over heat the moist earth; but there was already a vapour, a mist, about the ground; the sea was rough, tumbling about in great waves and breaking with a loud roar upon the stones. There were but few bathers and Mary watched those few in their vain endeavours to meet and escape the waves with amusement. She noted their curious garments, and smiled at the bag-like effect given to them by the wind. She thought curiously how devoid of vanity they must be to so divest themselves of any charms they might possess and appear unabashed in the broad daylight. Her swimming was not done so. She and Florrie used to go to the baths, where there was neither wind nor bystanders, and her garments were not fashioned in that curious style. She thought of her French costume, with its tight fitting drawers cut short above the knee, and the close jersey that surmounted it. Mary thought very complacently of herself in her bathing dress; she always admired the contour of her legs and the set of her head, that the round cut bodice with its sailor collar left exposed. From the bathers her thoughts took her to Alec, and she wondered what all this urgency was about. Then the idea came to her that she must find some opportunity to let Charlie know that his promise not to worry her did not imply his staying away altogether.

Really she thought it very silly and boyish of him to take her so literally. Perhaps he had gone home. She would like to see that fine old home of his; just to see for herself, once, the kind of life led by the country gentry of whom she had read. A life of calm and peace that had never known the cruelty of want, the miserable monotony of having to work for the very bread one ate, the terrible temptations of warmth and luxury. Such a life had been a dream to Mary before she knew Dr Phillips. The dream had faded before the satisfaction she had experienced in the comforts he had given her. All her dreams had faded, but she had been quite contented and happy. The last few days her content and happiness had vanished; why, she knew not.

Charlie was such a nice boy, and so fond of her. It was cruel to send him away without a word; and after his losing the tournament, too. Poor Charlie!

She sat there thinking these thoughts, and others even vaguer, for a long time. At least it seemed a long time to her, but it was short enough to those other two. But at half past nine Mary bestirred herself and went in to them.

She found Florrie weeping bitterly on the sofa. Alec, looking determined and masterful but, withal, not without a certain shadow of doubt upon him, was standing by the mantel shelf.

Florrie did not alter her attitude as Mary came in, but Alec seemed pleased at the sight of her.

146

"Do you young people know what time it is?" she said lightly, and laying her hand on Florrie. "What's the matter, little girl?"

"He says he's going away," sobbed out Florrie incoherently.

"No, I didn't. This is what I said. Just listen, Mrs Cameron, and see if I'm not right. Look at this," and he showed her a printed paper. "I went up to town to get a special licence. Florrie has promised to marry me. I have told her father I intend to marry her. All my arrangements are made, and now she says she can't." He sat down by Florrie and put his arm round her waist, and his voice, which had had rather an injured intonation, became more tender and appealing. "And now I say if she won't marry me I shall go to Australia. I'm not going to stay in England and be sneered at by all those people. Florrie, little girl, say goodbye to me."

But Florrie only cried.

Mary thought she was making a great fuss about nothing. Anyway he was asking her to *marry* him.

"Can't you make up your mind, Florrie?" said Mrs Cameron, not unkindly. But there was something of a sneer about the words.

"He wants me to marry him this morning," sobbed out Florrie.

"Of course," said Alec, "it is a splendid morning."

It was the Collings's treatment of him that had stirred up all his passions. His injured vanity had called aloud for retaliation. He had gone back to his hotel that evening raging against "the people," and preparing for revenge upon them. He had poured out all his story to Charlie, and Charlie, sitting miserable and disconsolate in his own room, chained by his promise, had yet roused himself to something like interest and had listened to and sympathised with his trouble.

Together they had hit upon this notable scheme of a runaway match; and Charlie had gone up to town with

147

him to get a licence. In the days that followed, Charlie had unbosomed himself to Alec and had found consolation, such as it was.

Alec had advised him, if he was really serious—at which supposition Charlie laughed bitterly—to go first down to Doveton Hall and see his uncle; then, when he had permission and everything was quite straightforward, to go boldly to Mrs Cameron and ask her once more to marry him, and, he added: "Make her give you an answer. It's no use beating about the bush. It's all rot to say she would have married you if you'd have won the cup. What do you think she cares about the cup? And as far as that goes," he said with uncompromising frankness, "you never had a chance, and she knew it; but she wanted time. You don't understand women, my boy. They never know their own minds. But just set to and bully them and they'll do anything you want; it's only a question of management."

Alec prided himself greatly on his management. In fact, he anticipated no resistance when he brought Florrie the licence and insisted upon her marrying him. But Florrie had displayed an amount of obstinacy as irritating as it was unexpected, and he had almost exhausted his persuasive powers when Mary made her appearance.

The idea of a runaway marriage at a registrar's office was an appalling one to this jealously guarded and well brought up Jewish maiden. The idea of losing her lover was equally terrible. Between the two agonising alternatives she knew no way to choose. The misery of her lonely and unsympathetic life with Ray, uncheered by hope—for Alec had said he would never see her more—contrasted with the terrors of an immediate marriage, and the abandonment of all her people.

She loved her father and her mother, her little brothers and sisters. How the Jewish people cling, and have clung to each and to their creed, is a matter of history. It was the strength born of generations of fidelity that kept Florrie from her lover's arms.

But she was very weak, miserably weak, and she loved him very dearly.

"Florrie, you must decide one way or another. It is nearly ten o'clock, breakfast will be over, and they will wonder what has become of you."

How could she go home at once looking like that, and face everyone's questions, and Ray's sneers? She would rather die.

"I can't go home! Oh! What shall I do?"

"Do, my darling, as I tell you. Nobody shall scold you. You'll see it will be all right."

A fly was soon at the door; but Florrie clung to Mary.

"You'll come with us, Mrs Cameron," said Alec, perfectly calm but desperately excited for all that. He half led, half carried the girl into the carriage, and Mary followed him.

They drove in absolute silence to the station. Florrie left off crying, awed by the situation, passionately admiring and clinging to her authoritative lover, yielding yet terrified.

Alec kept tight hold of her hand during the ten minutes' drive; his heart was beating fast with triumph. Perhaps he was thinking more of how Mr Collings would take the news than of anything else; but he loved Florrie and he meant to be very good to her and reward her duly for her obedience.

So Florrie was hurried into the train. She left off shedding tears. She had given herself up to Alec, and she waited on his words. She did not know what they were going to do next. Everything was void for her except the one thought that she could not have faced them all at breakfast, wondering where she had been, noting her tear stained eyes, cross examining her as to what she had done. The having nothing but cross examination and reproaches to look forward to till the

149

end of her days was a prospect she had dreaded too much. She had escaped from it, and now should look to Alec for everything.

He had a man waiting for him at the station with his luggage, and a reserved compartment. He had made all his arrangements, he told Mary, both at this and the other end for the 10.10 train. He could not conceal the triumph in his voice while he explained that he had calculated how long it would take her to consent, to such a nicety that they now had only five minutes to spare. He promised Mary—who didn't care a bit, by the way—that he would drive straight from the station to the registrar's office, and telegraph to Mr Collings immediately the ceremony was over. He got into the train, and stuck his licence prominently into his hat. His spirits rose to such a degree that he feared nothing; he put his decorated head out of the window so that all the guards and the passengers could see.

Florrie shrank into the remotest corner of the carriage and half wished, half dreaded that the train would start. She felt safe because Mary was there, unsafe because at any moment she might be missed. She dreaded to see her father's face; but Alec would almost have enjoyed waving his hat to him as the train moved slowly out of the station.

But Mary's was the only face he saw; and at the last a memory came to him.

"Mrs Cameron," he was serious for an instant, "you've been awfully good to me; may I tell Charlie you'll be just as good to him?"

It was the very opening Mary had been waiting for. But the train was in motion; she could not frame an energetic reply. She had no time for words at all, but she nodded and smiled, and Alec took that for an answer and conveyed it honestly to Charlie, who was waiting for him, with good natured, motherly Mrs Hailsham, to act as witness to the marriage, for even down to such details had Alec arranged his plans.

150

Book II · Chapter VII

The smile Mary had given Alec in response to his question still lingered upon her face as she turned to leave the station.

As the one train curved gracefully out, another came panting and puffing in, and the rushing porters, the calls for cabs, the crowd of people meeting, coming, and going impeded Mary's path.

She was in no hurry, however; she had made up her mind not to go home just yet; she would wait until the Collingses received their telegram before she risked their demanding their daughter of her. She smiled yet more as she pictured the scene at the Collings's when the news arrived.

Another thing, perhaps, that made her countenance so radiant was the feeling that came to her that Charlie would not linger long in London after he had received the sort of message Alec was likely to give him.

Her associations with Charlie were such as they might well make her smile. She dwelt upon his boyish, openly expressed admiration, the summer days that she had spent listening to the wash of the waves and exerting her intelligence to check the yet welcome advances.

It is sweet to be wooed in the summer, and Charlie was summer personified. So young and strong and ardent. What woman but must smile at such an idyll, however long it had been in coming to her. His fair fresh face, all innocent of the razor, the health and vigour that shone out from his bright beaming countenance. It was a pleasure to recall all this, and to feel that the summer was not yet ended; it would return to her.

There was a passenger by that incoming early

151

morning train who caught sight of the tall, lissom figure as it lingered near the gate. He feasted his eyes on it for a moment or two.

All the miles he had travelled since he lost her, he had never been able to shake off her image or disentangle himself from the meshes she had woven around him. He had striven, and striven vainly, to replace his former idol, Brain, on its pedestal; to displace Beauty, which held on tenaciously. But he had been ill. Everything had slipped away from him and faded, everything but Mary. And he had struggled no longer; he had done his work, made his last effort, and turned his footsteps home, back to the woman who held him in thrall.

All through that homeward journey Mary had been with him; weak and prostrated with fever, not the Benjamin Phillips that had left her; nothing seemed very definite in his mind save the woman who possessed his affections.

And now to see her here, waiting for him, at the end of his journey was as the realisation of his dreams.

He did not ask himself how she was to have known the hour and the day of his arrival; his deep content ignored such trivialities. She was here, and such a smile upon her face as could be but for him.

One or two moments he spent in satisfying his eyes, then he touched her lightly on the shoulders.

She turned from her dream of fair, vigorous Charlie, brimming over with youth and health, turned from dreams and saw reality.

Saw Benjamin Phillips gazing at her through his near sighted eyes, looking sallow and thin and sickly.

She stared at the sight. Rapidly a look passed over her face. Could it be repulsion? But as rapidly she recovered herself, and his defective vision spared him a pang.

"My darling," he said, "I have come back to you."

"You have come back," she answered, half

152

mechanically, and pressed his hand. Side by side they walked toward her hotel.

Mary had forgotten, ignored, put away the thought of Benjamin Phillips and his claims. And now her mind was in a tumult of feeling; she shrank from him involuntarily, she almost feared him, and his presence made her suddenly feel his claims were bondage.

She knew then, as they walked together in silence, that the thought of breaking those bonds had come to her, but with him beside her the thought faded. She stole a glance at him and noted that the youthful spring in his walk had vanished and the youthfulness of his expression had gone with it. She felt a thrill of dislike she had never felt before.

"Have you been ill?" was the first question she asked him after they had reached their hotel and they stood face to face in the sunlit room.

"I wrote you I had been ill; perhaps you didn't read my letters," he answered abruptly. An impressionable nature like Dr Phillips's is so easily cast down. His elation at seeing Mary at the station had vanished, as he realised she was not there to meet him; and it was succeeded by a feeling of weariness and depression.

The man was not himself. The Benjamin Phillips that had held Mary to his heart as he bade her goodbye on that early spring evening had been strong and domi-nant, and confident that all his powers were left to him, that this journey he was taking would sweep the cobwebs from his brain and enable him to reassign to woman her subsidiary place. The Benjamin Phillips that returned to her this morning was a mere wreck of his former self: he looked ten years older, there was grey amid the black of his luxuriant beard and hair, there were lines that had not been there before, around his eyes and on his brow.

Illness had robbed him of his strength. He looked at Mary and acknowledged to himself that she was

153

necessary to him. In his weakness he opened his arms to
her, and she submitted to the feeble embrace. Then he
asked for his child, and he had the joy of seeing Nita's
eyes sparkle as they met his, and her little hands seek
his, and his caresses, and he knew that he was loved by
her, even though she did not know he was her father.

And Mary unprepared as yet with any alternative,
taken by surprise at his sudden return, played her part
and disguised her feelings of repulsion with soft phrases
and gentle words. Benjamin revived slightly under
their influence and tried to shake off the depression and
illness which were the remains of his journey.

It was not only illness that weighed on him; he had
other troubles. Perhaps he would have been better able
to bear them had his health remained good; but it had
not, and he was cast down.

The woman and the child comforted him. It was not
until Nita went, after many a fond kiss, to her morning
sleep that he remembered to ask Mary what had been
her early mission at the railway station.

She was sitting by him, smoothing his hair with her
white hands as he asked her, and she told him very
simply the story of Florrie's love and its conclusion.

He sprang to his feet and gazed at her almost with
horror.

"Mary, Mary, do you mean to say you have actually
helped this unhappy girl to elope?"

"Yes, why?" She was astonished at his vehemence.

He could not repress a groan.

"Oh, child, what have you done? They will never
forgive you."

"Who? Mr Collings?"

"The whole nation," he answered hopelessly. It was
a fresh blow to him. He well knew the horror in which
this class of marriage is held by such Jews as the
Collingses, and he knew Mary would be the scapegoat.

He questioned her to try and elicit something on
which to hang a peg of hope, but there was nothing. It

154

was under her aegis they had met and under her aegis they had gone.

She failed to understand his despair. But he knew that at the very moment he most wanted her and the comfort and the help she and his child could give him; that at that moment he must publicly, at least, renounce her, or he would receive his share of the feeling in which she would be held.

He saw it all so clearly. The impotent rage of the Collingses, the sneers and evil tongues of those back-biting women. Mary would be blamed because it would save them from blaming Florrie, who was their own, and Murphy, whom their blame could not reach.

But energy succeeded despair. He would make an effort to save her, but if he were to do so he would need all his powers.

"What are you going to say when they come to you, as they are bound to, when they begin to miss her?"

"They have nothing to come to me for. Mr Murphy will telegraph to them as soon as the ceremony is over; then they will know all about it. Why are you angry, Benito? I am sure he will marry her."

"I am not angry, my darling. Was I ever angry with you? I ought not to have left you; it was my fault. Now I must go. I will see the Collingses, and come back again and let you know what I have heard after dusk. Goodbye until then." He kissed her on the lips, the first kiss he had given her since his return. It turned the formless vision of dislike into a positive and appalling fact.

He went to his hotel; he wanted time to think over the situation. It was not the return he had anticipated, but the necessity for exertion did him good. The trouble he had concealed from Mary, the trouble that had aided illness in lining his face and bleaching his hair, was one of money. He had over speculated. He had speculated, as he always did, rashly and daringly; then when the turn of the market came, when he should have seized the opportunity and realised, he was in bed struggling with that most depressing of maladies, low fever. He missed the time to sell; he waited for the market to recover and the market did not recover. Benjamin Phillips was a ruined man. All he had to look to was his professional income. Not only was that in a measure mortgaged but it never had been of late years sufficient for his requirements. Mrs Cameron's establishment cost him something like £2000 a year, his own modest household was not maintained under £1000, and his wife's money was not at his disposal.

When he commenced to earn a large income he had felt pride in writing to his wife's parents and settling her own income upon her. Since then she had inherited a fortune, and he had pursued the same course with it. He had always been a liberal man. His was that order of liberality that spends and gives uncalculatingly, and his wife's meanness passed unnoticed. But he knew, he who knew her so well, that it would not be without difficulty she would unlock her coffers, and he could not see his way clearly.

Now, as far as his professional income was concerned, it was large, but nothing like as large as it would have been in the hands of a business man.

For instance, he was an MD of London as well as an FRCS, and he was entitled to guinea and two guinea fees; but he had not taken this degree until he had been established in practice, and those patients he had attended for the ten shillings he continued to charge ten shillings to. His practice was largely among his own people. He was considered as a rich man; there was never any hesitation in keeping him waiting long for his fees or even, in the case of those that were not well off, in not paying him at all; and it was known he never asked for his money, and in cases of real illness he came just as readily, whether he had been paid or not.

All this pressed upon him now, and his path was by no means clear. The fact that he must go on living as a rich man, in whatever state his fortunes must be, was patent to him, but the "how" was very uncertain.

Added to this he did not feel well; the spring had gone out of him, his feverish nights continued, and he was growing thinner. He was conscious of an almost uncontrollable irritability, but he had attributed a great deal of his misfortunes to being without Mary and the child. He had commenced to look upon them as necessities to him, to imagine as he was travelling towards home that when he rejoined them some of the mists would be dispelled. He had rejoined them and the mists were deepening to fog.

He knew what would be said among his friends and patients when they knew what share Mary had had in Florrie Collings's elopement, and he knew equally well that he must side with her accusers, for they were not only his living but hers. True, he had contrived to be much with her before he had brought her among his people and endeavoured to provide her with some form of social life; but now he had got used to meeting her, to see her here there and everywhere in his daily rounds, and he knew it would be a hardship for him, and he would miss it greatly when it was so no longer.

He also dreaded the effect her solitude would have upon her.

What should he do to avert the coming disaster. Wait. But waiting was the very thing Benjamin Phillips did worst.

He decided on going over to the Collingses.

Book II · Chapter VIII

When the Collingses sat down to breakfast that morning they had first missed Florrie; they were not early risers, and it was then ten o'clock.

Ray said Florrie had gone to bathe with Mrs Cameron, but she did not know how long ago, because she, Ray, was only half awake; but it must have been about nine.

Mrs Collings said she supposed she hadn't had time to get back yet. The fish must be kept hot for her.

They all finished their breakfast without further uneasiness.

Mrs Collings went about her household duties, with two of her children clinging to her skirts, and forgot all about the absentee, and Mr Collings became absorbed in the *Times* which had only just arrived, and did the same thing.

But Ray had nothing to absorb her; at least nothing so absorbing as her jealousy of Florrie, and she watched the clock uneasily and spent most of the minutes at the window.

"Hadn't we better send round to the Queen's to see if Florrie is there?" she asked, at length, determined to be no longer alone in her doubts.

Mr Collings growled an inaudible reply. He was unused to be interrupted, and did not approve of the innovation.

So she sought her mother and repeated her question.

"Not come home yet? Yes, send round, of course. She has no right to stop out to breakfast without asking leave. I shall tell Mrs Cameron our girls are not brought up like that; as if they had no one to look after them."

"And if she's not there, mamma?"

"What do you mean? Be quiet, Teddy, I want to hear what your sister has to say. Where could she be?"

Mrs Collings was startled but as yet not alarmed, and no glimpse of the truth had dawned upon Ray's mind, although she suspected her sister of meeting Alec.

She mentioned this suspicion to her mother, and although Mrs Collings thought too highly of the way she had brought her girls up to admit them capable of clandestine appointments she was not comfortable in her mind until she had despatched a messenger to the Queen's Hotel.

"But that Murphy fellow has gone away..." she said, pausing in her occupation of feeding Teddy with her fingers off the bits of fish that remained in the plates on the yet uncleared breakfast table.

"Eastbourne is only an hour and a half from London," replied Ray sententiously, watching her mother curiously.

But nothing disturbed Mrs Collings; she had all her younger children around her, all clamouring for the titbits she had reserved for her youngest born.

It was an untidy room: the breakfast things still about, Mrs Collings in a greasy dressing gown and old slippers, the costume she reserved for her household duties, and the children not yet dressed up in their finery for the edification and envy of the public were dirty and dishevelled. The remains of their morning eggs lingered about their mouths and pinafores; their hair, in some cases still in curl papers, was innocent of the morning brush.

Into this Babel of dirt and untidiness walked Mrs Montague Levy, prim and neat, with only a scarlet bow in her bonnet to testify to her national love of colour.

"Good morning. Oh, there's Teddy! Well, I can't say he looks very delicate now. No, no, you needn't kiss me Teddy, your mouth is all over egg."

"There, there, go up to nurse, children, tell her she is to take you on the parade; you can put on your velvet

159

dresses. Aren't they a tribe? They always come down and have a little breakfast when we've done; it gives nurse time to wash up. Are you going shopping? I shan't be a moment getting my dress on; you'll wait, won't you?"

"Oh yes, I'll wait. Mrs Detmar is coming too, on her way to the Simmonses."

The dirty children trooped off to be made gaudy for their morning walk, and Mrs Collings herself went upstairs to emerge, in about two minutes' time, in a big black satin cloak that hid all deficiencies in the toilette beneath. A bird of paradise in her bonnet lit up the somebreness of this attire, and she carried a pair of bright yellow gloves.

"I didn't wait to change my dress, this cloak covers everything. Oh, there you are, Flora! I am quite ready. Are you coming, Ray?"

"Good morning," said Mrs Detmar, stepping from her bath chair into the house. There's a telegram for you coming up the steps; I just met the boy; I hope it's nothing that will keep you waiting, for I haven't ordered my lunch yet; I thought I'd see what you were going to do; you might come and lunch with me. I hate telegrams..."

"Oh, it wouldn't do to hate telegrams in this house," answered Mrs Collings, lightly. "We have two or three a day from the office, and sometimes more."

The bell rang, the brick red envelope was taken into the dining room, and Mrs Collings still awaited the return of her messenger from the Queen's.

But one minute had scarcely elapsed from the time of the delivery of the telegram before Mr Collings came into the room, with a white face, and the open sheet in his hand.

"Where are you, Tilly?" He scarcely seemed to see or know where he was. "Read that."

She looked at her husband's face and saw trouble, but not even then was she warned of the nature of the news.

To understand the feelings of these people on hearing of the elopement of their daughter with a Christian it is necessary to remember that they were Jews, essentially of the middle class and entirely unemancipated. They had not reached the level of the Jeddingtons; they were not ambitious. The world was nothing to them beyond "their people."

Added to this there was the degradation of feeling that their jealously guarded daughter had left all who held her dear, at the bidding of a stranger and an alien, one whom in their ignorance they invested with all imaginable evil qualities. She had deceived and abandoned them. They did not even know if he would marry her.

This was the wording of the message. Ray took it from her mother's unresisting hand and read it aloud. It was Alec's revenge.

Your daughter is with me. Will allow her to communicate later. ALEC MURPHY

There was no address but London.

"Well, I never!..." ejaculated Mrs Montague Levy in opened mouthed astonishment.

"I am not surprised. I always expected it of Florrie. I always said, if you remember, that she would come to no good end."

"There's Mrs Jacobs and Bessie. Let's call them in and tell them." The little perky excitable woman put her head out of the window and called them in.

Mrs Detmar and Mrs Levy could hardly get the words out fast enough as they communicated the purport of the telegram to the new comers, and soon the whole four of them raced each other with comments and ejaculations.

Mrs Collings went into shrieking hysterics and was helped to her room by her sister. But Mrs Lucas couldn't stay long to sympathise with her. She was

161

irresistibly drawn towards the downstairs room, where the gossip was going on, where all were comparing notes as to what they had thought and foretold.

It was something wonderful how they all enjoyed the

excitement. They stood at the window and called in all their friends as they passed on their way to the park, or the parade, or the shops. The children came in their bright garments and added to the confusion of the scene. Soon the room was full of women in reds and yellows and blues, with bright dark eyes and eager faces, with full busts and pronounced features, with voices loud and harsh.

Ray began to feel that even though her victim had escaped her there were compensations. She was the centre of interest: everyone surrounded her and cross examined her, and condoled with her. They wanted to know everything—Alec's means, his position. Did she think he would marry her?"

"No, of course he wouldn't, or he would have said so in the telegram. It was only revenge. He didn't care a bit for her."

"How shocking!"

"How terrible!"

"Mrs Collings would never get over it."

"That came of knowing Christians."

"It wouldn't be long before Florrie was back; he wouldn't keep her."

"Poor girl, she little knew what a fate was before her."

So wagged the tongues, while the clatter of plates as the unchecked children made their depredations and the sound of Mrs Collings's shrieks as they rang through the house added to the confusion and gave piquancy to the situation.

Mr Collings sat still through the noise and the stream of incoming people. He could hardly realise the news. If Egyptians had suddenly sunk to zero he could not have been more affected. Rage and grief made him dumb.

In such condition Dr Phillips found them as he walked in unannounced. How glad they were to see him and how they pressed round him, each one with her own version, each one trying to talk down the rest. He had been the one element wanting to complete their happiness. What did he think? What did he advise?

He went up to where Mr Collings was sitting and put his hand on his shoulder.

"Is this true, Collings?" he asked; and there was real sympathy in his voice and touch.

"Where's the telegram?" asked the unhappy man vaguely. Ray gave it to him.

They were silent in the room now, awaiting developments.

Mrs Detmar had sent for David, who came into the room now and read the telegram over the doctor's shoulder.

"This is a d—d bad business," he said. "What are you going to do? Let us go into another room and talk it over."

This was unkind to the anxious women, but as they went out the words the doctor had been listening for fell upon his ear.

Mrs Levy said, "Mrs Cameron must have known all about it."

Mr Collings caught the words also; and when Detmar asked him again what he was going to do he said he should go and ask Mrs Cameron if she had seen Florrie, if she knew anything.

Still the doctor felt all was going well, better than he could have expected. Nobody accused *her* of participation; at present no one blamed *her*. He felt he should be able to avert disaster.

He suggested waiting until Mr Collings had recovered himself a little, deciding to go up in the meantime and see Mrs Collings. Taking the lead into his own hands—and for once Mr Collings was glad to be led—he promised to go with him to Mrs Cameron's, and after obtaining all the information she had—although he expressed his doubts as to her having any—to go to London and ascertain if possible where Florrie was, and

164

if Alec had married her. But on this score he said he had no fear.

He did Mr Collings a great deal of good, and then he went to the bereaved mother.

He spoke to her tenderly, comforted her with brave words, and told her of many cases he knew where these mixed marriages had turned out well. He held out two hopes to her. Perhaps before the end of the day Florrie would return. Or even if they were married, perhaps Mr Murphy would go through the ceremony again in a synagogue. Anyway she was to bear up; there was her poor husband, there were all her other children needing care and watchfulness more than ever.

Had she looked after Teddy that morning? There was a suspicion of an east wind and she ought to see he did not go out without being properly guarded in flannel.

So he cleverly led her mind to other things, and while he talked he held his fingers on her pulse, not that he was counting the beats, but he thought it a soothing position; he had found it efficacious before. However that might have been she was calmed and quieted, and when at length he left her she clung to him and told him how she trusted him and begged him to find Florrie and bring her back anyway, married or single. Dr Phillips was the one person everybody could trust.

Then he prepared to go with Collings and interview Mrs Cameron, and the prospect was not a pleasing one to him, although his self confidence had in a measure returned through his success with the mother. He thought he should be able to carry the interview to a satisfactory conclusion and keep his hold both on his patients and his ladylove.

But the fates were against him.

Book II · Chapter IX

This is what had occurred.

When Florrie and Alec had arrived at Victoria they had been met by Charlie. Congratulations and hand-shakings followed, and introductions to Mrs Hailsham. A brougham was waiting to take them to the registrar's office, and while Charlie was assisting Alec to collect his luggage, the latter said lightly, "Your affair is all right, old man. Mrs Cameron as good as told me so."

Now what young, ardent, impetuous lover could resist this? Not Charlie. He saw them into the brougham, he hastily explained that he had an appointment, he basely left Alec without a best man at the last moment. He hurried back to the station and rushed to Eastbourne as fast as the 11.55 express could take him.

When Dr Phillips left Mary with a kiss upon her lips the full reaction against him set in steadily. Her mind was in a state of confusion and her usual calmness had forsaken her. The kiss that he had taken, the possessive embrace with which he had left the room, had turned the tide. It had swept away what little remnant of affection she had felt for him and proved to her without a doubt that her passion was not only dead but had changed to distaste, almost to hate.

The sole attraction Benjamin Phillips had ever had for her was purely physical. Remember that although he was an ugly man he had the advantages of perfect health, and a certain impressive vigour; a youth with all the additions of virility. There was about him an abundance of animal magnetism, and his touch, soft yet strong, had a singular galvanic power. Unconsciously one found oneself in elective affinity with him.

This youth and electric control had vanished with his illness. The Benjamin Phillips that had kissed her lips as he left her that morning was an ordinary slender stooping ugly man with flabby nerveless hands, and in place of the thrill she used to know was only the rough feel of a coarse beard scouring her soft cheek and a certain atmosphere of ill health that repelled her.

She thought of this, thought of having to bear with it and with him, and with the dark skinned sickly child, all the long future. She burst into tears, shuddering in her soul at the picture she had called up of a bondage growing daily more galling.

In this mood Charlie found her. Rushing into the room, full of hope and happiness, and ardent love, he found her in tears.

What more natural than that he should conjecture the tears were for him. What more natural than that he should sink at her feet, seize her hands, cover them with kisses, pour out his love in hurried words of devotion and homage.

The room was glorified to him, and the pale gold of his lady's hair was as the aureole of a saint. He confessed his unworthiness; He implored her to stoop to him, to raise him in the calm altitudes where she dwelt so purely. The look and touch of her ran like fire through his young veins. Her tears had humanised her; she did not seem so cold, so far off, as when she was smiling and deftly turning aside his love speeches. His heart was filled full with love and hope.

"My darling, you will stoop to me, you will be my wife!" he implored, his eyes swimming in eager tears at the prospect of his happiness.

Her tears had ceased to flow as she listened to the ardent young words and noted the hope in the young voice.

Charlie, youthful and strong and active, glowing with health and visions of coming happiness, was offering her—what? Love; not only love and comfort, but

167

marriage and that life of a country lady that she had dreamed of in her distant girlhood.

Then a dumb rage seized her, that all these good gifts should be out of her reach. Like another Frankenstein she was dogged by the wilful sin of former days, and happiness eluded her grasp. The shadow of Benjamin, coarse, ugly, ill, fell before her. For the first and only time in her life she lost all control over herself. An unreasoning hysteria seized her.

Her young lover knelt at her feet, offering her all she would so fain have taken. Between them stood the masterful shadow of that other one, barring the path. She burst into unpremeditated and unconsidered speech.

"Marry you! Marry you!" she said, and there was a wild and bitter laugh in her words. "I can marry no man, I am only a mistress, a kept mistress a... Do you hear?" She grew savage in her impotent madness. "You, who thought I was high above you and knelt at my feet to implore me to be your bride. Bride! I have never been a bride. Never a bride—Are you listening?—only an easy victim, and you... Why do you stand there dumb? Why don't you say something? You understand me? The woman you wanted to marry you, a common..."

"Oh my God, don't!" There were horror and anguish in his young voice. He covered his face with his hands and groaned. He had worshipped her, and this was what he had worshipped. He could not look at her. He shut out the sight.

And she... Her own words had almost sobered her. She gazed on the havoc she had wrought and subsided into an agitated silence.

It was this scene that Benjamin Phillips and Mr Collings met when they came to seek news of the lost one.

The doctor's quick eye took it in at a glance: the young man's look of agony; the woman, with the flush of rage on her cheek, the tiger light in her eyes. He knew she had this in her—this power of passion. He had seen it and been attracted by it, had even in times past felt a pleasure in looking at it that he might exercise himself to soothe it again, but now! Now it was very inconvenient. In this mood he could hardly hope to find her so ready to take a hint and aid him as he would have wished in hoodwinking the questioning father.

With all his talents of intuition he read the scene wrongly. He thought she had been repulsing the young man in anger at his daring, and his heart warmed to her.

Poor Charlie seized his hat and withdrew without a word or glance. That did not add to Mary's complacency.

"Mr Collings wants to ask you one or two questions about Florrie," began Dr Phillips diplomatically, giving Mr Collings a chair.

He telegraphed Mary with his eyes a policy of caution, but the message passed unheeded.

Her eyes and thoughts were full of Charlie and her impatience at the interruption was added to by the doctor's cool, impassive words. She felt he had ruined her life and was standing there mocking her for it—a fit return!

She did not sit down. She waited a minute ignoring the doctor's inquiry, trying to quell the tumult within her.

"What do you want to know?" she asked abruptly, turning to Collings.

"What have you done with my daughter?" he asked, roused by her manner and speaking insolently.

"Your daughter? What have I done with her? Saw her off at the station early this morning with her lover." And she laughed.

The laugh roused Mr Collings to fury, the more perhaps because Dave Detmar had come in and was standing listening to the words.

The doctor was powerless to interfere. He recognised

the hysteria in Mary's manner and awaited in dread what might follow.

Mr Collings' polish was but a very thin veneer, and Mrs Cameron's laugh struck it all off.

He flew into a tremendous rage and used some very ugly words. He stood up and got crimson in the face. He gasped, "You—you laugh! You do well to laugh! Where have you hidden her? Where have you sent her to? You know where she is! I insist upon your telling me. I'll have the place searched; I'll have the police in..."

"Come, come, Collings," interrupted Mr Detmar, who could not yet forget that Mrs Cameron was a beautiful woman, and his wife's friend. "Mrs Cameron will tell us all you want to know, I am sure, if you have a little patience."

But at this attempted control Mr Collings broke all bonds. "She—she tell me! Why, if it wasn't for her the girl would be here now. Where is my daughter? Will you tell me or won't you?" he almost yelled.

His manner was menacing. The two other men were powerless to intervene.

Mary faced them, the hysterical light still in her eyes, a mocking smile on her lips.

"I know quite well where your daughter is," she said slowly, dwelling on her words as if purposely to enrage him further. "She is safe in the keeping of a gentleman. She is a fortunate girl."

"You vile procuress, you shall pay for this!" he shouted. He made a step forward in his rage, as if he would have physically taken vengeance on her.

Benjamin started from his seat. With a gesture she waved him back, and he remembered what he had at stake, and with a repressed groan, he sat down again.

Her face was whiter than Collings's.

"Procuress!" he repeated, threateningly.

"Have you finished?" she asked him, raising her hand as if to enjoin silence.

170

There was a pause. Benjamin was in an agony of suspense, Dave Detmar curious and expectantly excited, Collings breathless, speechless with passion.

"Procuress, you call me," she began. "Well, suppose I confess it. Suppose I confess I am a procuress, prostitute, that I am lower still, that I am lowest of the low, viler than the vile. Suppose I confess all this. I do confess it. I am all this—more. Well, then." Up to now she had been speaking quietly, in a low voice, but here her eyes began to blaze and her figure seemed to extend. "Then, when I am all this, and more than all this, then I am too good company for you, and such as you." Here she made a comprehensive gesture, which included the doctor, and for which he felt bound to be grateful. "Jews, Jews!" she almost hissed this out. "The scum of civilisation. I know you now! Money dogs, pedlars, sharps. You—your company had degraded me, me, me! Do you hear? Jews!" Nothing can express the scorn with which she uttered the word "Jews."

"And now." Her voice, which had been monotonously even, rose slightly. "Leave my room! Leave it at once, I say!" She stamped her foot. "Not a word, not a word more..."—for Mr Detmar tried to speak. "Go, and if you've any sense left after your centuries of money grubbing be glad that your daughter has, at least, a chance of freeing herself from you. Go."

And they went.

Then she flung herself on the sofa and cried with all her might—hot angry tears of shame and disappointment. What had she told Charlie? What two scenes she had just passed through! What misery and degradation! And what must be the end?

But her sobs wore themselves out. There was no comfort in her position: the hard springs of the hotel sofa hurt her and the slippery cushion was no ease for her head. She sat up and tried to collect her scattered energies. First she walked towards the glass and rearranged her hair, and as she did so an envelope

171

placed in a conspicuous position before the clock caught her eye. She recognised it at once. It was her hotel bill, unsettled now for three weeks.

That little blue paper had an uncommonly sobering effect upon her. What had she done? She was shocked, appalled at herself. Good God! If Dr Phillips never came back; if, after all she had said against the Jews, he should leave her to herself.

Her money in the bank had come to an end in his absence. What would become of her? Visions of imprisonment for debt, of prosecutions for obtaining board and lodging under false pretences, flitted before her. Once before her allegiance to Dr Phillips had been restablished by such thoughts as these. But then she had done nothing against him; then at least she would not have had to reproach herself for her foolishness, her idiotcy.

And for what had she imperilled everything? For nothing but the momentary gratification of temper. Charlie—what was Charlie compared to all she had flung away?

And why, oh! why had she told him? Where had her thoughts been during this last hour? She failed to recognise herself. It was something apart from her well ordered mind, that wild hysterical outburst that had ruined her.

She looked into the glass at her wild eyes and white face. It seemed some mad and distorted dream she had passed through. She, generally so cool, so logical, had acted like some insane creature in an asylum. With her own white hands she had flung aside all that she thought most worth retaining.

First she cursed herself for her madness in telling Charlie; then she stamped her foot and execrated herself for estranging Benjamin.

If only she had not told Charlie she might have been able to cast off the bonds that chafed her, but now... Charlie would have none of her: she had driven him from her for ever by her confession. And the way that confession had been made! No extenuating circumstances; no story, so easily invented, of deceit and betrayal. Idiot, fool that she was!

And now what could she do? Her only hope, of course, was in Benjamin; but how get at him, how reweave her spells? The child...true, there remained the child and his love for it. For the first time she thought almost tenderly of Nita. He would never leave his child to poverty.

But he might take the child and leave her. Never, she resolved.

She sent for Nita and took the baby in her arms. It shrank from her in surprise and repugnance; the child she had never caressed looked up at her with the large black eyes that were Benjamin's.

"You love your mother, Nita. You wouldn't go away from your mother?" she asked, feverishly.

Nita only looked at her silently and startled.

Then Benjamin Phillips walked coolly into the room as if nothing had happened and said, "You were quite right and very clever to include me in your censure. But child, child, you have burnt your boats!"

Book II · Chapter X

Then he came and sat down beside her and embraced her and said, "Poor child! poor child!" over and over again, loving and caressing her with his voice, and his eyes, and his hand. And she sat, silent, quiescent, astounded, utterly unable to understand the nature of the man who loved her. It seemed she had no forgiveness to ask, and no future to dread, so she returned his caresses, and wondered.

"And to think I dared not defend you while that cad was abusing you, my poor darling, and it was all my fault. I should not have left you, poor girl, poor girl." He stroked her hair and lingered with his lips on her white cheek.

He was genuinely sorry for her. He had thought so much of her while he was away, while he was ill. He had thought of her—young, beautiful, and innocent. He had gone over her gentleness to him and the love she had ever shown him, and had reproached himself and felt she was after all fit for a better life than the one he had given her.

He had to sit still and listen while she was abused and insulted, and he felt he was to blame for it all. He must make it up to her somehow. He caressed her, and, once more safe, she loathed his caresses, disliked him, and misunderstood the generosity of his nature. She thought of Charlie, while her protector was filled with tenderness for her, while he thought regretfully of her position and tried to make her feel she was so much to him that he would compensate her with his love for all she might miss.

Perhaps in the larger knowledge that had come to him lately he saw that Mary's position *was* a sad one.

He did not repent of what he had done to her, nor did the immorality of it appal him. But he could see that the fresh start his successful mission had given him in his career was thrown away if the woman he loved could not share it with him.

On the one side there were all the ties of custom and expediency binding him to his Jewish brethren, his Jewish wife, his Jewish patients. On the other there was the knowledge that by only applying for it he could obtain the editorship and all the power of the new medical paper that was to be launched in the autumn. He knew that once installed in this position, and working as he knew he had it in him to work, all the ambitions of his early manhood and the prophecies of his early friends could be amply and abundantly satisfied. But—and in this large "but" lay the whole question—the post was scarcely remunerative. He must have money. Not for himself—his wants were few; and he might arrange matters with his wife...but for Mary.

He would no longer be able to spare fifteen hundred a year for he would not have so much altogether; and he knew besides that there would be too much strain upon his brain to permit of his devoting any large portion of his time to speculation and illegitimate money making.

Thinking of all this as he walked alone after having left Mr Collings at his own house and seen his patient once again, he heard the first rumbling of the storm that he knew must break over Mary's head. He heard the abuse levelled at her by the Collingses, to whom Mr Collings gave an unexaggerated account of his interview with her, and he was appealed to to confirm the general opinion.

He dared not, he literally dared not, refuse the appeal. Until he had decided for or against, his very living, and hers, depended upon the favour of these people.

He knew them so well, their jealousy, their gregariousness, their easily influenced opinions. If he, in the

175

face of her avowal that she was not what they had taken her for, became her champion it would be but the beginning of an end that would mean to him, for the present at least, ruin. It is wonderful how rapidly things are disseminated among a sect that can make or unmake a reputation by their force of gossip.

It was impossible for him to risk the loss of all those daily guineas that fell into his hands as Mosses, Levys, Jacobs, and Benjamins called daily in Portsdown Road to be relieved of their ailments, having been told by Mrs Aaron, or Joseph, or Marks, or Lucas that Dr Benjamin Phillips was the only man that could cure them.

Sexually the Jews are not an immoral race, and the god of respectability has a prominent place among their household idols. The mere hint that their immaculate doctor, a married man, was on too friendly terms with a woman of doubtful character and his reputation would be dead.

So circumspectly must he behave that no hint of his intimacy with her should get abroad.

He had been thinking of all this before he had rejoined her, thinking of the difficulties of the position, almost, not quite, seeing a possibility, a necessity, of life without Mary. But then he had gone back to her, gone into the hotel to take the taste of that terrible scene out of his mouth and found her sitting subdued, her lovely eyes tear stained and his daughter in her arms.

She had brightened visibly as he entered. "Poor child, how she loves me," he thought. "Poor Mary." And he caressed her silently; and his heart swelled with love and pity. She put the child on his knee as if to plead her cause. He understood the intention and drew them both closer to him. These two weaklings looking to him for strength and sustenance could not be gainsaid. He loved them.

And while he was thinking thus, Mary was disgusted by the weakness of his tender embraces, she shuddered at his fevered breath full upon her soft cheek. She was

176

all the time mentally comparing him with Charlie, in his robust youth.

"What are you going to do?" he asked Mary, at length.

"Do? Nothing at all, Benito mio," she replied softly. "Now you have come back to me I feel quite safe. What would you have me do?"

"Don't go away again, Doc-doc," whispered Nita and flung her thin arms round his neck. He clasped her closer and his heart grew fuller as he thought of their dependence upon him, and vowed to himself that come what might he would never forsake them. And this vow, and the fear of how much he might have to sacrifice to retain them, bound them to him with a stronger bond.

His brain was not very clear; he did not seem to be able to think very clearly or coherently about the difficulties before him. But just the same as during the onset of his illness in Egypt he had not been able to disabuse his mind of the impression that if he saw Mary he would be cured, so now that a relapse was threatening him he felt he must secure himself in the possession of these two.

A vague idea came to him that if it were not for that invalid woman in Ischl he could have made Mary his wife and defied the world with her by his side; but the thought faded.

He felt weak, and he knew that his illness was still lingering about him. The questions of the future must wait. In the meantime he must arrange with Mary as to her immediate plans. Then he would go to lie down at his hotel, hiding his weakness and combating it by his strength of will.

He thought she had better go back at once to town; it was no good lingering in Eastbourne. She would find her position impossibly uncomfortable, and he could do nought to alleviate it. In fact, as he explained to her, after the child had left them he must pretend to side with her enemies. In public, at least, he must avoid her.

177

"The best thing you can do is to go back to town. I suppose the house is in order, or can be made so in a few hours. Go home either this evening or tomorrow morning. I'll come to you as soon as possible. Trust in me, my dear. There's nothing to be gained by remaining, except recrimination and arguments and possibly more insults. You see, you were so very ardent in your observations this morning, and it will be all over the place by now; you know what a gossip Detmar is."

"I wonder Mrs Detmar hasn't been to see me. I should have thought her first impulse would have been to come and try to find out first hand 'all about it.'"

"I daresay that was her first impulse; but when she heard you despised her and hers and all the rest of it she probably thought it best to remain away. Besides, I fancy the Collingses will make a point of all their friends taking up the cudgels to avenge their wrongs on you. It will suit them to consider Florrie as the innocent victim of your evil machinations."

"Very well, then I'll go back to town tomorrow or the next day."

"Why not tonight?"

"Because I want to see for myself if you're right." Which was not candid. Mary could not leave East-bourne until she had at least found out whether Charlie had left, what he had done or thought.

And so Dr Phillips found it impossible to move her from her determination and at last gave up the attempt wearily. They then discussed the future and made their plans for meeting. Dr Phillips asked Mary what she thought of moving, going into another neighbourhood and thus letting her friends lose sight of her entirely.

But Mary did not fix upon anything definitely. She did not want to commit herself until she knew what Charlie would say to her. In fact, she wanted nothing just now but to find out what had become of Charlie when he left her in the morning.

Every caress of the doctor's—every evidence she saw

178

in him that he considered himself bound to her eternally, one spirit and one flesh—made her the more determined to see Charlie, to ascertain beyond doubt if it was indeed too late. If there were no chance of reinstating herself in her former place in his esteem. If there were no outlook in her future but Benjamin, Benjamin as she began to think of him, feeble and sickly, with nauseous fondlings and slow springless movements.

Book II · Chapter XI

She could think of no better scheme than to go to the park as usual that evening, for she thought if he still lingered in Eastbourne with the desire of seeing her again it was there he would expect to find her.

She dressed herself very carefully by the light of the two candles, critically observing herself in the glass and taking a long time to make her choice between a plain black cashmere, almost nunlike in its simplicity, and a more becoming costume of brown cloth and grey astrakhan. Finally she decided that under the circumstances the black would be more effective.

"Idiot, fool, that I was!" she thought. "He will think I am one of those women who are downright bad. I shall never be able to persuade him it was only hysteria, though if I can see him and get a chance I daresay I shall be able to improve matters."

And while she was adjusting the black straw bonnet, neatly tying the velvet under her white chin, critically regarding her *tout ensemble*, she tried to concoct some history that would serve to rehabilitate her in Charlie's eyes.

Then she walked alone to the park, her tightly fitting dress exhibiting in all their beauty the slender curves of her figure, her small neat bonnet and black veil completing a picture of decorum and propriety. She had a book in her hand; she meant to sit down where the light should clearly reveal her to anyone searching and where reading should be an excuse for any conspicuousness there might be in the position.

But when she arrived at the park gates she found the evening had threatened rain, so that the band played in the covered skating rink instead of in the open air. This

suited her purpose even better. She took a seat just
outside, under the glass verandah, so placed that she
could see all the visitors as they entered the park, and
they could see her.

And fortune favoured her more than she was aware

of, for Charlie—miserable, heartsick, with his young heart still on fire, shocked as he had been by this terrible disenchantment—was there a long time before her, and stood watching her with yearning eyes.

Then began the trial that Benjamin had foreseen. Mr and Mrs Detmar came slowly down the little hill that led into the concert hall. They passed the shining row of electric lights, they passed the trees, undulating in the breeze; they passed, without a bow, that solitary black figure with her eyes modestly cast down upon her book. After them followed the Montague Levys, Mrs Lucas, and Ray Collings—Mrs Collings's feelings kept her at home. Gone were all the cheery greetings and the intimacy that almost made greetings unnecessary. With their accentuated noses in the air and their heavy features fixed into an expression of utter unconsciousness they passed on into the darkness and left the woman sitting there alone.

There had been a crowded meeting at Mrs Detmar's that afternoon, and the whole question had been thoroughly threshed out. There were no card tables brought out; cards were not even thought of, so exciting was the topic they had met to discuss. There had been tea, and cakes of all descriptions, and the Babel of many tongues.

Mr Detmar came in among this assembly of women and caught the last word that fell from Mrs Levy's lips.

"Mrs Cameron! I won't have Mrs Cameron's name mentioned in my house. She is nothing in the world but a ..."

And he used a word that is not usually mentioned in the presence of ladies; but in the gravity of the occasion it was overlooked, only Mrs Montague Levy feebly and fretfully remarked that "for her part she thought he might have managed to express it differently. But there, there was a great deal of wickedness in the world, and as far as she was concerned she never had any opinion of Mrs Cameron. Look at her hair even: it was

182

most likely dyed. She didn't know anyone who had that coloured hair natural to them."

Mrs Detmar thought no one could blame Dave for using the word; after all it seemed Mrs Cameron had used it of herself.

The incident reminded Mrs Jeddington of a story twenty years old, which she proceeded to tell, to the obvious weariness of the company, who had all heard it before, about a girl whom "we had all received and who was supposed to be the adopted daughter of Mr Solomon, but it turned out afterwards that she was only living with him, and called him papa in public just to deceive them. He was dead now, but he had not been buried among Jews: they never forgave him the trick."

Then some association caused Mrs Lucas to say reflectively, "I wonder if Dr Phillips suspected anything."

It was the only moment he stood in jeopardy; but it was only for a moment. Mrs Detmar answered indignantly, while all the ladies looked at each other in startled silence.

"Of course not. How is a doctor to know anything about his patients excepting what they tell him? He knew her through attending Mr Cameron—I daresay an assumed name—through his last illness. How was he to know they were not married? Dave says he was quite overcome when he heard her, and turned quite white. It was a great shock to him; anybody could see that. Dr Phillips isn't the man to even suspect anything of that sort and keep it to himself."

Reassured by their leader, they branched off into an interlude in which all said a few words in praise of their trusted doctor. How he respected women, what a good life he had always led, even before he was married. How, whenever he had anything...well, anything *particular* to attend them for, he was always so delicate and so considerate; more like a woman than a man. And as for his conversation, no one had ever heard Dr

Phillips even make an improper allusion. Then they all thought of hand pressures and tender sympathetic glances. Mrs Lucas felt thoroughly ashamed of her suggestion. She subsided into silence when the virulent gossip broke forth again and like a nest of hornets they buzzed and stung around the decaying reputation of this woman, who but yesterday had been their bosom friend.

Mrs Levy and Mrs Detmar rivalled each other in bitterness, and there was no depth of depravity to which they didn't suggest Mary Cameron had stooped.

Their race prejudices reawoke with vigour: her Christianity was blamed for all her misdemeanours.

"That settles the matter as far as I am concerned," wound up Mrs Detmar, when she could make herself heard in the Babel of voices. "That will be the first and last Christian who ever darkens my door."

"Or mine," "Or mine," echoed the satellites.

Only Mrs Jeddington, conscious of treachery in the camp, could not take the same vow; and after she had delivered herself of the one stock anecdote which was always produced when general or specific wickedness was discussed, she subsided into silence, feeling in her honest vulgar soul a sense of pity for the mangled Mary, and a strong opinion that Florrie's elopement was not entirely the result of her machinations.

As for Soph, she listened and sneered. She had begun to despise "the people," she envied Florrie, and she felt an urgent desire to have a long conversation with Mary and ask her many questions about inner secrets of that wicked fascinating existence she was supposed to lead.

Before the afternoon séance concluded Mary Cameron's fate was sealed. They would not know her.

So she sat on alone with her book by her side as one by one they passed her in silence. Her soul grew hot within her, her cheeks flushed crimson, and her hands trembled. She despised them, she despised them all; these egotistical people with their narrow lives, their crude customs, their vulgar manners. How ill bred was the way in which they were all grouped near her now, loudly talking and ignoring her!

She despised them, but for all that they hurt her.

It came home to her a little, sitting there alone and neglected, that she had turned against her sex. So easily had she fallen, she scarce realised it was a fall; the years had rolled by empty and dull. Philosophy and Benjamin had taught her that it was only an imaginary distinction that placed an unloved wife above a beloved mistress.

And yet, and yet...this despicable people despised her.

Her cheeks flamed and her thoughts grew hot. Benjamin! It was Benjamin Phillips who had brought her to this, betrayed her with his false philosophy, tempted her with his wealth.

She hated him as she sat there, and Charlie, who had brought freshness into her dull domestic life, came not to her.

Sitting there, apparently reading, while the music penetrated through the glass and the people passed and repassed her in the enjoyment of the keen sea air and the company of their friends, a perfect storm of angry feelings was rending her bosom; her face was set in hard white lines.

And miserable Charlie, watching her with longing eyes, as the moth watches the flame, and seeing her seated alone, deserted, and despised, felt by the leaps and bounds of his heart that his passion had died no sudden death at the shock of his knowledge; felt all that was youthful and passionate within him, yearning towards her in her solitude. He hated and raged against all who had deserted her, against anyone who should trample on his poor fallen goddess. What could he do? Mingled emotions kept him spell bound in his place. He loved and feared her more than ever, but it was a different love and a different fear.

185

He wanted to go to her and comfort her but he dared not trust himself near the witching of her smile.

What she had told him seemed to have put her beyond the pale of possible wifehood, and yet some thought he could never have found words for reddened his ingenuous cheek. He took a few irresolute steps towards her, and she saw him and raised her eyes to his.

The look she gave him was the perfection of acting.

It was full of unutterable sadness and humility. It was but a second her eyes were raised; a dumb pleading was in them. Then her lids fell, her head drooped a little. The picture of a forsaken and repentant Magdalene.

He reached her side and stood silent beside her for a moment, full of contending feelings. Then he took the vacant chair, and she thanked him with a look.

It was enough; her heart beat high with hope. He who had sinned not was filled with embarrassment, unable to speak, his sympathy for the shame she must be feeling over mastering every other sentiment or power.

But triumph overmastered all her anger, calmed her, and gave her back her self possession. The task before her was difficult; she wanted to prove it not impossible. She had to unsay her words of the morning, or put a different interpretation upon them. She had to regain, as nearly as possible, her lost position in Charlie's eyes.

After all it was he who spoke first.

"Do you mind my coming to sit here?" he asked; then stammered on, uncertain of his ground, "There are so few chairs, every place seems full tonight."

She sighed, and the sadness of her expression wrung his heart with pity for her.

"It is good of you to speak to me at all." Then she looked at him, and he saw through moisture into the dark blue depths of her eyes. "Look, they have all abandoned me." With a gesture she indicated the immaculate Children of Israel, who were even then

186

engaged in commenting on her brazen behaviour and transferring their theories from Alec to Charlie.

"You told them," he faltered.

"I could not sail under false colours," she answered tremulously. "Perhaps if you knew all... Perhaps if I had had even one friend..." She stopped, overcome by her emotions. Then she said passionately. "Don't forsake me, Mr Doveton. Don't let me feel I am quite alone in the world; it is too terrible." He noticed the nervous interlacing of her fingers.

How her appeal moved and thrilled him! "Forsake you, forsake you!" was all he could stammer out. But under shelter of the night—the light having all at once amiably vanished—he laid his hand on hers.

For the moment they were almost in total darkness.

"You will be my friend?" she murmured, and clasped the hand he had given her.

"I will; indeed, indeed I will," he answered and emboldened, pressed the hand he held.

As suddenly as it had gone out the electric light flashed up again and revealed the tableau to the doctor, as with his slow step he passed along on the grass.

Mary knew he saw her. Rapidly as they unclasped hands, it was too late. She hated him, she was glad for the second that he saw them, glad that she had the power to bring that look of pain into his eyes; but she was also annoyed, for she knew she must not quarrel with him yet.

He passed her, just raising his hat in greeting, scarcely looking at her. The Jews saw and were satisfied, and when he joined them treated him to a dissertation on her viciousness, and her insolence in brazening it out, and conjectured whether Mr Doveton or Mr Murphy, or both, were her lovers.

Dr Phillips listened. He said very little, and they could see that the shock of knowing that the woman who had been his friend and his wife's friend had discovered herself as she was, was too much for him.

187

They sympathised with him, wondered what Mrs Phillips would say, and anticipated how horrified she would feel.

There was no other topic they could discourse upon. The exposure of Mrs Cameron had blotted out everything else.

They were no longer surprised at her self betrayal. They could see she was tired of respectability. "Just look at the way she sits there before us all talking to that Mr Doveton when she ought to be hiding her head, ashamed to show herself among decent people. The park authorities ought to interfere."

Only Mrs Jeddington said, "Poor little Nita. Doctor, isn't it sad to think of that little child, to think of her growing up in such surroundings? If only she'd been a boy, now, it wouldn't have mattered so much."

"You know," said Mrs Montague Levy in a half whisper, "I think Nita is very like Mr Murphy; they are both so dark. I've often wondered that such a fair woman should have such a dark child."

This was not pleasant for the doctor to hear. The wild unrest that pursued him, and had ever pursued him since this fair haired boy crossed his path, was raging within him now as he saw Charlie and Mary still in converse, side by side. From the very first moment he had seen the youth he had had an instinct against him. Each time he had met him this instinctive dread and dislike had deepened, Why was he here tonight with her if he had correctly interpreted that interrupted interview of the morning?

Dr Phillips felt so miserably weak; he felt he could bear no more trouble. The agueish fever was on him again this evening, and he could scarcely command himself to appear as usual among his patients.

' He soon left them, and the park. Again gravely saluting Mary as he passed.

She went home satisfied. The Detmars and their friends would have been even more shocked if they had known how contentedly she had gone home after they had overwhelmed her by their disapproval.

In very truth she forgot all about them, and the incidents of the early parts of the evening. Her mind was full of her conversation with Charlie, and she felt she had done well.

She had told him nothing; but she had played the part of the injured woman, once the betrayed girl.

Nor had she given any details; her ready imagination had not yet fixed upon the exact colouring of the picture she would present him with. In the meantime he was to be her friend. Some day she would tell him—All! This she had promised him.

He had been no less respectful than heretofore in his manner, perhaps a shade more distant. He seemed to feel a separation; that her confession should make him, if he would retain that precious gift of friendship she proferred him, more chivalrous and deferential in his manner.

But she trusted to time and to her woman's wit to cure him gently of that and to teach him that he might find balm for all his sufferings.

She had fully made up her mind now that she would throw over Benjamin Phillips and marry Charlie Doveton. She would be a lady, and use her beauty and intelligence to better purpose than for the entertainment of a sickly Jewish doctor.

But to do this she must have time. And to secure time she must secure Benjamin and must resign herself, at least for the present, to submit to him and continue in her old course of behaviour towards him.

All this was repugnant to her, not on account of its immorality, for that weighed very lightly with her, but because her splendid physical organisation shrank from his ill health.

She shuddered when she thought of his feeble embraces; she began to look upon him as a vicious and ailing old man. She had noted the feebleness of his step, the added stoop in the shoulders, and again he had compared unfavourably with Charlie's vigorous youth.

And then Nita was decidedly a drawback. Charlie might find Nita anything but an acquisition to that little ménage she was planning for him in the future, and to her Nita would be as ever a burden and a disgrace.

If she could only persuade Dr Phillips to adopt Nita. She thought she could manage it; she saw difficulties in her path but her hopes made light of them. She was full of hopes tonight and felt a glow of self satisfaction in her conduct during this long and eventful day. Everything had turned out well.

She had got rid of all her so called friends, just when they might inconveniently spy upon her actions and report them to the doctor. The confession she had made to Charlie had not estranged him; and perhaps after all it would prevent there being any difficulties later on. Certainly he had not renewed his offer, but she felt that was only a question of time.

Then as to Benjamin Phillips, she must let time and circumstances guide her, only remembering that it was absolutely necessary that he should be kept satisfied until such time as she could conveniently do without him.

A more utterly heartless and shameless decision could not have been arrived at. She settled her part and set herself to play it with consummate skill. To keep the two men apart, allowing one to supply her needs until such time as the other should definitely give her not only his means but his name, that was her task. She thought it all over in the train going up to London next day and congratulated herself on her prospects.

190

Book III · Chapter I

And Dr Benjamin Phillips ?

He also returned to town. September was approaching and with it the great fast that draws the wandering Jews back into the shelter of their synagogues.

He came to meet his wife. Her ten weeks' cure had been completed, and he was at home to receive her.

The cold, clean, comfortless house looked less home-like than ever without the inanimate figure of its lethargic mistress. It was clean, but there is comparatively little comfort in cleanliness. He wandered into the dining room. The shining mahogany, the chairs in their stiff array, the table without even its usual decoration of literature, the wire blinds that were fly blown and looked like prison gratings, even the oil painted pictures of his father and mother in law failed to bring comfort to a man suffering from the effects of a low fever.

The autumn skies were dull and cheerless. He took up his position by the window to watch for his wife. He had found a telegram saying that she would be home at four, and that her father and mother would accompany her.

He waited for her, unanxious, unheeding, as one waits for those whose arrival is no pleasure. He had not seen Mary again since the evening when she had been in Devonshire Park with Charlie. He had not dared, he had been too closely surrounded. But the picture which the sudden flash of electric light had revealed was still present to his mind as he stood there watching for his wife.

All around him was dull and cold and cheerless, and

even the jealousy he experienced knew an antidote in the languor and torpidity of the fever.

He felt miserable. The picture of Mary sitting hand in hand with Charlie Doveton, comforted by him in her desolation, added only a dim pain to his weakness.

Failure! That was the burden of his thoughts. His money troubles—so strong were his race instincts—pressed upon him the hardest. His first act when he had returned to town was to send Mary a large cheque. The smallness of the balance left at his banker's made him feel sick.

He had overridden many difficulties in his career, had financed and finessed himself out of worse troubles than these, but he had never felt as he did now.

In reality things were not so bad with him. His debts were trifling, his wife's income sufficient to pay expenses, and his professional earnings large. But he had not been used to ask his wife to pay expenses, and his pride shrank from it. He could not bear the fall he imagined he would suffer in her eyes.

The causes of the gloom and depression under which he was labouring were almost entirely physical. The remains of low fever, in addition to an empty, half warmed house, and overstrained expectation ending in disappointment.

He was not fond of his wife's parents. They were two stout old commonplace Frankfurt citizens. It did not cheer him to think of them sitting at his board and entertaining him daily with their gossip about people of whom he knew nothing, and cared less.

He groaned in spirit over it all and then, sick of the dismal skies and the muddy streets, went back to his study, flung himself in utter weariness on the sofa, and went to sleep.

So when Mrs Phillips and Mr and Mrs Strauss arrived in their noisy four wheeler with their luggage, tired from their journey, there was no one but the servant to receive them. And Mrs Phillips was sorely troubled that her father and mother should see her husband was so negligent.

It ruffled even her placid temper a little; and when the doctor awoke, and the two met about an hour later, she commenced to mildly reproach him.

But she only commenced. It took her, poor dull unloved wife, only half a second to see that it was not well with this honoured husband of hers. She marked, as the other woman had marked, his dropping gait and dulled eye, and a sudden rush of tenderness came over her, and the love that the commonplaces of years had almost smothered welled up again in her heart.

Her reproaches died on her lips as he kissed her and sank heavily into a chair, feeling almost too weak to stand.

"What's the matter with you, Benjamin?" she asked almost sharply in her anxiety. "Have you been ill?"

"Ill! no! What put that into your head? Do you think because you're better I must be ill?"

He spoke irritably, but even his voice was altered, and his wife was not to be set at ease by his denial.

She watched him all that evening as he played host to her people. She saw how ineffectual were his efforts to be genial and courteous as usual. She marked his vain attempt to conceal his languor and indisposition, and that night, after he had gone to bed, she stole into his room and found him in the unresisted grasp of the fever. He had succumbed when he thought himself alone; and his moanings and restless movements were outward signs of the illness he could no longer master.

This woman—whose life had been for so long one of constant invalidism, whose Ischl cure had only brought her home with the knowledge that her malady had reached its climax and that an operation of dreaded severity was her only alternative to a horrible death—was full of pity and care for the man who was her husband.

She could not fathom him, she could not understand

193

why he should conceal his illness as if it were a crime, but she could and did understand how to nurse him and soothe him, surround him with the thousand and one comforts a thoughtful woman can bring to a sickbed.

Morning dawned and found the doctor unable to struggle any longer. He could not raise his heavy head from his pillow. The fever of the night had exhausted him, although the gentle tendance of his wife had saved him the intolerable thirst and the misery of a solitude peopled with the phastasmagoria of fever that had tortured him before.

He had never been ill since his student days, when he had caught the smallpox whilst studying by special permission at Darenth. He had been nursed in the hospital; that is to say he had had his food and medicine brought to him at stated times and, for the rest, had been allowed to lie still on his hard bed and count the weary hours between the visits of his attendants, longing the while for the cup of drink they generally placed just beyond his reach.

He had a different nursing now. During the few days that followed her return home, Mrs Phillips never left the bedside of her dear husband. He even found his mother in law a comfort, for the two women between them gave him what he had never known, sympathetic and loving care.

His illness was soon diagnosed: intermittent fever, than which few illnesses are worse, whether for patient or attendant.

The house was besieged by his friends. Mrs Phillips's life was made a burden to her by the numerous letters she was forced to write to the inquirers who would not take a formal answer from the servant.

Israel melted with sympathy, and half the synagogue would have sat up with him by night or nursed him by day. But Mrs Phillips would not give up her place by her husband's bedside.

It was her hands that spread the damp cool linen over

194

his fever racked brow. She was always there, responsive to his slightest movement and ready with the draught, the cooling drink, or the carefully prepared nourishment.

Perhaps it was through having been constantly ill herself, perhaps it was only through the mighty power of a good woman's love, but from whatever cause, Clothilde Phillips was the perfection of a nurse and waited upon her husband with absolute devotion.

Three weeks he lay ill, the while her life was bounded by the four walls of the sick room. And perhaps they were the happiest three weeks she had spent in her married life. He was dependent on her, she was everything to him, and she loved him and yearned over him, giving him all the love she would have experienced for the child she had never borne and all the devotion she felt for the husband who had never been truly hers.

He was never in actual danger, so she was spared the anguish of doubt; and at length the fever abated, the nights were passed in normal sleep, and Benjamin was convalescent.

He enjoyed that sense of happiness which cessation of pain always brings. He thanked his wife for her care of him and thanked Mrs Strauss for aiding her. He felt very grateful, too, to his brilliant colleague who had devoted so much time to his case.

His frame of mind in the first few days after the fever had left him was gentle beyond expression, so long it seemed to him he had suffered that he could feel nothing but gratification at the return of comparative comfort.

"He is such a splendid invalid," his two nurses said. He took with avidity cupful after cupful of all the food they prepared for him; he was anxious to get strong again. Knowledge came back to him slowly, and remembrance of the precipice on the brink of which he had stood.

The first day he felt strong enough he asked for the cards of the people who had called. Mrs Cameron's was not amongst them. He could not conceal his anxiety, and he turned to his wife for information.

"Have you heard anything of Mrs Cameron?" he asked.

"I heard she had assisted Florrie Collings to elope and that Mr Collings had found out she was never married to Mr Cameron, but I did not believe it, poor thing, and I told them so. But I've not taken much interest in that or anything since you've been ill, Ben, darling," she answered tenderly.

"Has she sent round since I've been ill?"

"Oh, yes! Nannie and Nita have called every day. That dear little child, Ben! She burst out crying one day when I was telling Nannie what nights you have had. I just hugged her for it, the darling. She is so fond of you. If you feel strong enough may she come up and see you this afternoon?"

No proposition Mrs Phillips could have made would have found such favour in her husband's eyes.

The little one came into the room on tiptoe with an exaggeration of caution that would have been comic had it not had its tragic side when one considered the fragility of the little being who was so careful lest her too heavy tread should disturb the man's repose.

She crept up to him slowly, almost shyly, Mrs Phillips watching her the while. One moment Nita stood by his sofa and put out her hand to him. Then her lovely eyes met the hollow eyes, the sunken cheeks; she burst into tears; he leaned forward and gathered her in his arms, and she lay and sobbed upon her father's breast.

"Dear little thing," said Clothilde, wiping her eyes. "She is so soft hearted."

"You can leave her with me," said Benjamin, straining her tightly to him. "I will mind her, and Nannie can have tea in the kitchen."

Nita's tears were soon over; but the doctor still held her in his arms with the strongest emotion. She was with him for a long time that day and every day during

196

his convalescence, and gradually it became an institution for Nita to come and sit with Dr Phillips while Mrs Phillips took rest.

In fact, to an experienced eye Mrs Phillips looked infinitely more ill than her husband. Her obesity had increased to such an extent that locomotion seemed pain to her. She moved slowly and with obvious effort.

The doctor had not yet noticed her state, nor did he for some days.

In the meantime he got well quickly, and Nita's visits roused him gradually to take interest in his surroundings.

He would try to lead the child to talk to him of its mother, but in this he was ever unsuccessful. Some instinct kept the baby dumb on that one topic, but of all else that concerned her, of her little daily life with its infant joys and infant cares, she would prattle to him unceasingly.

Book III · Chapter II

Benjamin was now well enough to go about the house, and to talk of resuming his professional duties. For the first time he noticed his wife's exceeding feebleness, and spoke to her of it. He was very gentle and loving with her now. The tenderness he had always had was deepened by gratitude, and he still wanted her in many ways. Mary's image was a little dim to him still; although Nita was nearer to him than ever.

Clothilde burst into tears when he spoke to her of her health. She was happy now and dreaded what was before her. She had tried to forget it, to regard it as so immeasurably distant that it might be ignored; but this could no longer be.

The doctor in Ischl had told her she had a tumour, which must either be removed or she must die.

The poor woman wept bitterly when she told her husband; and Benjamin Phillips, who had suspected the truth many years ago, felt all his professional instincts awaken.

The commonplace cretonne covered drawing room was transfigured to the suffering woman; for to Benjamin she became for a minute no longer the dull wife but the interesting patient.

He calmed her and comforted her with voice and touch and manner. He told her again and again to have no fear. He put the operation before her in a new light. A few days during which she would be almost entirely under the influence of chloroform or morphia, and then she would gradually awaken to find her sufferings over for ever and herself in such health as she had been a stranger to for many years.

He drew a consolatory picture, and she brightened

visibly. Then a thought struck her. She bent forward and whispered him one question, with an appeal in her eyes.

How could he answer her? Professional morality warred with an impulse of pity. What not make her happy for the time being? As usual with Dr Phillips, impulse gained the day: he answered her affirmatively and left her contented. She looked forward with hope instead of dread to the operation from which her trusted husband predicted such bright results.

This semiprofessional conversation did Benjamin good. It awoke him from his dream of convalescence to the practical questions of life; and with this awakening came the desire for Mary. So wonderfully allied seemed the good and bad genius of this man that his new tenderness for his wife reawoke in him all his passion for his mistress.

While he was talking to and soothing his wife, looking down upon her as she lay on the sofa in her fat unstudied misery, a vision of Mary came to him and softened his tone and deepened his pity. When she had whispered him whether the operation would affect her hopes of children, and he had lied to her, his child and the woman who was the mother of his child, and the thousand and one little remembered endearments of past time, made him especially pitiful to the woman who would never again know love dalliance—who never had known it as he knew it.

Looking upon women as subordinate beings made but for one purpose, born with but one mission, he always classified them into two categories. Either he said to himself, "This woman has love before her," and his feeling was one of affectionate interest, or he would think, "She has outlived passion," and his pity and sympathy showed involuntarily in voice and manner. Such unsubstantial caresses being in his eyes a kind of substitute for those they had lost.

But all thought and feeling had lain dormant during

199

his illness, except gratitude to the people who were helping to make him well. Now he commenced to be himself again.

The household resumed its wonted aspect, save that Mrs Strauss took the place of Mrs Phillips in the housekeeping department, and Mrs Phillips became the central figure of interest.

Everyone had missed the doctor so much during his illness that he was more than ever in request now he was again amongst them. The gentleman who had acted as his locum tenens had not won their favour, and the doctor found his practice more than restored to him.

All were very much interested in Mrs Phillips's condition, and the doctor was overwhelmed with inquiries and suggestions. Florrie Collings and Mrs Cameron had passed quite out of the general field of view, as first the doctor's illness and then the operation his wife was to undergo monopolised the public mind.

Mrs Detmar did her best to upset Mrs Strauss's and Mrs Phillips's peace of mind by telling them of cases she knew of people dying after operations, and she advised them not to have one performed. "Trust to time," she said, and proceeded to make observations too ignorant to chronicle on the nature and habits of tumours.

Mrs Collings came too, tearful and broken in spirit. Her resentment against Florrie was deep and grew deeper every time Mrs Lucas or Mrs Montague Levy made some sneering remark about "well brought up girls." But Mr Collings was yearning for his favourite daughter, and the Collings's ménage was rendered uncomfortable by this difference of sentiment among the elders. Mr Collings wanted to forgive his child and to receive her again; but Mrs Collings dwelt on the bad example that would be to the others, so the doctor's advice was sought for, and the dreary dispute was argued over and over again. Only Mrs Cameron's name was never mentioned; she had died to them all and they ceased to mention her, glad that their discreditable

200

share in having entertained her in their chaste houses should be forgotten.

But Benjamin Phillips found he had not forgotten Mary Cameron.

He pulled the check string one day and ordered the coachman to Brunswick Place with a keen rush of pleasure at the thought of again seeing her.

It was in the foggy dusk of an October evening, and he trusted to his good fortune not to be seen.

The long interval since he had seen her and the events and doubts that had intervened melted into an indefinite past as he was shown into the draperied drawing room and found her as before, lounging alone in the twilight.

She was dull and alone. Under the circumstances, that she was willing to resume her former relations with Benito goes without saying, and he found her no different from what she had ever been to him.

A subtle difference there was, but Benjamin saw it not. She was distrait, a little uneasy. Her glance wandered over to the door, a passing hansom made her start. The sound of a distant ring turned her cheeks white.

She was more impatient than ever with Nita, but she disguised her feelings better, and his claim on her attention withdrawn for a while, she retired a little, and left the father and the child to their small confidences and little caresses.

The child had grown; the broken baby accents were gone. It was an eagerly interested child whose eyes flashed rays of bright intelligence into Phillips's. The dark eyes greeted and frankly questioned him as he told the old old stories that had soothed her baby couch.

Question followed question as the delighted father helped to draw out more and more the powers of the developing mind.

"Nita must be taught to read," he said, "then she can see all these pretty stories for herself."

201

"I can read," answered the little one eagerly, getting off his lap and hastening away to find her book. There was a rushing sound upstairs, then a little cry.

"Good God! she has fallen down," exclaimed the doctor, rushing towards the door.

"She often falls," said Mary calmly, keeping her seat by the window.

And she still sat unmoved when the doctor re-entered bearing the sobbing child.

"Oh Nita, Nita, be a brave little girl. Don't cry, Nita, and Doctor will kiss the place to make it well."

"It won't make it well," sobbed the child. "I know better now."

But her sobs gradually ceased, and she showed him the book she still clasped in triumph.

Mrs Jeddington had given it to her at Eastbourne; it was full of beautiful pictures of animals with big letters opposite their names. Nannie had told Nita the letters, and Nita had wearied her with "what's this" and "what's that" until now, two months from the day she had received the book, Nita could read every word of it. Really a remarkable accomplishment for one four years old.

Benjamin Phillips was delighted. He had lost or forgotten his own ambition, but he felt it reviving in him for his daughter.

He turned to Mary for sympathy. Her words were warm, her manner cold; but that scarcely damped his enthusiasm. He sent for Nannie and gave her a sovereign; so pleased was he.

In the perseverance and brightness of the child the man saw the ghost of his boyhood, and long after the child had left off reading and was playing in the most babyish manner with a kitten that had strayed into the drawing room, his mind was full of her eager voice and he drifted into a dream of the future—of the time when she should be his pupil and all the world of science should open before her.

He roused himself from his dream as Mary sat still silent.

"Well, child," he said, kindly. "I suppose you have been very dull these last few weeks?"

"Very," she said, drily. She was racked with impatience. She did not know how long the doctor would stay, and Charlie, dear, indefinite Charlie, might come in at any moment.

"But Nita is quite a companion now, isn't she?" His face was bright with the pleasure she had given him. Mary, who was not used to seeing a pure emotion in the doctor, looked at him with surprise.

The doctor caught the glance.

"She is an exceptional child," was his apology. "I suppose now you will teach her yourself?"

"Indeed I shall not." Mary's impatience was making her forget her caution. "My teaching days are over for ever, thank God."

"I don't think God had much to do with it," he

203

answered, for her manner jarred on him. "You might at least give me the credit of that."

She laughed, recovering her temper.

"Quite right," she said. "But seriously, Benito, you don't expect me to teach her." She laid her hand on his arm and the caress turned the current of his thoughts.

"No, no, of course not. But now tell me..."

"Mr Charles Doveton," announced the servant.

The doctor sprang to his feet, and the two men faced each other.

Mary was equal to the occasion.

"You know Dr Phillips, don't you, Mr Doveton?" she said, easily. "Nita has not been well again; but the doctor assures me I need not be uneasy. Oh, must you go now, Doctor?" she continued, holding out her hand to the doctor, who was still standing. Then she rang the bell.

Dr Phillips had but one course open to him. He took the proferred hand, ignored his rival, and said, looking Mary full in the eyes, "Yes, I must go now, but I will look in again later."

"If you think it necessary," she replied, still in the same tone, but not meeting his eyes.

Then he left.

Alas! Mary was no longer a happy or a contented woman. She was playing for a big stake and the game was not going entirely in her favour.

She had encouraged Charlie all she dared. She had spun him a long fictitious tale of a desolate infancy and a betrayed girlhood. She had filled in all the details with a lavish hand. She had done all she knew to make the young man forget or look lightly upon her position.

But up to now she had failed. Since the day the lad had learned from her own lips what the woman was whom he had worshipped no word of love had passed his lips.

He could not give up seeing her. Daily his footsteps,

204

half unwilling, turned in the direction of Brunswick Place. Daily he spent long hours chatting, lounging, reading, sympathising with the beautiful mistress of that cosy drawing room.

But farther she could not get. It was as if an indefinable barrier, bearing the word "unclean," was between her and him. The lad, who had been bred in the country, could not embrace the sin of the city. All the passion of his dawning manhood drew him towards her. All the instincts of a refined nature warned him to beware.

He dallied with the temptation he could not resist. The holy part of the boy's first love was extinguished; but that which was unholy yet violent and vivid glowed fiercely. Yet she could complain of no want of respect: by no word or gesture did he overstep the social boundary that separates the sexes. She led him on by melancholy, by half unwilling words that told him she yearned for sympathy, by some dubious expression that hinted at a dawning love.

His vanity was flattered. Nowhere was he happy save in her society, and no thoughts came to him that were not rose tinted by her image. Yet something held him back, and the words she ever listened for had not yet fallen upon her ear.

She calculated her chances and knew that she must seize him in some moment when he was off his guard, in some position wherein his passion might master the remains of his prudence.

But that moment had not yet come, and Benjamin Phillips had met him there. Her tact had saved her, but she well understood she was on the edge of a precipice. Once Charlie Doveton recognised that instead of an inexperienced girl who had sinned, repented, and atoned he had to deal with one still in her sin, even the fascination she exercised over him would scarcely survive the knowledge.

"Your doctor does not like me" were Charlie's first words when the door closed. "Did you see the look he gave me?"

"He knows my unprotected condition," sighed Mary; as she gave him a glance of mingled sweetness and sadness. "He does not know you, nor what you are to me."

The young man blushed.

"I hope I am a good friend to you. Anyway I am not a blackguard to take advantage..." Here he got confused and Mrs Cameron helped out the situation with a deep sigh.

She laboured very hard, poor woman, and it seemed really a pity that she found it such up hill work.

But Charlie could not make up his mind. It was a situation in which he had no precedent to guide him. Would she marry him, notwithstanding? Could he ask her? Ought he to do so, considering how she trusted in his friendship? His uncle... But then he never could forsake her; she had told him he was her only comfort. Fancy, her only comfort! Then his strong young body would yearn for her until the longing was pain. It was wonderful that with all the youthful passion there was in him it had taken her so long to lead him into the toils.

It was his country life—the innocence of the fields—that had been his safeguard. But the victory, if slow, was sure.

Book III · Chapter III

Dr Phillips left Mrs Cameron's in a strange state of mind. He had held Mary as sacred to him and had trusted her as implicitly as good men trust their loving wives.

Once before his jealousy had been aroused, causelessly, he had owned afterwards to himself, but now he could no longer think his jealousy causeless. Charlie Doveton in Mary's rooms! All at once that scene he had witnessed in Devonshire Park, Eastbourne, which in his illness he had forgotten, which had seemed to him as only one of the many fevered dreams he had suffered under, came back to him in a flash of remembered pain. And Charlie's expression, as he had seen it this afternoon, was one of impatience at finding an intruder. He, Benjamin Phillips, Mary's Benito, an intruder— and in Mary's drawing room!

For five long years his home and his heart had centred in this woman, and in the indifference of security he had put similar hope in the future. He recalled Nita's little performance that afternoon; her mother sitting at the window, her father holding her in his arms. Truly it was a domestic picture. It was with a shock he remembered the woman was his mistress and his child a bastard.

Charles Doveton was at home in their house; he, Benjamin Phillips, an intruder! The basis of his mind admitted of but one interpretation of the situation. Mary had deceived him; and he who had deceived others all his life writhed under the pain of this and could scarcely bear the agony the conviction of her faithlessness inflicted on him.

He sat in his study, as he had sat that night after the

dance at the Collings's, in fear and wretchedness; and this passed anguish seemed joy in comparison with what he was feeling now. That had been but a slight stroke that had served to rivet closer the chain that bound him; this, this heavy blow must break it.

Break it!

The drawing room—that drawing room whose every chair and every curtain fold memory held dear; looking back on hours of absolute happiness—the sofa they had sat upon together, the little chair the babe would bring beside her father to perch herself on, the soft shadows and draperies enfolding all! His nervous hands were clenched tightly together as the possibility faced him that this one corner in the world that lay at his heart's core might be blotted out to him for evermore.

He had never trusted a woman, but he had trusted this woman. The jealousy tortured man forgot how he had consoled himself before, forgot everything but his present pain. He cursed that illness of his, during which he could keep no guard over his interests.

His vivid imagination gave him fresh torture as he pictured Charlie in his place and enjoying all those delights Mary held for him; playing with her yellow hair, kissing the curves and dimples of her neck and shoulders. It is an agony such as none but a nature that is at once passionate and jealous can know; nor then until they love. And Benjamin Phillips loved Mary. Picture after picture came to him as he sat there in the twilight, in the gathering gloom, and every remembered bliss doubled every pang as he saw that fair boy's face usurp his privileges. It was not coherent thought; it was nothing but suffering; he held his throbbing head in his hands and groaned.

"If you please, sir..." said the servant, opening the door.

"I can't be disturbed," said the doctor harshly. "I can't see anybody; I am busy. Shut the door."

"It is only Mrs Cameron's little girl with a note."
And she handed it to him.

"Mrs Cameron's little girl," he repeated. The words
broke through the mists in his brain.

"Let her come up."

Mrs Cameron's little girl—his little girl. The one little
girl in the world that was his, and was dear to him, and
loved him, and looked to him for love and sympathy.
Nita, sweet little clever baby Nita, in whom he could
trace with keen delight all those thousand and one signs
that told him she was his: the little supple fingers, the
dark eyes that were almost as a mirror to him, the eager
mind that brought him back his innocent boyhood.
Nita—Mrs Cameron's little girl!

He took the child on his knee. He burst into tears as
he felt her caressing him and softly kissing his cheek,
and murmuring, "Dear Doctor, dear Doctor, Doctor
mustn't cry. Doctor's got a headache like Nita has, and
then Nita cries." She laid her little warm hand on his
forehead and crooned over him, with tender loving
ways.

He kissed her again and again and held her close to
him. Here was his comfort, here was his home, and he
could not and would not give them up.

"Nita loves Doc-doc?" he asked her in the old baby
language.

"Nita loves Doc-doc," she answered and buried her
face in the thickets of his beard.

He still held her, as he read her Mother's letter—a
loving letter, asking him to come to her.

"Come with Nita; Mother's kind to Nita when
Doctor is there," she said, jumping off his knee and
trying to pull him along with her.

"Isn't Mother kind to you when I'm not there?" he
asked, detaining her.

Nita's dark eyes swam in tears.

"Mother hates Nita."

209

"Nita! Nita!" said the doctor, shocked even now at the remark.

Nita bent and kissed his hand in a strange unchildlike way.

"Come," she said, and without giving himself time to think he went with her.

Mary had prepared for the interview, knowing she had had a narrow escape and feeling that it would need all her wit to reinstate her in her former position.

She was in the small boudoir, which adjoined the bedroom, her yellow hair unbound, a loose white peignoir enwrapping her, reclining in a position of easy abandonment on the blue satin sofa, in the glow of the fire.

Dr Phillips' jealousy was at white heat, yet he could not withhold his tributary glance, so fair did this woman look, so blue her liquid eyes, so white her skin, so rich the golden gleam of her hair in the firelight, and so seductive the unconfined curves of her bosom.

Now for the first time Dr Phillips was undeceived in her, as a short time since Charlie Doveton had been undeceived in her. But the revelation had a different effect upon the two.

Dr Phillips in his study, away from the witchery of her presence, had writhed in an agony of jealousy, had been convulsed with despair at losing her and all she meant to him. But Dr Phillips in her presence, knowing she had deceived him, even doubting in his heart her practical faithfulness to him, yet felt the blood in his veins bound buoyantly, his heart throb wildly, his desire for possession so strong that he determined she should yet be his and his absolutely.

What had he despaired of and agonised over? Bah! Did he not know women? Let him try his craft against that of this puny boy who had dared to rival him. He looked at her silently, thinking by what means he should rivet her to him with such bonds as she could never rend asunder. But relinquish her—never!

210

Benjamin Phillips felt his youth reviving, and his pulses beat high.

They looked at each other in silence. Then Mary smiled with a smile full of meaning.

Frankly cynical as Benjamin Phillips was at first—urging his suit, not by passion but by teaching her that it was expedient, and pleasant, and natural that she should take the good things of this world if they were offered her—very soon after she had accepted his protection this cynicism had vanished. She had borne him a child and since then had been to him as a precious and honoured wife. He had not treated her or looked upon her as a mistress otherwise than by loving and caressing her more than is usual from a husband towards a wife of five years. They had never discussed the dubiousness of their relations. He had never been disrespectful to her or treated her lightly.

Now they met, for the first time after he had learned to doubt her, and he had looked at her questioningly. She answered the question with a smile. And what a smile! One that put virtue to shame; that of a courtesan detected in her wiles. It was bold, it was challenging, it mocked at the idea that anything else was to have been expected. Her smile put them at once on a different footing. For the first time in her presence he remembered she was but his mistress. It was not as a husband would have spoken that Benjamin Phillips said, "So you have taken another lover?" She did not wince at the question, nor repel it, as she might well have done; but with that smile still upon her lips she answered laconically: "Why not? Five years is a long time."

"A long time." And Dr Phillips sighed, thinking it over.

"Come and sit down," she said, moving back her drapery and making room for him on the sofa beside her.

It was she instead of he who took the initiative just now. The doctor was taken aback for the moment, had

211

not formed his plans, and found her even more fascinating in this mood.

What would have repelled Charlie attracted him. He took the hand she held out to him, and the loose sleeve falling back revealed to him the plump white arm. He held it critically, thinking the while, and she who thought she knew him, and had adopted this pose in full belief it would help her achieve her purpose and give her both liberty and the means to enjoy it, began to doubt.

"Very fine," said the doctor slowly. "You are a handsome woman, Mary. You might succeed in your new career...for a time."

She had the grace to blush. She had adopted this role but did not like it thrust upon her in this coarse style. Coarseness was always abhorrent to her.

"What career?" she asked with innocent unconsciousness.

His glasses dropped and with his dark eyes he gave her a look, and the look was the fit reply to her smile. For Benjamin Phillips was a man, and a man of the world, and Mary Cameron was after all only his pupil and he had not taught her all he knew.

She quailed beneath his look, his sneer at her innocence. All at once she missed what she had lost when he had respected her, even while she was not respectable.

He still held her arm, stroking the white flesh with his supple fingers.

"Don't," she said, trying to withdraw it. "You make me nervous." And indeed she was nervous and afraid too.

"How long has that young man been your lover?" he asked, without noticing her request.

"He isn't my lover at all," she said, quickly changing her tactics.

Dr Phillips's eyebrows went up in polite incredulity. "Why make a mystery of it?" he asked. "I am really curious."

212

"I am not making a mystery. He has never been my lover...I wish he had," she muttered.

Observing her critically he came to the conclusion she was speaking the truth, and his heart felt lighter and he felt more secure than ever in his power.

"What do you want that I have not given you?"

"A name, respectability, marriage."

"And you thought that Mr Charlie Doveton would marry you? Good heavens, you women are credulous."

"Why not?" she flamed up angrily. "He would never know."

The very piece of information Dr Phillips was anxious to secure.

"So he does not know of your—well, I don't wish to hurt your feelings, but to say the least of it—somewhat dependent position." He looked round at the blue hangings, the silver toilet accessories, then down to the silk stockings and small satin shoes.

"No," she said, as sullenly as a captive.

"I fear it would be my duty to inform him, before I attended at the church to give you away. I suppose you had arranged for me to give you away?" he asked, still maintaining his calm interested tone.

He exasperated her, maddened her, but she was helpless with him. Suddenly he released her hand, looked at her a moment, took her full in his arms and kissed her passionately two or three times, then released her entirely and walked to the other end of the room.

"So you are sighing for respectability, after we had decided it was an unnecessary incumbrance. Well, I think you are wrong. Still it was very clever to think of entrapping young Doveton. I admire you for it. The idea was positively brilliant; but...you underrated me, my child. That is where you made your mistake. You are mine, you have always been mine, and mine you will remain."

213

She sat silent, and so masterfully he spoke that she felt it must be true, and her dreams almost faded away.

"Mine for ever. No wedding bells and orange blossoms and white satin dresses; no troop of fair bridesmaids and village maidens strewing roses; no lilies, though I think lilies would be most appropriate in your path. No, you are my mistress. Do you know, I had almost forgotten you were my mistress? My kept mistress! And you thought to escape me in a bridal veil."

He was speaking in a cold metallic tone, but inwardly he was raging with mad jealousy and yet madder love for this base woman who had enthralled him.

And she heard the rain outside and the wind howling in the chimneys, and she too looked at the luxurious warmth around her, and feared him because he could force her to exchange the one for the other. Charlie? She could not go to *him*; that would mean double ruin.

She feared Benito, she had never seen him like this; he looked capable of anything. He could put her out now at once into the dreary cold of this wet night. How should she act? She called up all the resources of her womanhood, and they seemed inadequate. She was not repentant; on the contrary, she longed with all the strength of her being to have been able to say, "I will go," and to have gone to Charlie, but she was not sure of Charlie. Would he receive her? She hated her jailor with an intense hatred, and she rapidly made up her mind as she lay on the sofa watching him while he uttered his cold keen phrases; she made up her mind she would for the present dissemble, and conquer his coldness with her warmth. But later, when she was secure, when her plans were safely laid, then would she take her revenge, and he should suffer.

She put her hands before her face and burst into tears.

Now this tender hearted man could not bear a woman's tears. Were not women ever made for lightness and love? He wavered, he had wanted to punish her, but her bent golden head, the sobs that convulsed her, the sight of a tear that was trickling slowly along one small hand, down the finger just to the dimpled knuckle, moved him. A little further and it would reach the wedding ring which he had given her. He must stop its progress.

He took her hands away from her face gently and gently wiped away her tears with his own pocket handkerchief.

"Poor little woman!" he said tenderly, "was I unkind?"

She didn't stop crying all at once, but allowed him to soothe her, and rested her head on his shoulder and let the rough beard exacerbate her cheek, and caressed his hand.

He repented his harshness, doubted even the evidence of his senses. Impossible that she could have ever tried to repel him by her cocotte-like airs, ever meant to persuade him that her favours might be for more than one. Mary, dearest, sweetest, purest of women. He begged and implored her not to cry. How of all men could he, through whom she had lost that respectability she longed for, have made her weep by his harsh reminder?

And when her sobs ceased, and she lay quiescent in his arms, he still caressed her, and felt all the strength of his love rousing under the touch of her silken hair, under the spell of her warm smooth skin, her sweet breath meeting his as he hovered over her ripe lips.

"My darling," he murmured, hungering for the assurance of her love, "if *I* could have given you marriage you would have preferred me to anybody. Would that I had been able!"

"I love you, Benito!" she murmured falsely, and wound her arms around him. "If I wanted to be respectable it was because I wanted you to respect me."

"But if *I* could have married you?" He listened

hungrily. Some weighty thought was in his mind; he wanted this woman, wanted her mightily; holding her in his arms thus, and yet feeling insecure of his treasure, he listened.

"Nobody would have been anything to me but you," she whispered softly, and their lips and eyes met. But his hunger was unsatiated.

He was trembling when he released her, but calm with the calm of resolution.

"Mary," he said, and this time he avoided her eye, "*I will marry you.*"

Startled, she looked at him. She thought for the moment he was going mad from love of her.

"Your wife..." she said.

"My wife is dying. She is to undergo an operation tomorrow, from that operation *she will never recover.*"

"Do you perform it?" she asked. And looked at him curiously.

This time he met her eye steadily.

"No, it will be performed by one of our first surgeons, but... it is hopeless."

A strange silence fell between them.

Dr Phillips did not allow himself to think. The operation was to be a serious one that sometimes ended fatally; but Dr Hiram Slate, who was to perform it, had reduced the danger to a minimum. Still she might not recover; then Mary would be his and the child would be his, and in respectability after all she would find her happiness—the happiness he could not give her now. Golden visions of wife and child floated before him. He trembled with excitement.

Mary wanted time. Time during which, if her beauty and her skill availed her, she would have secured her future.

So she endeavoured to satisfy Benjamin Phillips by her answer. Yet he went out from her presence with his brain inflamed by her beauty and his jealousy, on fire with his unsatisfied passion, mad with fear of his rival, who could give her marriage!

216

Book III · Chapter IV

As he walked to Portsdown Road that night, over and over again the phrase repeated itself to his straining ears: "She will not recover, she will not recover."

He walked quickly, but not quickly enough to outdistance that damnable iteration. "She will not recover, she will not recover." He could not go home and hear it there. He turned back into Regent's Park and stood again on the bridge where Mary had first given her promise to him.

He had done this thing carelessly. A beautiful intelligent girl, her finger tips showing out of her darned gloves, her skirt shabby, her boots large, old, and shapeless. Her face, whose fairness he alone could then see, was pinched with hunger and cold, and a line of discontent between the eyes marred the beauty of the brow. That was what he had seen then. A young girl, poor, discontented, beautiful, and alone. What end to this in the Great City? One patent, natural end; and he but aided her to fulfil her destiny.

He had not loved her; he had not meant to love her, save with that easy love which springs up and flourishes and decays, and has no aftermath. That was the love he had meant for her, but instead of it had come an absorbing unholy fascination that gripped him as in a vice.

He stood on the little wooden bridge and gazed down into the black waters, and they seemed to him to reflect back the white face and golden hair of the woman he loved.

The air was chill and each little gust as it blew past him penetrated through the turned up collar of his coat and froze him into misery, murmuring, "She cannot recover."

He had said it, and now the words mocked him. "She cannot recover."

But she could; and he knew it. She could and would recover, and then Mary was lost to him, and the soft little kisses that Nita left upon his cheek; for Mary and Nita would belong to Charlie Doveton.

"Sooner than that, sooner than that..." and the miserable man gazed into the black water. Ah, if he only had Charlie here now! Just here on the little wooden bridge, with the dark quiet waters flowing beneath it and nobody by. He clenched his hands as if tightening on some resisting body. Then there came another little gust and whispered, "She cannot recover."

She must not recover! His brain was working. She *must* not recover. And yet—and yet... Purpose was growing on him. Charlie was not here; there must be a victim. Himself? No. He was of use in his generation; could save life, was a man, and could add his quota to the good of a coming race.

Clothilde. Poor Clothilde! How in all her pain and all her fear she had tended him and sat by his sick couch. He could remember his grateful feelings as she held the cup to his fevered lips; as she smoothed the hot, crumpled pillow under his aching head.

And her hopes. And the lie he had told her. If she recovered ("She cannot recover," muttered the breeze) it would be to disappointment, to a life time of regret, perhaps even to a recurrence of her disease. Poor Clothilde! He took off his hat, and his imagination recalled the feel of her plump white hands as she stroked his hair. She loved him and believed in him so.

"One, two, three!" rang out the great church clock. Three o'clock, and this time tomorrow the operation was to be performed. He had seen it done a hundred times at the operation table at Bart's; had crowded round with the other students, forgetful of the woman stretched there in her agony, eager only to watch the

218

clever fingers, deftly cutting and tying, carefully holding back.

He had been clerk, then dresser, and then full assistant to Hiram Slate. He knew his skill, his care, his pride in his low death average. Few of these cases that he had seen had died. One after another he had seen the patients progressing favourably day by day, until at the end of a month they left the hospital relieved of their burdens, with gratitude in their hearts and praises on their tongues. Many a woman who was also a breadwinner he had seen restored, when apparently past hope, to her family. He had gloried in the new science that had saved them, and carefully and jealously done his part in dressing, in preparing, in assisting.

Once he remembered they had lost a case. The poor woman had come into the hospital after many delays and many hesitations, full of fears, with a large pendulous tumour they had promised to relieve her of. Her daughter had come in with her, although it was against the regulations; and the girl had sobbed and clung to her mother and there had been a scene in the ward. But he, Benjamin, had sympathised with the child, had explained the operation to the mother, and had assured her of a speedy convalescence.

And partly because the woman was still young and passably pretty, and partly because of the child that had clung to her, there was much interest shown in her case by the students, and the nurses, and even by some of the staff. She had shrieked and sobbed when she was carried on to the table, and it was a long time before she could be brought thoroughly under the anaesthetic.

Then Slate had operated and everything had gone well. Benjamin had not acted as assistant, it was not his turn, but his place was taken by a youth who had never before seen an operation and whose nervousness almost caused him to faint.

The operation had gone well and all seemed sat-

219

isfactory; then symptoms of blood poisoning had set in and finally the patient had sunk and died.

Benjamin standing there on the bridge gazing into the water saw next the post mortem room, bare, close smelling, with its band of eager students. There lay the woman, white and cold and lifeless. He remembered the look on the youth's face when, the abdomen being opened to discover the cause of death, one of the sponges used to clean out the wound was found—left by a culpable mistake that had cost a human being's life.

The matter was hushed up, but the youth had left the hospital. He could not bear the looks of his fellow students, nor perhaps the reproaches of his conscience.

Hiram Slate had a qualified assistant now, and he always counted the sponges himself. So why did this incident recur to Benjamin with such dread distinctness?

Tomorrow—no, today—it was his wife he should see in this cruel position, awaiting in agony the result of the ordeal. His wife, Clothilde, who had nursed him and tended him in his illness.

If...the dawn was colder than the night; he shuddered again as he pressed his icy hands to his head. If...by any chance an accident should happen... What accident? Hiram Slate would take every precaution, he and his assistant. Then the woman would be left quiet to recover from the chloroform, the nurse in the room, probably the mother also.

What accident could happen? Well—for instance they would not let her quite recover consciousness. She would be given half a grain of morphia. If by mistake they gave her a grain, or say a grain and a half, that and the chloroform she had taken...

"Oh Mary, Mary!" he groaned aloud. Why had he ever met her?

He knew whither his thoughts were leading him. His horror at himself knew no bounds. He was no longer cold, he was burning; he was wet through with perspiration. He drew back shuddering as his own white face, reflected in the water, met his glance.

He roused himself, he tried to forget the phantoms he had been conjuring up, but he could no longer drive them back; they haunted him until their persistency hurt his head like the heavy thud of a hammer.

The streets were deserted, he met no human being as he walked home, there was nothing to distract his mind from the thoughts and the visions that absorbed him. Something of horror was on him, but that he might have shaken off. It was having to think of the details. And then his vivid imagination would wander from the scene of the operation—*that he knew now would be the last scene in the poor woman's life*—to other scenes where the doomed woman was kind and loving and considerate of him.

He could not go to bed. He walked up and down his room, the little room that he had kept to himself, and the closeness of it shut him in. He could not breathe in it so thick were the phantoms that peopled it. He threw open the window and let the cold air blow in upon him. It was of no good; nothing was of any good. For the time being at least he found it impossible to so utterly falsify all the good that nature and education had implanted in him as to set himself to compass the murder of an innocent woman without feeling a horror at the act.

He was half horrified at himself for comtemplating the deed; half disgusted with himself for shrinking from such a natural solution to his difficulties; but his thoughts led him instead of permitting themselves to be led. He wanted to dwell upon his future with Mary and his child, but he could not get his imagination past the operation of the morrow. Over and over again he pulled himself together and conjured up the vision of his love. Over and over again the vision slipped away from him and left in its stead the curtained four poster and the white motionless figure that he would see tomorrow. He

221

could not shut it out; it was destroying his nerve and his resolution and incapacitating him for the work he had to do.

"Her will is made in my favour; a clear £1000 a year and all her savings..."

That was the next thought. It had been hovering dimly about him all the while; now it flashed fully revealed into sight and sickened him.

"I shall not do it for money; it isn't for the money. I shall go mad if this goes on..." He pressed his slender hands to his forehead: it was burning.

Again he felt the affectionate movement of his wife's hands and cursed the imagination that was playing him such tricks.

That was how he had passed his night, and the morning found him nerveless, flaccid, feverish, with dark lines under his eyes, and trembling powerless hands. He was in the same clothes he had come home in. Sleep had not for a moment enfolded him in kindly oblivion.

His cold bath, his change of linen, his morning cup of tea refreshed him somewhat, and then he went to his wife's room to bid her good morning as usual.

The poor woman was racked with anxiety and terror about herself. Her mother, who had spent the night with her endeavouring to keep up her spirits, had succumbed to the communicated fear and was crying quietly on the sofa.

Benjamin could not but be moved by the sadness of the scene. He forgot his breakfast; he forgot that he did not feel well. With the devotion and self oblivion that characterises the heaven made doctor, he set himself again to the task of comfort.

His cheerful manner gave strength to the dishevelled old woman on the sofa, and she got up.

"I'm not crying about you, Clothilde," she explained, "but I've been awake all night, and it has given me a headache. I am quite happy about you; ain't I,

Benjamin? From today you'll never know the meaning of pain again," as she tried to follow his lead and reanimate the sinking woman.

"Never know the meaning of pain again," repeated Dr Phillips, half mechanically, bending over to kiss her brow.

The caress soothed her even more than the words. "Promise me you won't leave me all the time, Ben," she asked feverishly. "Hold my hand while it is being done, then I shan't feel afraid."

He promised. The close smell of the sick room floated before him and almost deprived him of consciousness; he was faint from overstrained feelings and want of food. It seemed to him that this close sickly smell would always mean "his wife" to him now. Still, he kissed her again before he left her to go to his breakfast, and then he kissed his mother in law and told her to keep her spirits up. There was nothing to be frightened about. All would go well.

"All would go well," he repeated to himself in a dull way as he left the room. "All would go well."

Book III · Chapter V

All did go well.

Punctual to a moment the great doctor arrived bringing with him his dresser and meeting on the doorstep the gentleman who was to administer the chloroform. The nurse was already installed. All three men looked serious; every case of ovariotomy meant to them an increase or a loss of professional status. It was against Hiram Slate's rule to operate anywhere but in his own small private hospital; but Dr Phillips was his professional brother, and had been his pupil. Slate, from his knowledge of him, felt that the patient would be as carefully tended as if he had supervised everything himself.

He noticed Dr Phillips's agitation, sympathised with it, and thought more highly of the man for its display. He had known him so cool when the game of life and death was being played, and his wife was not the shuttlecock.

"Don't remain in the room, Phillips," he said to him kindly. "It isn't necessary, and you don't look fit for it. I needn't tell you everything will be done carefully."

The doctor looked pale, almost white, against his black beard, and his voice had an uncontrollable tremor in it. He half hesitated, but only for an instant.

"I've promised my wife to be with her," was all he said. He would have liked to convey his perfect confidence in Slate, he would have liked to go through his ordeal with unflinching countenance, but nature for the moment was too strong for him, the issue too tremendous. On the failure or success of that operation something depended which made even him for the moment flinch from what was before him.

Then he found himself in the room. The dressing table had been utilised as an operating table. Every preparation was far advanced. The terrified woman looked as if her last hour had come. She turned to him as her only refuge, her only hope. He could say nothing, his voice was gone, but he pressed her hand. He bent his face over hers for a moment, and his was as pale; through the glasses his eyes looked haggard and bloodshot.

The anaesthetic was administered. The unconscious woman lay at the mercy of these men. It looked like some scene from the inquisition—the bound woman, the sacrificial knives, the torturers with their grave pitiless faces.

Benjamin Phillips took up his position in the corner just behind the bed curtains. Some fascination compelled him to watch every step of the operation. His eye took in every sickening detail, his ear heard like cannon shots every ejaculation, every whispered order.

When the chloroform first began to take effect, the muscles to relax, the face to lose its strained expression of anxiety, some sort of prayer rose to his mind; his heart almost stopped beating. If she should take too much! Then the apparatus was removed and she lay unconscious but safe. He watched, half hoping—for if accident should kill her, then he...half fearing—for it would be horrible to see the woman who had tended him in sickness die like this, bound and helpless.

When the first incision was made, and the blood spurted out, he hid his face in his hands, his head sunk on the bed, he could barely repress a groan. It was as if the spirit that had been dodging him all this time in darkness had sprung suddenly in naked hideousness into the dreadful light. It was the bloody spirit of murder he saw, and at the sight he hid his face in his hands and he groaned. The room seemed to reel before him, and around him; he was miles away, floating on the Thames with Mary, but the river and sky were red, and Mary's white hand as he held it was sticky and soft with jellied blood. Then he heard the songs of the birds and the murmur of water; till the one changed into groans and the snap of the scissors and the other into the splash of the sponges as they fell into the basin.

Often and often as he had seen this operation performed, never had it seemed so long, so interminable. How still the room was; had anything gone wrong? He could not look up.

"A simple sarcoma," said Hiram Slate. "Come, come, Phillips, it is all over. Rouse yourself, man."

The face Dr Phillips raised was white, and tense, and anguished. No one had suspected him of such deep feeling for his invalid wife, and the assistant, who was a soft hearted young man, had tears in his eyes when he looked at him and would have liked to shake hands with him and tell him how beautifully everything had gone.

"Most successful!" said Slate.

"Wonderful!" echoed the gentleman who had spread the veil of unconsciousness over the sacrificial lamb.

"Marvellous!" repeated the assistant, gazing at Benjamin with soft tearful eyes. "Beautiful!"

Dr Phillips looked dazed... "Most successful," he repeated. He seemed not to know the meaning of the words; it was as if he were talking in his sleep.

Dr Slate led him gently from the room.

"Compose yourself, Phillips," he said when he had seen him safe into the study and had forced a glass of sherry on him. "What has come over you, have you lost your nerve, man? I am going back to the patient; you rest here; it is all right, could not be better, we shall have her about again in a couple of months."

Dr Phillips tried to smile his thanks, but it was a very sickly smile. Then he was alone; he groaned aloud. He drank another glass of sherry. He tried to brace himself up again.

"We shall have her about again in a couple of

months...most successful..." "She cannot recover..."
Somehow or other the two phrases met and jangled.

"Good God! What has come over me? I must pull myself together, what am I dreaming of?"

He had only overrated his strength. The doom he meditated for the poor woman had shown itself to him in a definite and ghastly shape in the broad light of day, and he shrank from it. Easy to see a picture of freedom, and an absent form. Terrible to see, as in an allegory, the victim on the altar, bleeding from the sacrifice.

It was over. The sacrifice completed and the victim saved. Saved... How could he help shuddering, for he knew she was saved, and he was doomed. That it was impossible to ignore, to forget. The horror and repulsion were physical. He called on his brain for assistance, and by the time the doctors had rejoined him he was grave and composed and quiet; only his soul was still shuddering within him. A faint hope came to him as they entered; perhaps she was worse, perhaps...but no, their bright faces told him.

Then followed another long hour while prescriptions were written and instructions given. Wine was offered and accepted, and in the grave professional talk that ensued Dr Phillips seemed to throw off his fears and his depressions; he talked eagerly and clearly.

"You ought to have done really good work, I never could understand why you took to general practice; you were fit for better things," said Dr Slate.

"There is yet time," answered Phillips very gravely, as one who sees a light beyond but an abyss between.

"Oh, there is always time," answered the other, "but I must confess I should like to see you work out and publish that little alteration you suggest; it would create quite a sensation. But goodbye for the present; I'll be in again in the morning; she is safe with you and the nurse until then; we've given her a pretty large injection of morphia. So there will be nothing to do but

227

to keep her quiet; she will hardly suffer at all...
Goodbye."

"Goodbye, and thank you very, very much."

Once more at the mention of morphia Dr Phillips felt
himself growing white and his heart throbbing
violently, but he roused himself to say goodbye. Only,
as he closed the door and the brougham drove off he
drew his handkerchief across his forehead and it was
wet with perspiration.

Providence had not intervened; nothing had intervened; all he had gone through was nothing. Before
him, not behind him, lay the task his unsteady nerves
were unfitting him for.

He shrank from it. A doubt came into his mind. A
doubt of himself and, strange to say, of his constancy to
Mary when naught lay between him and her. He knew
himself, he doubted, he hesitated. He was in his
laboratory. Something he had taken from his drawer—
taken slowly, slowly—he placed in his waistcoat pocket.

"Poor Clothilde. How frightened she was."

He sat down to think it over again. Perhaps some
loophole would present itself; perhaps he could find
some other outlet. What a whirl of thoughts and
figures! They would not let him think but jostled
together in his mind and confused him.

The fat German woman upstairs, with the faint smell
of illness that had lingered about her so long, why
should she cling to him and suffocate him and drag him
down with her weight? That witching smiling woman
with her yellow hair, with her light laugh, her warm
skin, why should she tempt him? Her yellow locks
entangled themselves in his hair, in his hands; her
witching face, with its downy skin and blue eyes, was so
near his own that his pulses throbbed with the delight.
And Nita, sweet little baby Nita, that woman child of
his whom he could see grown up, and watch in her
gentleness and her love for him and her clinging little
ways!

She had come upstairs to him when he lay ill. Mechanically he too went upstairs, thinking of the little feet that had paused on each step, and held on desperately to the banisters, and then broken into a trot when she came to the even ground of the landing.

"Dear Doc-doc, get better," she used to say to him, laying her little soft cheek against him and caressing him with her eyes as she lay in his arms. Dear little Nita!"

He was already opposite his wife's bedroom. He thought he might as well see how she was going on.

Softly he turned the handle of the dressing room door. The nurse was there, with her white cap and apron and her turned down linen collar, looking so clean and so capable.

"Couldn't be better, sir," she answered cheerfully, "she's gone off as peaceful as a lamb."

"Perhaps I'd better not disturb her then," he said, slowly, hesitatingly. "I'll come up again in an hour."

"I'll ring if there is any change," she answered, going on with her work of immersing and clearing away the soiled linen and sponges. "But she'll do nothing but sleep for the next four and twenty hours at least."

So he, still hesitating, closed the dressing room door. "I wonder if she has pulled the blinds down," he said to himself as he stood on the landing. "I might almost go and see." But it would be a pity to disturb nurse again. He went in by the other door, the one to the left of the bed. He went in very softly; it was so necessary she should be kept quiet. The blinds were down.

He drew aside the curtain that surrounded the bed and kept the draughts from the door away from it. She was sleeping a little heavily, her white round face showing dark amid the whiter pillows, her arms outside the counterpane, her expression still anxious and troubled. He stood over her, his glasses dangling from the string touched her as he stooped. A movement, a heaving breath that spoke of pain, warned him, and he

229

placed them in his pocket. His fingers touched something else in that pocket.

He thought of his wedding night.

"Poor Clothilde, she will be in pain when she wakes," he thought. Something like a sigh escaped him, but he doubted no more. It was, after all, only an experiment he was going to try. He wanted all his nerve. A movement in the dressing room roused his attention. Rapidly he drew behind the curtain; the open door beyond it would secure his retreat. But there was no need. The room was empty save for that tall dark figure behind the curtain, the bound form on the bed that had been his nuptial bed.

A few quick, quiet deft movements of the slender nervous hands about the arm that lay on the counterpane. It was heavy, almost like a dead arm, but warm and soft and white, save for one little mark. A curious look came into Benjamin Phillips's face. He stooped over the little mark and touched it with his lips.

"Sleep well, Clothilde, poor Clothilde," he murmured, and left the room.

Book III · Chapter VI

Some hours later, when the household was wrapt in slumber and only the indistinguishable sounds of night broke the absolute silence of the house, Benjamin Phillips was roused from his sleep by a loud and hurried knocking at his bedroom door.

He had slept; the knocking mingled with his dreams. One nail! Two nails! How hard they were hammering at her coffin!

"Who's there? What is the matter?" It had woken him at last, and he sat up in bed to listen. His dream had been vivid; it still made his heart beat fast.

"It's me, sir. Make haste, sir; I must go back. There's a great change." The nurse was speaking in a hurried, frightened voice.

"Go back at once to your patient. I'll be with you in a moment." So strong are the habits of a lifetime that Dr Phillips could forget the significance of the summons and was only the doctor hurrying to his patient.

Two minutes had hardly elapsed before he was in the sick room. The dimly burning night light was the only illumination. The shadows were dark. The patient lay behind the curtains in a double obscurity. She was breathing heavily with a long drawn stertorous sound, distinguished at once by the doctor.

"Bring me a candle. When did this begin?" he asked abruptly.

The nurse was crying. "You have been asleep?" he interrogated her sharply.

"Rouse the house," was his next order. "Send for more help. Let Mrs Strauss know."

In the meantime he worked hard and conscientiously to arouse the patient from this terrible sleep. He worked like a good doctor with all his brain in his endeavours. At the back of the brain lay the *knowledge* that all his endeavours would be useless, but he did not lessen them. It was not acting, his endeavours were real; he did all that the most eminent of the profession could have done to save a patient dying from... congestion of the brain.

The symptoms were those of congestion of the brain; there was no doubt about that. Morphia poisoning had the same symptoms, and it might be that; but anyway he was following a correct line of treatment. He forced himself to forget how his wife lay there, killed by... He only recognised a patient in her death struggle with an unknown foe.

He worked vigorously. To her head he applied ice bandages; and warm flannels to the feet and legs. He sent for a mustard plaster for the back of the neck, took out his lancet reflectively, and thought of the advisability of cupping. And in this he acted quickly, honestly, intelligently.

But it was no use. Almost before the other doctor had arrived, the hard, laboured breathing had ceased; she lay in a deathlike calm, except that her eyes were widely dilated. She seemed to gaze at Dr Phillips with accusing glance.

"Congestion of the brain?" said Phillips interrogatively in a low voice to his colleague. "Hyperaemia?"

"Have you a stomach pump in the house?" was the reply. "If not, send at once to the hospital."

"A stomach pump!" said Benjamin, astounded. "Why she was operated on for ovarian tumour yesterday!"

The pupils of her eyes were contracted to the size of a pin's point; the icy wet towels Dr Phillips had bound around her head seemed to have no effect.

"Did she have opium?" asked Dr Symes.

"Yes, after the operation," answered Benjamin lightly, in a tone almost of contempt at the question.

233

"And who administered it ? "

"Slate himself. "

"We will try the effects of an emetic, and you had better send for Slate at once. "

Dr Symes was an old man and in no way distinguished, yet Dr Phillips obeyed him mechanically. It was a relief that matters were taken out of his hands. He didn't allow himself to think; he only obeyed, and tried as far as possible to avoid seeing those terrible distended eyes, to avoid hearing the heavy, crushing sobs that broke from her aged parents as they helplessly watched her struggle.

Long before the emetic could be procured both doctors could see it would arrive too late. The feeble beats of the uncountable pulse, the irregularity of the heart, the pinched look round the nostrils, the hue of the skin, all told them that the end was imminent.

"Open the shutters; let us have more light," said Dr Symes.

The grey dawn of the morning crept in and showed the tear stained cheeks of the bereaved parents, the empty medicine bottles, the face of the unconscious woman lying back amongst the pillows, her brows damp with the dews of death, her wide open eyes gazing into vacancy.

Reverently and gravely Dr Symes passed his hands over them and closed them.

Then Dr Benjamin Phillips burst into loud uncontrollable weeping, and bending over the inanimate form kissed it and embraced it with passionate abandonment.

The poor old people, seeing their only daughter lying there dead before them, could yet find pity in their hearts for the bereaved widower. They tried to draw him gently away from the corpse. Weeping they yet endeavoured to comfort him and induce him to leave her.

Dr Symes was speaking to the nurse quietly in the

corner. Suddenly Dr Phillips tore himself away from his dead wife.

"You have killed her," he shrieked to the nurse. "You have let her die. Symes, she must have seen this coming on for hours."

"That is," said Symes quietly, "if your theory of brain congestion is the right one."

Benjamin flung himself on the sofa in a renewed agony of grief. Sobs and lamentations filled the room.

"Phillips," said Dr Symes, with a grave and judicial calmness, "you have of course my fullest sympathy in your sudden loss, but I wish you would try and rouse yourself for the moment. I want to find out how this has happened; otherwise"—here he hesitated half a second—"I am afraid I cannot give a certificate."

The curiously complex mind of the emotional widower was stirred again to action by these words. He had no fear: to give vent to all his emotions by a burst of tears had been a luxury to him. The tension was over. At the words of the doctor he sat upright on the sofa and said, as if only half comprehending, "A certificate..."

That theory of congestion of the brain, started by Dr Phillips, when to him at least the cause of death was written in such legible letters before him, had roused a vague suspicion in Dr Symes's mind and somehow or other made his sympathy with Dr Phillips of the most perfunctory character.

"One will be necessary," he returned drily.

The two men went out of the chamber of death to discuss the matter, and in the discussion, the sending for Dr Slate, and such like matters, Dr Phillips's excessive grief moderated. He was grave and sad, but he gave way to no further bursts of tears or passion.

It was all over for him. His wife was dead; Mary and Nita would be his in the lovelit future he saw before him; all his present task was to see that everything went quietly. He did not formulate any fresh theory of death once Dr Symes had doubted the congestion of the brain; he calmly awaited the opinion of the great man who had performed the operation.

Meanwhile the blinds were drawn down, and the dread news flew through Jerusalem.

It was a great disappointment to Dr Slate when he arrived and saw the failure of the work of his hands.

He questioned the nurse very closely. He questioned both Phillips and Symes. Then he made a minute examination of the corpse, and reserved his verdict for an hour while he talked it over with Symes.

In the meantime Dr Phillips suffered. He locked himself in the study and bore his suffering, which occasionally amounted to an agony of apprehension, in silence and alone. He reviewed the act he had committed and saw in it no flaw, no loophole where detection was possible. Still, he could not avoid strong throes of doubt and fear.

His proceedings had been so simple that he *knew* everything was safe. Still, he saw difficulties, and his agitation was too great to allow him to go and sit with his mother in law as he would have wished.

What would be the medical verdict? It mattered little to him actually. Inquest or no inquest, nothing could ever be proved; but still he was feverishly anxious for it all to be ended, for the doctors to go, and the funeral to be over, and the Strausses to return to Frankfurt. He wanted to enjoy his freedom.

The furnace of doubt and fear and anguish he had passed through had flamed itself out. He had been able to sleep after it; the first part of the night he had slept calmly and well. The sleep, and the tears, and since then the good breakfast he had eaten had reanimated his brain. He could think clearly and he saw that she was better dead; better for him he meant, and now that he had done the deed and was free he almost wondered it had never occurred to him to do it before.

The deed fascinated him. Half a grain of morphia had

236

been injected so that the poor woman should not awaken too soon to her suffering. He had simply, while the nurse was in the dressing room, in the *self same place* added one grain to the previous injection. It had been a delicate little operation, done in the half light under the constant danger of the nurse's re-entering. But it had been done, and done so well that the keenest eye could detect but the one spot. Of this he had assured himself when he had been first summoned to the bedside. He had slightly miscalculated her strength and imagined she would simply sleep until her sleep knew no waking; but he had been prepared for the emergency and it had not overwhelmed him.

And now, though he could not repress the rapid beating of his heart and the occasional shivers of apprehension that shot through him, he could see a certain fascination in the simplicity of the act, and deep in his heart lay the consciousness that he did not repent; nay, rather—so safe, so easy had it been—that he positively gloried in his own ingenuity and skill.

He unlocked the door when he had thought things out, and flung himself on the sofa, posing for the doctors when their conclave, which they were holding in the dining room, should be over.

He did not look like a murderer. The broad forehead with its thick masses of black hair, the beard, moustache, and whiskers all in one, with the slight stoop and short sighted spectacled eyes, left an impression of something benignant and kind. The slenderness of his hands, through which you could almost see the working of the nerves, added to this general impression of tenderness.

Dr Symes looked keenly at him when they entered, and his formless suspicions were almost dissipated by the expression he saw; almost, but not quite, because suspicion once sprung to life never dies but by a lingering death. He had failed in persuading Dr Slate of the necessity for a post mortem, failed in showing the

237

great man any cause for withholding judgment. So having neither reason nor support for his doubts he perforce abandoned them now and for ever.

Dr Slate drew a chair up to Benjamin's, who rose to greet him, and delivered himself of his opinion. He gave it absolutely, because he was not in the habit of being contradicted; and he, encouraged by his pupils and admirers, had come to consider himself infallible.

"Your wife died, my dear Phillips"—he laid his hand on the man's arm, and felt it trembling—"from the effects of the chloroform she inhaled and the morphia we injected. Her peculiar constitution would evidently not permit of her assimilating the doses. You must take comfort in the knowledge that all human skill had been employed. It was an accident no one could have foreseen, no one could have guarded against. You will have the entire sympathy of the profession."

And so it was ended. It was all over.

Book III · Chapter VII

It was all over.

But callous as the man was, far from repentance as were his thoughts and his conscience, he could not at once make up his mind to go and reap his reward. He remained in Portsdown Road during the next few days, with the blinds down and the sound of weeping ever in his ears.

The Jews mourn for their dead for seven days after the burial has taken place. Dr Phillips sat in the gloomy dining room, the blinds closely drawn, on a low backless seat, in the company of his wife's parents for one whole dreary week. All day long his friends flocked in, their ostensible object to comfort the mourners, their real motive gossip. Mrs Strauss related over and over again the minutest incidents of the death scene; between her sobs she would describe the heavy breathing, the open eyes; with her handkerchief hiding her face she would tell of the clammy leaden hued skin, of the nerveless fingers trying to clutch at the bedclothes.

Then—in the midst of "How dreadful!" "How sad!" "What a terrible shock to you!"—someone would say something about the operation, and there would be a little surging movement; chairs would be drawn more closely around Mrs Strauss and some sympathetic questioner would say, "And do you think it was Dr Slate's fault? Do you think the operation was badly done?" or else: "These operations so often end like this. Still it must be a comfort to you to know you had Slate; they say he is so clever. Did you say it wasn't done while she was in bed?"

And Mrs Strauss would be lured from her grief to describe in her broken English as much of the operation as she had seen from the dressing room door. The more morbid and the more revolting the details, the closer were drawn the chairs and the more eager was the attention. Only Mrs Detmar confessed that it made her feel faint, and she moved away to talk to the doctor in his deserted corner.

Deserted; but by his own choice. They could not make him talk; he really could not give them all these details they sought for with such gusto. It was an ordeal he did not feel he was called upon to face, so he took refuge in the intensity of his grief and maintained his demeanour of reserved yet terrible trouble. This was not amusing, so after the first greeting which, in accordance with custom, runs, "I wish you long life and no further trouble," they left him to listen to the mother's loud lament.

But Mrs Detmar was determined to make him talk. She took a chair and planted it close by his stool. Thus hemmed in, he had no remedy, and she had no idea of reticence on any subject that interested her he braced himself up for a painful ten minutes. But he was agreeably disappointed.

"I am not going to talk about your wife," she began. "Of course it's very sad, but she had been an invalid a long time and you couldn't have been at all surprised. Besides, I don't want to dwell on any of those subjects just now..." and she looked at him meaningly.

Truth, to tell, Mrs Detmar was again on the eve of requiring his services, and the object of her interlocutions was to ascertain when he meant to return to the ordinary avocations of his life.

This was the first time the question of the immediate future had come before him.

"I am not sure that I shall be able to go on practising," he said slowly, thinking as he spoke, "but my colleague, Dr—"

"Thank you. If I don't have you I'll choose another

doctor for myself. But why shouldn't you go on practising, you must do something?"

Nobody but Mrs Detmar would have questioned the doctor in this fashion, and he was hardly prepared for it yet. His days had been spent in receiving these visits of condolence; his evenings were occupied, also according to custom, by large prayer meetings held in the same room and joined in by all the Jewish men in the neighbourhood. He had not yet had time to formulate his plans. He was actually at a loss for a reply. She went on. "You can't go on mourning all your life; and really, doctor, I don't want to be inquisitive but I suppose you haven't got enough to live on without doing anything."

"No," answered the doctor briefly, hardly hearing the question. Then he roused himself, put his slender hand on Mrs Detmar's jewelled wrist, and said, "But you may be sure, if I am in England, that I will not leave you alone through your illness." And he looked at her so kindly through his glasses that she felt Benjamin Phillips was indeed a man to be trusted. In this way he got rid of her, for after all she had no thought but to secure her own immediate object.

Somehow or other that little incident had an influence on Dr Phillips. He had thought vaguely of going away, or giving up practice, of doing a hundred and one things that would have been as reasonless as possible. Now he decided he would stay where he was and work on as he had been doing, except he would use all his leisure time in consolidating his position and extending his influence.

He decided he would gradually give up his general practice in order to become a consultant. He could afford it now, for both his wife's income and her accumulations became his.

He would not marry Mary for twelve months. He thought he could rely on his talents to force his people to accept her at the expiration of that time, if he carefully paved the way in the interval.

These seven prescribed days of mourning had been very long and dreary ones to him. He could not so throw off the habits and restrictions of a lifetime as to bury the woman and then go out and ignore the dead. He kept the seven days the laws of his nation demand, submitted to the evening prayer meetings, and the addresses of the clergyman, who drew tears from his audience by his vivid word pictures of the empty hearth, the desolate home, God watching over the bereaved one, and time, the great comforter, bringing him resignation.

All those coarse, black browed men, with their hats on and their prayer books in their hands, muttering in Hebrew their responses, were moved even to tears by the eloquence of their pastor. But Benjamin Phillips sat with his face buried in his hands and gave no indication of his feelings.

The week seemed endless to him. He missed the inanimate figure that for so many years had presided in the house. He forgot sometimes the object of the gathering and waited impatiently for his wife to come and help him to entertain these people. From such hallucinations he awoke to long for the time when all this mummery would be over, when his mother in law would return to Frankfurt, and he could begin to live the life he had planned.

Mrs Strauss would come to him in the morning, before the day began, to ask if she should order cake for the people; if she should offer them wine or tea; what were the English habits at "shivas"—for so is the mourning week called—and he, to whom all details of domestic life were abhorrent, felt overwhelming and unreasoning vexation at the questions.

Then, curiously enough, it annoyed him that Mrs Strauss could take an interest in all these matters, could gossip about them with every fresh comer. He would say to himself that she could not mourn her daughter much, that her grief could not be very deep if she could concern herself over the cinnamon cakes and the butter cakes and the raisin wine, and it vexed him that she was so callous. He felt it a sort of slur upon her—upon that poor patient woman who had been such a good wife to him and tended him so well in his illness.

One day, in his irritation, he said something like this to Mrs Strauss, and was surprised and doubly angry when the poor old woman cried bitterly at being accused of heartlessness. After all she was old, and had been separated from her daughter for many years, and knew that she must soon rejoin her, but still she sobbed at the doctor's words, and he had to retract them and soothe her.

So the incident passed; but it was repeated to her friends in the afternoon.

"He wondered how I could think of the cakes with my poor daughter so cold in her coffin; but someone must see to the cakes, and there is no one but me."

"Of course, of course, dear Mrs Strauss; everyone knows how you must grieve; but you could not have all these people here and not give them so much as a biscuit or a cup of tea. But men never understand these things, and poor Dr Phillips, you must make allowances for him. She never let him know anything of household matters; she kept every little worry from him. Why, I remember when they changed their cook he never even knew it until one day he said the fish seemed rather badly fried, and then she told him. He never can get over such a loss, such a wife as she was to him, poor dear! One can see how he grieves. You'll find he'll never rally from the shock, never be the man he has been, poor fellow! I pity him from my soul. And he had such hopes from the operation."

So said Mrs Jeddington, and she but spoke the general sentiment.

An endless week to Benjamin. A week of coming and

going and ceaseless bustle. He had no time for thought except during prayer hour in the evening; then, his face between his hands, he would try and bring before his mental eyes the picture of the life he would lead with Mary and his little daughter.

But the picture never came. In its stead would rise the wraith of that buried woman. He would see that still and silent room in its dimness, and his nostrils would be filled with the sickliness of its many odours. He would see the thick heavy arm on the counterpane, and once more his sensitive fingers would be groping for the puncture that he must repeat. He could even feel again the soft down of the flesh as he gently manipulated the place. How neatly he had inserted the needle. He never could keep down that little throb of gratified pride as he thought of his own dexterity. It was so quick, so painless, so easy. Another thing that puzzled and beset him was the kiss he had pressed upon the place.

It never could have been passion; his wife had never even in the earliest days of his married life managed to inspire him with that. What was it? Not affection, not pity; fear and remorse found no place in his breast. It was only a mere physical nervousness that had unhinged him before the deed was done; but in the doing it and in the knowledge of the freedom that the having done it gave him, there was nothing but satisfaction and pride; deep seated professional pride in his manual skill.

Why then had he kissed the place? That was a question he never could answer satisfactorily. He half despised and half admired himself for the curious impulse.

This constant brooding over his work had an obvious effect upon him. He knew himself to be a man who had performed under unfavourable circumstances a most delicate and successful operation. The longer the time that passed the more pride he felt in his achievement.

244

His self confidence, that had languished in Egypt and almost died in Eastbourne, rose again to splendid heights.

Before the week of mourning was ended, before God's rain had had time to fall upon the grave of the woman who had been his wife, he began to see before him the intellectual good of an unshackled career. He could not conjure up, as he would have wished, visions of Mary and his child, but there came to him unbidden, unwished for dreams of greatness and success. He sometimes felt dazed with the light, as a man relieved from a lifelong prison.

Still he could not quite shake off a consciousness of some indefinable trammel that yet precluded him from soaring; some throb of nature warned him; some clinging thought brought him down again to depression and a nervous impossible dread.

He was reminded for the first time—it was when he was but a lad of sixteen—he had failed to keep the great fast day that is enjoined upon his people. Overcome by an irresistible hunger, he left the close synagogue where he sat with his hat on by his father's side, and had gone, on pretence of feeling faint and wanting the air, down a little back street until he came to a baker's shop. With terror at his sin, yet with an appalling relish, he had devoured a bun; then looking from side to side, oppressed by the dread of discovery and agitated with the deadliest fear of consequences, he had sneaked back to his place, his cheeks crimsoning again and again at the memory.

And all that year at every mischance—when it had rained upon a holiday; when he caught the measles the day before he had to go in for his matriculation; when he had come out second instead of first in his examination—he had said to himself, "That is because I broke my fast." And the shame of it had clung to him like an uncleanliness that cannot be washed away.

He had quite got over that feeling about the great

fast day and now treated it as he did the other mummeries that kept from mischief the women and children of Israel. He only recalled the memory of it in order to assist himself in his philosophy.

"I have got over that," he said to himself, "and I shall get over this; but I must give myself time. What one counts a sin at sixteen one knows at twenty was but a natural instinct. What one shudders at thirty I suppose will be accounted quite a virtue at fifty.

This was his reasoning, but it was faulty in one link: he did not shudder now at his sin, he could only not get rid of it; it clung to him sometimes and dragged him down from the heights whither he had ascended to survey his prospects.

He thought perhaps Mary could exorcise the demon, and he went to her—after the week had ended and the blinds had been pulled up, and the Strausses had returned tearfully to Frankfurt.

He was drawn to her by a sudden impulse one day. It was the day he first saw his wife's bank book. That stung him more than anything; the figures in the book reproached him.

He had not done it for money; the terrible reward he saw there defiled him in his own eyes. He had never had a mean thought. He hated profiting like this by his action. He was debased by this reward for his justifiable action.

Book III · Chapter VIII

Mary had received the news of Mrs Phillips's death with absolute terror. There was no room for doubt in her mind, nor would all the inquests and postmortems in the world have satisfied her of the doctor's innocence.

He had murdered his wife in order to put her, Mary, in that wife's place. If she had hated him and shrunk from him before, now she loathed him with a bitterness and fear that were beyond words.

She passed a week of dread; that week he had not come to her. One thing only upheld her—Charlie's attentions. They had increased rather than diminished since Mr and Mrs Murphy had returned to town. He had had to champion her with Florrie and Alec, for Florrie and Alec had heard rumours as to her past, and perhaps the very fact of championing her had aroused his chivalry.

Whatever may have been the cause, the effect was to lengthen his visits, to increase the irresistible fascination that drove him to this woman, whose image had shut out, already, all considerations of home and of duty.

She felt—and women have a sure instinct in these matters—that her game was won. It needed but an effort, a short time more of acting and finessing, and the day was hers. A future of safety and an end to the shifts, the dissimulations, the uncertainty of her present life.

"I shall hardly know how to be natural again, I have acted so long," she thought. And the mask was still on when Benjamin came to her.

The mourning hatband, the black garments, added to the sombreness of his dark appearance. But his eyes had a new lustre in them. He did not kiss Mary, and for that

247

she could not be sufficiently thankful. Neither did he for the moment allude to his wife's death, but he commented on the weather, and the superiority of Mary's wood fire over coal, and he sat down very near it and warmed his hands by the blaze.

She hated to see him cowering over the fire thus, looking so much at home. She hated it more when Nita came down and sat on his knee, and she looked at them both together and thought of the bar they were on her life. Father and child were alike abhorrent to her. She nursed her wraith in silence.

"At length I have a right to my home," he said, clasping the little one close, not raising his eyes from the fire.

Mary shuddered, but his back was towards her.

"Would Nita like a papa?" he asked her; and his voice was not quite firm as he listened at the same time for the answer.

"No," answered the child decisively. "Nita only wants doctor." And she hid her face caressingly on his shoulder.

"Dear little girlie; you must explain it to her, Mary; I can't."

The glow of her affection penetrated him and warmed him more than the fire. He hardly noticed Mary's silence; he was so absorbed in the comfort of the scene, in the warmth of the cosy room, and the love of the little girl on his knee. Every line of the soft little face was so dear to him. He had a hunger of love for her, a womanly love and yearning over the baby fingers and the round little contours, the droop of the lips.

"My little girlie," he murmured,

So the hour went on. Then it was Nita's bedtime, and the doctor carried her up to Nannie in his arms, and watched while she was being undressed, and sat in a low nursery chair while she splashed her nude limbs in her bath, and shouted with laughter over the failure when

she tried, with the big sponge, to wash her own little
baby face. He saw such beauty in the tiny dimpled
limbs and quick unceasing movements, he could not
tear himself away. And when at length Nita, warm and
glowing from the bath, attired in her little white
nightgown, her dark hair demurely plaited back, knelt
at his feet, and folding her little hands, said, "Our
Father which art in Heaven," with all a child's
innocence and faith, the happiness and joy in his heart
almost overcame him, and his glasses grew moist and
dim. He drew her again on his knees, feeling acute joy
in the touch of her slender body through the thin linen.
Never had she seemed so wholly his.

"I haven't finished my prayers," said Nita, wonderingly.

"Finish them here," he said.

"But I must kneel."

So she knelt again. "God bless mamma and Doctor
and Nannie, and God bless Nita and make her a good
girl for ever and ever, Amen."

"Now Nita's done."

Nannie didn't interfere; she was folding up the little
clothes and putting away the bath.

Benjamin Phillips, his eyes wet with pure emotion,
put his daughter into her cot with womanly tenderness
and stayed by her holding her hand and telling her baby
stories until the long lashes lay motionless on the sallow
cheek and Nita slept.

Meanwhile Mary, left alone cursed her fate, and told
the servant that when Mr Doveton called she was to say
her mistress had gone to bed with a bad sick headache.

"You ought to have been upstairs with me,"
Benjamin said, "you would have enjoyed seeing her
splash about in her bath; but then, I suppose it is
nothing new to you." He never could quite realise that
she did not spend her leisure hours in communion with
the babe. So closely associated, so intertwined were

249

they always in his thoughts that it had become impossible for him to think of them apart, and he always mentally saw them together.

"You will dine with me?" she asked, and strove to make her manner warm.

They were in the drawing room; but Dr Phillips's eyes were still moist, and he was thanking God mutely for his little daughter.

"Yes, my darling, yes. And soon, very soon, our home will be together; no going out in the cold nights for me; no question of what people say for you. Mary"—he was still standing, looking into the fire, not at her—"ours will be a very happy life, I think. No woman has ever been to me what you have been. One episode of my life is closed for ever. Before I turn the leaf, look on it. "There must be no secrets between us. You know"—his voice was unsteady—"what I have done for you and my child. I have earned my reward, God knows; nothing can come between us now. My child"—he went to her, put his arms about her, and gathered her to his heart—"I have always been good to you, have I not?" He looked softly and tenderly into her eyes.

"You have always been good to me," she repeated impatiently, avoiding his eyes, and struggling a little in his embrace.

He loosed her.

"Why is this? he said.

"It is so soon after," she answered with downcast eyes.

The blood rushed to his head. He turned from her and sat down. A silence fell between them and she waited.

"*You* should not have reminded me," at length he said bitterly.

A little fish, a cutlet, a bird, a glass of wine, relieved the tension of the situation. Benjamin could live in the hour and ignore what was beyond. He became happy with his present and his future.

250

Mary could play her part well, as long as he did not touch her, but she shrank and shivered at the feel of his hands.

Those cool cruel fingers! As they touched her she quivered from head to foot. She seemed to see them tightening around the throat of his wife. She trembled as she imagined those small supple iron jointed fingers working relentlessly about their helpless prey. She saw in them doom and the crushing influence of his indomitable will.

She felt her courage sinking, but rallied, and dashing the pale phantom from her mind she grasped her woman's weapons...

"No, no, Benito, don't touch me," she said, playfully eluding him as, dinner over, he attempted to draw her down beside him on the sofa. "You say we are to be married. Well, now we are only engaged. You must be on good behaviour for three months, or"—here she looked at him archly—"I shall break off the engagement."

"What, not a kiss for three months?" he said, smiling indulgently. "Come, my fiancée, that is too hard."

She smiled back.

"Let me see if you are strong enough to refrain. After all, you deserve a penance..."

He turned grave; she had struck home. "He deserved a penance." The words cut him; he had no longer any desire for her caresses; she had awakened a train of thought too bitter; he began to feel the impossibility of ignoring this incident.

At first he did not reply. He leaned back in the chair, thinking, with knitted brow.

"Sit down there, Mary," he said, indicating a seat on the opposite side of the hearth. He spoke slowly as if weighing each word as it fell from him.

"I think we had better talk this matter out. You are quite wrong when you say I deserve a penance..."

251

He paused.

She did not reply, but she looked at him. His pose was easy; he was gazing into the fire with thoughtful eyes. Little more than a week ago he had deliberately, in cold blood, murdered his wife. He sat there before her strong and confident and easy. What manner of man was this with whom she had lived all these years and whom she now felt she had never known. What would he shrink from, what would he not do? He who had done such a deed, and now... claimed a reward.

"Listen." She was listening, watching, waiting. What was he going to say. What justification was he going to offer?

"Do you remember, years and years ago, when we decided, you and I, that it was fair and justifiable for us to live together? I could give you comfort, you could give me love. We said that it was right and we have lived in accordance with our conviction. The righteousness of it has come home to us more and more in the years, as I have known all you are to me. But she—she was ill and would never have been well; she would only have awakened to pain. She sleeps. It was my hand that gave her that sleep. Now I can take to my hearth and to my home the woman and child who God and humanity have taught me are to be the completion and crown of my life. He gave me you and that child. I have had no other child. He sent no tie to bind me to that other woman but He bound me to you, and you to me, and the child to us both for all eternity, and I thank him for it."

"Benito, what on earth has come over you? What do you mean by God? What God?" She was bewildered by this new phase. The Benjamin Phillips she knew had laughed at the ignorance, the helplessness, of those who must have a God to reconcile them to themselves and to their fate.

He roused himself again and spoke no more of religion. It had been the child's prayer that had moved

252

him thus and imbued him transiently with some vague idea that there might be a deity to whom an apology for his action was due.

The doubt thus engendered in his impressionable mind had been defined by Mary's reference to penance. Calling reason to his aid he justified himself to a creator whose existence he disbelieved in. Proving that if there was a wrong anywhere the Supreme Being was responsible for it.

And by so doing he cleared his moral atmosphere and went far to dissipate those clouds that had hung about him and obscured the daylight.

Mary insisted on keeping up that pretence of an engagement, and Benjamin, with the enjoyment of a lad, set himself gaily to the task of this mock wooing. And she defended herself with a woman's wit, and concealed well her nervous horror of him and his touch.

"And now we have finished all grave conversation. You must come and sit beside me, and we will talk about our honeymoon."

He made room for her on the couch beside him; but she shook her fair head coquettishly.

"You are on parole," she said, holding up her finger in the way one says "hush" to a baby. "You stay there, I here. We are only just engaged, and I am shy."

Benjamin smiled at her.

"Do come!" he said coaxingly. "This sofa is too big for one; I am quite lost in it." He put his arm around the back of it. "See how comfortably you will rest there with your head on my shoulder. It will be a much harder test if I don't kiss you then."

But she still shook her head. The doctor, taking this only as a challenge, got up and went towards her.

She felt her heart beat fast as he approached her. She drew herself back, and it was only with an effort she could still laugh lightly as he put his arms around her.

But still she laughed, pushing him back with both hands against his chest.

253

"No! No! Certainly not, it is not fair," she said struggling against him.

But he was stronger than she, and notwithstanding her struggles managed to reach her lips and press his own to them.

She could barely repress her shrinking, her fear, her abhorrence as she strove against his embraces. And he, thinking it all but a joke and doubly enjoying the possession of the resisting form, kissed her again and again, using all his strength to keep her close to him and all his influence to make her respond to his passion.

But she was stiff and unyielding. Suddenly he remembered that scene in the boudoir when he had treated her as a mistress, and it came into his mind that it was this she was resenting. She was to be his wife. He must respect her. He must treat her differently. He released her; and with every nerve quivering from the intensity of repulsion she had felt she sank, white and trembling, into her chair.

"My darling," he said gently, looking down upon her with a tender smile, "I must beg your pardon. You will forgive me. I shall not offend again." Then he knelt at her feet, and took her cold hand in his.

"My child," he said softly, "put away from your mind for ever the remembrance of that night. Sweetheart," he whispered, "tell me it is dead and forgotten. Forgive me for it, *my wife*, I was mad with jealousy. I had no excuse, I know that now."

And as he pleaded with her his cheeks flushed at the remembrance that he had treated her as his mistress, and that night would ever stand out in her memory, and degrade her in her own eyes, and be between them.

She rallied her forces, although it was difficult so long as his hand held hers, and said, as if still half in jest: "Very well, let that be the treaty between us. I will forget that evening, but only on condition that until I am your wife you shall treat me as your fiancée. Mind, no kisses."

254

She never had had a harder struggle than to maintain her smiling demeanour whilst he was still holding her, whilst she hated and feared him with such repellant force. He rose from his knees, his eyes dwelling on her charms with a lingering pleasure.

"Well child, it shall be as you wish," he said, and sighed. "I will woo you, and win you again, and we will have a new bridal. All our past shall be buried."

Then, with an effort, he flung his past from him and played the lover gaily and well, and Mary too, the moment she was not forced into personal contact with him, threw off her repugnance and jested and played with him lightheartedly.

Book III · Chapter IX

This gaiety and light heartedness clung to him as the days and weeks went on and made his work light and his brain clear. He was in the state of mind that the Scotch call "fey." He saw further and more clearly than he had ever seen. He worked with such vigour and such pleasure that it seemed to him he could not get enough to do.

The charm he had over his patients intensified, and the men with whom he came into contact at the medical meetings he once more began to attend found in Benjamin Phillips all the dash and brilliancy of genius.

He limited his visits to Mary with the pleasure of a child who reserves some delightful titbit for a future enjoyment. He kept up the farce of an engagement with her, playing his part with spirit and evident pleasure. He was alternately respectful and familiar. Sometimes he would implore her to have mercy on him, to curtail the time, to make him a happy man. Then he would seize her suddenly in his arms, kiss her familiarly, and ask her with mock seriousness whether she was not tired of this play, whether she was not in very truth yearning for her wedding morn. Then, without waiting for an answer he would rush away, appearing the next evening with a rose, carefully hidden in his hat, that he would present with trepidation after a great deal of assumed doubt and nervousness.

All this fooling gave him keen delight. It was part of that youth and energy that came to him as the dawn of his future seemed daily nearer and more roseate.

His mornings he would still devote to his patients, but he had accepted the subeditorship of the new medical paper, and in the afternoons he wrote.

His articles were brilliant, daring and original. They served their apparent object in bringing the new paper into notice, but there was a want of depth in their science—perhaps a want of feasibility in the theories. They were written easily and quickly. They attracted attention; they brought the man who wrote them prominently before the public, and Benjamin Phillips revelled in the disputes, the challenges, the arguments he had to engage in, to meet, to refute.

Seated in his well worn study chair, smiling under his beard even as he wrote with a quick pen and ready phrases, it was his great delight to let Nannie bring Nita to him of an afternoon, to perch her up beside him on a high chair he had brought for the purpose, and to alternate his literary labours by guiding her hand as she made her pothooks and hangers, or by telling her in simple language some deep paradoxical fairy tale, laughing at her bewilderment when he rose beyond her comprehension, kissing her little lips when they pouted their baby confession of ignorance.

These were happy days to Benjamin. His dual personality seemed to have died with his wife. He was once more young, happy, single hearted. But his youth had known the want of money; this second youth of his had enough and to spare. His first youth had known the restrictions of parents and guardians; he himself was now a parent, and his own guardian.

His sin never visited him now. He had put it from him when he made his defence before God.

Nita of an afternoon, Mary of an evening—his time was fully occupied and his life seemed to lie cast in pleasant places. His dead wife would return to him sometimes, often, because, notwithstanding the complications her existence had given rise to, he missed her in a hundred little household ways. But when he thought the matter out he could always see that he had done well. Her life—according to his conception of woman's life—was over and there was naught before her but pain for the present, disappointment for the future, and uselessness for ever.

He had not sacrificed her without compunction; he remembered that clearly. She had had no unnecessary pain; she had simply drifted to death down the stream of Lethe.

"Nita, little Nita, would you like always to live with Doctor, to call him Papa, and come and play with him in the morning as well as in the afternoon?"

"Nita would like to stay." And she put her arms around him and embraced his shaggy head.

"Call Doctor 'Papa,' Nita, just to see how it sounds," he said coaxingly.

"Dear Doctor Papa," she answered. And this remained his title—a title that grew sweeter to him each time it fell from the baby lips.

He found she interfered somewhat with his work, this quiet little mortal, who, with all her quietness, demanded a constant attention, who would sit on her high chair and put a little hand across his manuscript as his quick pen traversed the pages.

"Look, Nita's fingers inky!"

"Oh, but Nita shouldn't ink her fingers. Naughty little Nita!" he would scold her laughingly. But the train of thought was interrupted and the smudgy page gave so much pleasure to the child that he was forced to leave off writing lest she should try to make the next page equally "pretty," He had no heart to scold her but would tell her more stories instead, or carry her over to his washstand to wipe the ink off. There nothing satisfied Nita but to turn the water on herself and see the basin overflow, which was an amusement of which she never tired; the mess on the carpet delighting her almost as much as it disconcerted her awkward parent.

For Nita was, after all, only an ordinary little affectionate baby and had all the capacity of her kind for mischief; and under the spoiling—which means the love—that she had now for the first time in her life she rapidly developed her repressed child life.

And Benjamin Phillips's gaiety and light heartedness, his pleasure in living, the fullness of his days, knew no abatement. He was in love with his fatherhood; he had no presentiments and no regrets; and as for his ambition, that could wait.

So much work a week was required of him, and so much he sent. After all, anything would do. Most people who read only half understood and for the rest, well, he could explain it next time when they wrote and asked him what he meant.

Book III · Chapter X

"I can't live without you, Mary, my darling! Forgive me; I have tried so hard; do not send me away; do not turn from me. My own, own injured darling, forget all the past. Marry me; let us be happy; I love you—I love you."

Charlie was at her feet, kissing her hands, imploring her to become his wife.

Mary was triumphant. The fire burnt low in the grate, and they forgot to ring for the lamps. Charlie's scruples and caution had vanished, and he was pouring into her ears his love and his longing.

She leaned back in her chair, and the sweet curves of her face dimpled into smiles. One hand she had surrendered to him; the other, soft and white, lay on her lap.

He held the hand she gave him so graciously and kissed it with his ingenuous young lips, blushing at his own temerity. He was her slave, and the first kiss he pressed innocently on her cheek riveted his chains beyond all hope of freedom.

He sat looking at her with swimming eyes, afraid to break the charm by approaching too near. He kissed her gown, her fan, anything that was hers. He longed, yet dared not, to kiss her lips.

She was happy. After Benjamin Phillips's half cynical respect and assumed bashfulness; after his pretended wooing, of which she could always see the mockery and divine the sneer, Charlie Doveton's timid advances appeared to her the ideal of love.

Listening to him as he poured out his love, she began to see the beauty and the charm of goodness. She began to feel herself really an angel of virtue and to think of

Benjamin as a seducer and a murderer, the villain who
had ruined her life. Almost ruined her life; but now
Charlie was going to save her from ruin. Dear, good
Charlie, who feared her while he loved her and whom
she loved!

She thought this afternoon she really did love him.
His large sunburnt hands and fair, freckled face were
innocent and charming to her. Her eyes dwelt with
pleasure on his broad shoulders, even on his thick neck,

and the warm colour that was always suffusing his honest face.

He illuminated the room with his freshness and youth, and the afternoon hours passed quickly while she listened to his vows, and thought of herself as really the angel he mistook her for.

Her smiles were sweet and caressing; the scene and hour had transported Charlie at once into paradise.

How he fondled the hand she had given him. The mock respect and bashfulness that Benito had assumed with her lately was now hers in very truth. Soon this devotion would bore her and this meek lovemaking pall, but she did not think of that now; she thought only of her own charms, and her smiles were sweet and frequent.

"Dear, dear Charlie," she said.

"Nannie says will you please go up and see Miss Nita, or else send for the doctor." So spoke the servant, opening the door.

Now the introduction of Nita's name at any time or in any conversation was sufficiently provoking, but just now it was unbearable. The child had never entered into Charlie's calculations; he did not know her; had hardly even seen her.

"What is the matter?" she said, not rising from her chair. Charlie had risen and was standing quite close to her.

"Don't go away!" he murmured, "I can't spare you."

"These old servants are always so fussy," she answered sweetly. "Tell Nannie that I will send for the doctor in the morning," she said to the servant. "She had better put her to bed now, and I will come up presently."

Dr Phillips was going to a meeting that night; it was one of Mary's rare holidays, and she had used it to good purpose. She meant Charlie to dine with her tonight, and in the warmth of the after dinner hour she would make such arrangements as would precipitate matters a little, and give her at the earliest possible date the happiness she coveted.

It was too bad of Nita to interfere in this way. If she sent for the doctor she would have to send Charlie away. But then she knew Nannie was not fussy—quite the contrary.

"I will come up presently," she said again. "You can tell Nannie." Her mind was made up, she must complete her conquest.

And she did. The cosy little dinner and warm room, the lights that flickered in her yellow hair, and the seductive contours revealed by her liberal tea gown overcame any lingering scruples in the lad's mind. He grew impassioned, eager, until his eagerness over-matched hers. He pressed, and implored, and even wept that she should promise him a speedy marriage.

Coyly, with becoming modesty, she yielded, drawing him on point by point until his demands increased as he became more and more excited by her beauty and the sweet abandonment of her attitudes.

It was late before Charlie tore himself away. Then Mary, in all the glow of her newly found virtue and happiness, stayed a little by the dying fire, dreaming of the time when her new life would have begun and in calm and contented happiness she and Charlie would live their idyllic existence.

When it came across her that she had promised to go up and see Nita she put the thought from her. She felt that her emotions were pure and that anything that reminded her of Dr Phillips was disgusting and repulsive. Her lips smiled all the time she was undressing, at the idea of Charlie's devotion.

Meantime Nita tossed and turned on her little cot, and her eyes burnt brightly. She moaned, she called for Nannie, for doctor, for drink; she wanted to get out of bed and sit on Nannie's lap. Then again she thought she would like to go to bed again. Would Nannie put her back ? Poor little Nita's bones ached, she had a pain in her side, and her head felt strange. She felt so hot and she was so miserable. Then she cried, and crying made her head worse, and her eyes were burning, and she didn't know where to turn for comfort or ease.

And Nannie—who did her best—took the little restless form on her motherly lap, tried to comfort her, gave her drink, and kept the rough hair from tumbling over the flushed face. Nannie spent that long night, during which she sat on the low chair and tended her little charge, in alternately trying to soothe her patient and thinking hard thoughts of the mother who had kept from her the aid of which she stood in such sore need.

Sometimes the child fell into a little doze, and Nannie would prepare to go to bed and think it was all over. But even before she had got her stiff old limbs into bed Nita was awake again, worse than ever, crying with pain, drawing every breath with difficulty and making the difficulties worse by her sobs.

And some baby instinct seemed to tell her what it was she wanted. She moaned out for Doctor to come and make Nita well. She cried out mother was keeping Doctor away, mother hated Nita. She tossed and turned and flung her little thin arms about, and kicked off all the warmth of the bed clothes, lying now in this position, now in that, trying for the ease that never came to her poor little body.

Nannie did her best, but her best was very little, and by the time that endless night had passed, and the morning had dawned with its grey fog and bitter east wind, poor little Nita seemed to herself to have gone through an age of suffering that would never leave her.

But as the early morning came on, some merciful stupor intervened, and Nannie, in her happy ignorance, seeing restful sleep in that fevered semiunconsciousness, went to bed and slept off the fatigues of the night until the risen sun had dissipated the grey dawn.

She never heard the spasmodic cough that occasion-

264

ally broke from the labouring chest of the child. She never even heard the paroxysms that shook the tender frame, and the call for her that Nita put forth before she sank again into stupor. The babe suffered alone, while he who would have given the world to save her was nowhere near to mark the fevered lips, the agonies unrelieved that his skill and science could have spared her.

What that babe went through in those long hours God alone could know. The physical agony, the terrors of loneliness while Nannie slept, and that weight on her chest and eyes, her limbs, her back, seemed to hold her when she would try to rise and wake her; that terrible thirst when her lips were like wood and her tongue seemed all shrivelled up and stiff in her mouth; when she struggled and moaned and coughed for breath, but breath came to her less and less, and the weight grew more and more, and she could not move or call out, only cough; and Nannie never heard her. And all this time, in the little mind, some dim feeling told her that if Doctor's quiet hand were laid on the iron weight she could rise and all her pains would be over. The bed was hot, the sheets were on fire, and everything was burning her, but she could not move, and somebody, somebody —it must be mother—was digging a sharp knife into her side and turning it round and round until she wanted to shriek; but she had no breath to shriek with, and so the knife kept turning and the pain growing worse until there was nothing left but that pain; and she could only moan with her poor little eyes tight shut, until ever and again she would drift into unconsciousness with her baby fingers clenched in agony and the fever demon crimsoning her sallow cheeks.

And when Nannie at length got up, and wearily—for Nannie was an old woman, and it was five o'clock before she had got to bed—went over in her night dress to look at her charge, she saw the red cheek and red lips and closed eyes and said, "Poor little thing, I daresay she'll sleep late this morning after the night she's had. I wonder what was the matter with her. Another tooth, I suppose, but the doctor won't like not to have been sent for."

Then she dressed herself, prepared Nita's bath, went into the day nursery, pulled up the blinds, made Nita's porridge on the spirit lamp, boiled the kettle for her own tea, laid the breakfast, dusted the room, even looked round to see if all the favourite toys were in their places, and the picture book within easy reach. And still Nita slept.

Nannie ate her breakfast in the front room, and moved quietly so that the child shouldn't wake. But she was an old woman, her ears were not so sharp as they had been. She had almost finished her breakfast before a sound reached her from the bedroom. Then she hurried in to find... what? Only a little flushed nightgowned figure struggling for breath in a terrible paroxysm of coughing, that seemed as if it would burst the veins standing out on the forehead, that would break the shaking and gasping chest.

Nannie acted on her own responsibility then, and sent a cab for the doctor. The doctor was out on his rounds; it would be one o'clock before he returned.

More long wasted hours while the little lamp of life, that lamp that never can be refilled, burnt quickly away.

Then he came.

As far as Nita's pain was concerned it was almost over. She lay upon her back, her breath coming in gasps, eyes shut, face swollen, unconscious; ignoring his presence now and for ever.

One glance from those keen eyes. Alas for the gift of rapid prognosis! He saw plainly the Angel of Death holding possession of the cot. Saw him sitting in majesty and knew that no skill or ingenuity of his could dethrone him.

But two days ago the child had sat by his side, laughed with him, fondled him. He had had no warning. Yes—he remembered now in a dull way, as he stood still by the door, paralysed by the knowledge that had struck him dumb—he remembered how Nannie had said she had a little cold and cough. But in his gaiety and high spirits he had taken no heed.

Too late!

He moved to the bed. He sat down by it, but his eyes were gazing before him into vacancy, fixedly staring at the fate that had so suddenly overtaken him.

"What shall I do, sir?" said Nannie.

Benjamin Phillips looked down on the cot—its occupant unconscious now and drifting fast.

"You can send for a doctor," he said, his voice harsh with emotion; but not stirring to help her.

Too late! Nannie left the room to obey his order. He was alone with the child. How could he order or act? He saw death, against whom availed not all his weapons of duplicity, of sophistry, of philosophy.

He sat on, mute and stuff and dumb, when the doctor came. He sat on while poultices were applied, while one remedy after another was tried, and baby Nita sank from unconsciousness into death. He sat silent, his eyes dry and hard.

Nobody spoke to him. Nobody tried to rouse him. Nannie sobbed. The doctor, a stranger, saw no cause to sympathise with this motionless figure, who was "no relation," as the mother had told him. Mary came into the room only once. She had chosen to believe it was not so serious as the doctor had said; that it was only a scare such as Benito had once before had about his precious offspring.

Charlie had been in during that long afternoon and sympathised with her over her child's illness, but forgot his sympathy, as she did the illness, in the endearments and arrangements that filled all his mind.

The afternoon slid into evening, the evening into

267

night. Almost imperceptibly the spirit glided from the frail body, and none could tell the moment of the final separation.

"It is all over," said Nannie. "She's gone." She put her handkerchief to her eyes and wept for the baby who had gone out into the emptiness and the cold.

Benjamin did not weep. He staggered up from the chair he had sat in so long and stumbled out into the darkness whither his little girl seemed to have gone.

His mind was an absolute blank. The shock had numbed him. Instinct led him home, and he passed the night, still dumb and vacant, sitting by the empty grate in his study, wondering where the fire had gone ... whether Nita was with it, and warm ... He was shivering.

Book III · Chapter XI

Benjamin passed through the next few days in the same state of stupor. He was hardly suffering; he only felt numbed; and he went through his duties, made the funeral arrangements, and took his lonely meals in the gloomy dining room, in mechanical semiunconsciousness.

He only saw his patients, and prescribed; he did not speak to them. He went through his necessary tasks and no more, with a grey, aged look on his face which began to show furrows and wrinkles. He seemed to be living in a dream, automatically, to be acting an empty part. He could not write; he would sit down of an afternoon, pen in hand, the empty high chair at his side; and his pen would fall from his fingers and his eyes wander into vacancy. So he would sit until the servant brought him dinner, or, chilled and shuddering, he rose and went to bed, and lay awake through the night hours, his eyes still fixed, his brain still dormant.

He saw nothing before him but emptiness; his arms, outstretched in the darkness, never gathered aught but shadows into their embrace. He was always alone on a high bleak mountain under a black sky, set apart from the rest of humanity, who worked and loved and suffered miles and miles beneath him. Everything was dark, empty space and he a lonely figure face to face with eternity. Even that distant humanity that toiled beneath him he could not always see. Some bitter wind arose, laden with black clouds and hid that also, leaving him lonelier, colder, bleaker, on that height of solitude, with empty arms and the blackness around him.

No figure of wife or child came to him in his isolation. Every rift in the clouds only showed a blacker darkness and an emptier void beyond. Yet there were times when his anguish grew greater than he could bear and he strove to shriek aloud only to find his voice as hollow as the vast spaces that moved about him. There were times when meteor-like a pale golden head would gleam for an instant against the blackness of the night, would gleam for an instant and disappear. These momentary flashes saved him. They were the symbols of hope, unnamed, unknown, that kept him from flinging himself down from the firm ground to be whirled hither and thither for ever by the storm clouds of the abyss below.

His thoughts had grown no clearer when the day of the funeral arrived.

It was cold and drizzling when he got to Brunswick Place. Already the black nodding hearse was at the door, and the one funeral carriage that would more than hold all those who mourned for little Nita. So steady and quiet his demeanour, so grave and composed his look as he stood at the window to see the little coffin, undecorated by a single flower, lifted in; so self possessed the way in which he handed in Mary and then stepped after her into the carriage that was to take them to the burial ground that Mary, saying to herself that he cared for nothing but her, that even the loss of the child could not make him suffer while she was by his side, hardened her heart against him and waited the hour of her deliverance with impatience.

They stood side by side, and the drizzling rain fell steadily upon them both as the last token of their union was placed in the damp yawning ground and the minister gabbled hastily through the words which were the last spoken for Nita before the earth shut her in for ever.

And the rain, as it fell upon Benjamin, seemed strange to him after the endless clear cold space in which he had dwelt, but the gleam of the pale golden head that he had seen seemed to be charming for him a way back to life.

270

"The grace of our Lord Jesus Christ, and the love of God, and the fellowship of the Holy Ghost be with us all evermore. Amen."

Dr Phillips offered her his arm and together they left the ground. The sight of the damp hole in which he had left his delicate baby daughter awoke him to the consciousness of his loss and of his pain. He drove back in silence with Mary to Brunswick Place. No tear came to relieve him.

Mary, watching him behind her black veil, said to herself, "He does not care. So long as he has me he does not care." And she hugged to her heart the thought that she had done for ever with this dark silent man and that the tears she had lightly shed in the churchyard set the seal on the black pages of her old life.

Thus she thought as she sat beside him in the brougham, and it seemed to her as if she were going from darkness into light. Then the thought came to her and gave her pleasure, that she had yet to tell Benjamin.

"You are mine, and mine you will ever remain," he had said to her that night, which seemed so long ago. Almost she smiled as she pictured her revenge. Yet there was fear at her heart, and she dreaded the moment when they should reach home.

The drive seemed very short to her.

"Mary!" He turned to her when they had reached the drawing room. He was yearning for human love and sympathy in his trouble. He held out his arms and his voice shook. "Come to me, comfort me. God help me..." He broke down and covered his face with his hands.

She stood over him and looked at him.

"How can I tell him?" she thought; and her revenge seemed no longer so sweet.

"Forgive me, darling," he said brokenly. "You must want comfort as much as I do, but I have suffered... Come!"

She did not move. He looked up; his glasses were dim

271

with the first tears that he had shed, but something he
saw through them checked him, as he rose to go to her.

"Mary..." There was doubt, and fear, and a new
strange pain in his voice.

She answered sullenly, still standing in her mourning
garments.

"Well, what do you want of me?"

What did it mean? No light dawned upon him. He
only waited, confused, fearing he knew not what. Still
he answered gently, thinking perhaps the pain of her
loss had overpowered her.

"I want you here," he said, rising and trying to draw
her to his heart. "I want to comfort you, and I want
you to comfort me. We must be all in all to each other
now, my darling"—this so sadly—"We must help each
other; there is no other help for us."

"None for you perhaps," she answered, avoiding his
embrace and his eyes.

"What do you mean?"—in a shocked, amazed
voice—"We are one."

She laughed, actually laughed, in a harsh unusual
voice. Her revenge seemed very faint though, and she
wished it were over. Something akin to shame had
touched her.

"It is all over between us; the last act of the comedy
is played."

"All over between us!" he repeated blankly, not
understanding. "My wife."

"Mrs Charlie Doveton," she corrected, still in the
same harsh manner.

"Oh, my God!" he moaned. "Oh, Clothilde!"

There was a moment's silence. "How could you, how
could you, Mary! I have loved you so."

"How could you expect me to love—a murderer?"
Even she paused as she brought out the word; but it
seemed to revive him.

"And you can call me a murderer, you—you, woman,

who can forsake the deathbed of your neglected child to deceive its father by this shameful intrigue."

He spoke abruptly; the taunt seemed wrung from him. Looking at her, the woman who had called him murderer, the woman on whom he had lavished his all, he saw as by a sudden revelation the utter vileness of the thing he had pressed so close to his heart.

And from her, stung by that contemptuous taunt of his, something of the veil she had enfolded herself in fell away. Her newly found purity and virtue seemed to flee from her. Her neglected child, the two men she had deceived; something of her own baseness she saw and shuddered at. The pleasure in her marriage fled for ever from her tainted heart.

"Forgive me, Benito!" she said, longing for him whom she thought the stronger in wickedness to take up the burden of her sin, and let her go free. "We can still be friends," she faltered; "Charlie..."

"Silence!" thundered the emotional doctor. "How dare you offer me your shameful self? Have I fallen so low that even you could think there is no depth I would not stoop to gain you?"

But he could not maintain his righteous wrath as the consciousness of her baseness came to him. He had lived so long with this woman that all his actions and thoughts had become tainted. In that sudden flash of knowledge he saw the blackness of his past. And the blackness that had surrounded him since his child's death he knew was the blackness of sin and not of sorrow.

In that terrible moment he knew the nature of the woman he had loved. His voice was hard with self contempt as he said, "The day when your child was buried; did you choose it for your wedding morning? The day she lay in agony and I was called too late, did you sit here—here in my chair, on my sofa, in the clothes that I gave you—toying with your lover while

273

she gasped for breath? Or did you...did you perhaps laugh with him over her sufferings as you saw the last link breaking that bound you to me? Did you, in my house, mine—who have loved you and gone down into the depths for you—did you coldly leave to her torment that one thing you had that was so precious to me? She choked as you kissed him. She writhed in convulsions as you sat on his knee. She died—and you wound your arms about him and went to him—a bride! And Clothilde, my wife, she, too died for you!...and you played with your lover! *And I loved you!*"

That he had loved her; that was what stung him. As she sat and listened she almost saw what a vile woman it was he was portraying.

"I didn't tell you to murder your wife," was her faint excuse.

"You...you didn't tell me! Why, *you* murdered her! You got the poison, you filled the needle, you made the puncture, *you* murdered her as surely as she lies rotting in her coffin. And you sit there, more rotten than she, and say you did not tell me to kill her! Was I sane or mad when I came to you that evening, and you played with me like the...the...the wretch that you are and tempted me through that viler part of my nature which had been revealed to you? Was I sane or mad as you lay there on the sofa, supple and warm and seductive, with your dimpled limbs and siren lips, and told me you loved me but hated to live in sin? Woman! You are the murderer, not I. You sent me from you; you knew well on what errand. Was there no spark of human nature in you to call me back and say, 'You are already too late?'... God help me! Why should I reproach you? You had acted as a creature of your kind. It is I who have been blind and deaf.... Oh, my poor wife! My poor Clothilde!'"

She had begun to cry in the middle of his speech, but this time her tears did not move him. She was frightened at him, and in her shallow soul dreaded the vengeance he would take on her.

"That is Charlie's knock," she said, looking at him piteously through her tears.

"He is coming to fetch his bride from here?" And the doctor looked round at his household goods with his bitter sneer, recovering from his rage as he saw how it only affected her to this extent; seeing how little she was moved to real shame or regret, how she only dreaded his vengeance.

She cried yet more.

"You will tell him?"

In the light of his new knowledge she sickened him.

"Nothing," he said abruptly. "I will tell him nothing. I will leave you to your happiness. To your respectability born on the grave of your nameless, neglected child."

And as he passed out, Charlie entered to greet his bride, to wipe away the tears he would think fell for her child. To enter with eager feet on the terrible path that had led a stronger man to ruin.

The doctor, lifting his thoughtful head, saw him pass in and glanced at him with pity.

Book III · Chapter XII

This last interview with Mary, in which all his emotions had been so cruelly overwrought, arrested for ever the insidious influence that had so nearly proved fatal to the intellectual life of Benjamin Phillips. The love that had reigned in his breast and overpowered every other sense died a natural death when the woman in whom he had rested all his faith flung at him as an excuse for her infidelity the word "murderer."

The recoil was tremendous. He had for the moment forgotten his philosophy and his reason and had said hard things to her, giving utterance to the rush of emotions which her conduct provoked.

He had not said anything to her, however, that was undeserved. As he went out from her presence, leaving her with the tears on her cheeks and her new boy husband only waiting for him to leave to kiss them away, he somewhat regained his old attitude of mind, and instead of resenting he despised and pitied.

Mary was not worth his anger. He was conscious of a new and intense feeling of self contempt as he noted the glance of confidence that passed between those two—the woman who had been so nearly his wife and the boy he could not but pity, knowing him to be her husband.

He despised himself for that there could have been any rivalry between this brainless country bred lad and Benjamin Phillips, philosopher and physician, over the possession of this heartless, white skinned woman.

"Thank God I didn't marry her," was almost his first conscious thought as he felt a gradually increasing relief in his newly found freedom. And he pitied Charlie who had married her; and very soon laughed at himself bitterly when he remembered what wild feelings of hatred he had felt for the youth, who after all had done him such a good turn.

The sense of relief at his freedom, and of gratitude for it, did not come to him all at once. He had to pass through a stage of loneliness when, although he did not regret Mary—for he never had another tender thought of the woman—he yet found his life empty without her, and the days passed slowly and seemed to lead nowhere. The motive spring of his existence was broken, and his actions had no sequence.

It was at this time he again missed his wife, who began to be constantly in his mind. He regretted her, not that he felt remorse—his strange conscience never troubled him in that way—but he missed her and he wanted her. The absence of woman about him fretted him and he grew irritable under the constant unfulfilled want.

This was all that avenged her. The unrest of the doctor, the loneliness he felt when he wandered into the cretonne covered drawing room and saw no figure on the sofa, the dreary look the heavy dining room had for him as he ate his badly prepared meals in its cold solitude.

The house in Portsdown Road began to haunt him with its dullness, its four stories of windows out of which there looked no face. The lack of beauty it had always had grew to something oppressive and un-bearable now as he went from his cold, empty library to his cold, empty bedroom, as he passed down the staircase where no one met him or sat in the morning room where no one faced him.

But when the consciousness of the life he was leading came fully home to him it was the precursor of an alteration.

Benjamin Phillips was no weakling to sit down and drift into misery because a woman had died; because a

277

woman had been false. He roused himself and began to reopen his books to force more of his brain, that was rusting in disuse, into his literary work.

And when he had aroused himself to this extent and began both to write and to think logically and clearly, it dawned upon him that the stillness of the house and the loneliness of his life could not be entirely due to either Clothilde's death or Mary's marriage.

Where were the patients that had disturbed his morning hours? Where was his case book and the slate in the hall that had been so rarely empty? And October—was not October the month in which he had promised to attend Mrs Detmar? He turned over the leaves of his engagement book. Yes, the beginning of October, and this was the end. What did it mean? And Mrs Montague Levy? Her health must have improved very suddenly; it was two months since he had been called for to her.

He had been going so introspectively about his day's work that it was a long time before he noticed the gradual lessening of that daily labour. And now that he looked with awakening consciousness on the situation, he saw that it was his Jewish patients who had deserted him; those who had been friends as well as patients seemed to have discarded his services.

This knowledge came to him with an almost incomprehensible bitterness. He could not accept it all at once. He even went to the synagogue one day, that large synagogue in Bayswater where he and his wife had been made one. He sat out the long Hebrew service, thinking his strange thoughts of the events that had happened since then, of what that day had been the commencement.

And when the service was over and he had placed his tallus and his prayer book in their places, he had waited in the body of the hall for his coreligionists as they passed out.

He stood so that all, as they filed out, must see him,

must almost touch him as they passed. His slender stooping figure, his grave dark face with the gold rimmed glasses, could scarcely be mistaken; they could scarcely ignore him. He stood there among his people, having joined in their worship. He half defied, half despised them as they passed him one after the other. But his heart was very sore for he had loved them and he was one of them, yet they left him standing alone in his mourning, a solitary figure that might have been an alien in their midst.

He knew then that somehow or other it must have permeated amongst them that Nita had been his child, Mary his mistress, that this was but their just resentment.

The justice, however, he did not admit; for he could still look upon what he had done philosophically. His philosophy only failed him when he saw himself standing up, an outcast in the midst of this big family, round whom all the fibres of his life had twined themselves.

He watched them pass him one by one, and found comfort in noting the ungainliness of their walk, the brilliancy of their cherished Sabbath clothes, the smug satisfaction which glistened greasily on their coarse features and loose lips.

Watching them passing him, talking in little eager groups, inviting each other loudly to luncheon or to the evening game of cards; watching the children decked out in their satins and plushes, the little boys with the sharp Jew look dawning upon their faces, their frizzled hair, their shining clothes; watching them there he saw for the first time all their faults, magnified through the glass of his resentment.

Saw, and felt the bitterness of the Jew who feels an outcast among his fellow Jews became in his breast a fierce resentment. It wounded him doubly that they *could* wound him, these people who were so immeasurably inferior to him and whom he could even despise.

279

He walked up the street to his lonely home, giving them no further look, passing the minister, as he had passed the congregation, without appeal from their judgment or their condemnation.

He knew himself then as the outcast Jew. The Jew who—though a larger world may honour him and his name be much in the mouths of men—is yet cast out from the hearts of his people. It is partly this intolerance, which they carry into small matters as into large, that is thinning their ranks and driving day by day a larger number of their once united body into the vast ranks of the unacknowledged, there to be absorbed into the multitude, and their very name of Jew forgotten.

And Benjamin Phillips, as others like him, from the outcast Jew became in time the Jew hater. Apart from them, he began to see their faults more clearly; their virtues, the clannishness, hospitality, generosity, of which he had used to boast, when no longer practised towards himself were obliterated by their bigotry, their narrowness, their greed.

It irritated him to see them walking about the neighbourhood, that new Jerusalem which they have appropriated with their slow and characteristic walk. It stung him to see them using the public thoroughfare as a meeting house, congregating in Clifton Road, in the gardens of Sutherland Avenue, in Warrington Crescent, in their free familiar communion in which he had no longer any part.

Such of his practice as had lain among Christians remained, but the neighbourhood became haunted to him: he felt his powers of thinking and of acting wane under the constant irritation of being surrounded by a family of which he had ceased to be a member.

This was the crisis in Benjamin Phillips's life. He might, by remaining in Portsdown Road and attending to his religious and professional duties, gradually, after many years, by dint of hard struggling and many humiliations, have regained his lost place among his people. Or he might, being now independent—although he had not as yet touched Mrs Phillips's money—give up his practice and try to fulfil, in the higher branches of his profession, the ambition that had once been his only hope.

At this juncture Dr Slate stepped in and decided his fate.

"You have never been the same man since your wife died," he said to him when they met in consultation one day, forgetting their unfortunate patient while enjoying each other's company. "You look as if melancholy had indeed marked you for her own. You want a change, man! Why don't you go out for the journal again? I can't help wondering at your settling to general practice in Maida Vale, with all the opportunities you have had of doing better."

Dr Phillips was indeed looking melancholy, thin, and pale. The life he was leading was weighing on his spirits and depressing him in every way.

"What can I do?" he answered. "It is too late!"

"Too late, too late! nonsense, man! Give up your practice, move down west, call yourself a consultant, apply for the vacant surgeonship at Bart's. They've not forgotten you there yet, and your newspaper friends can help you. It is absurd for a man of your abilities to devote himself to a midwifery practice that would scarcely satisfy a student."

"I have my literary work."

"But it doesn't suit you. You are doing it badly, too—putting nothing in it. You don't mind me telling you that. What you want, and what you can do, is surgery, and plenty of it. There, I must run away now. I have a very pretty case of pyosalpinx. I wish you could see it with me; but I suppose you have some confinement or other imminent. Think over what I've been saying, and remember you can rely upon me for help if you decide upon going back to the hospital."

281

"You are very kind," answered Benjamin, touched by this interest in him.

"Not kind at all; you are wasting your life."

"I will think over your advice."

"Do! You'll not regret it."

The two men clasped hands cordially. The elder, who ascribed Benjamin Phillips's obvious unhappiness to the loss of his wife, was earnestly desirous of rousing him from his depression. He had never ceased to regret that incident which had lost him his patient, and he had been so much impressed by it that he had devoted a whole chapter in his forthcoming work on abdominal operations to "The Extraordinary Susceptibility of Certain Constitutions to Morphia, with Notes on a Fatal Case."

And Benjamin Phillips, listening to the man who had been his master, began to feel perhaps life was not yet over for him and to rally his forces for a struggle against the past.

He succeeded, as a man like Benjamin Phillips is bound to succeed. What his skill and his reputation failed to accomplish for him was secured by his diplomacy and Machiavellian talents. Once free from the toils, he rose rapidly, and the Benjamin Phillips of today is a prominent light in the medical world. His Judaism has fallen from him like a discarded garment; he is scarcely known as an Israelite; he scarcely acknowledges the title.

What he suffered, or whether he suffered in that separation, he confided to no one. What he regretted, and what he had cause to regret, remained a secret in his breast, but ten years from the date of his freedom he dwells in honour among his contemporaries, an outcast from his people, outwardly happy on the edifice he has built up.

See him as twelve o'clock strikes entering the wards of his hospital, with his large and eager following. His shoulders are more bent, his unthinned mass of hair is

grey, and his high brow is furrowed with thought. His eyes are still bright, and the gold rimmed glasses add intellectuality to the appearance of "one of the first surgeons in England."

As he stops beside the hard, narrow bed, the patient awaits his verdict in affright, for Benjamin Phillips is known as a most uncompromising operator, but he is soon reassured. Benjamin's manner is as gentle as ever, and his influence as magnetic.

"You will soon be well," he says kindly, and passes on. The patient sinks back on his pillow satisfied, but the students are disappointed.

The rage for surgical interference which is overriding the pharmacopoeia and demoralising the physicians of today has no keener champion than Benjamin Phillips. A terrible curiosity to unveil the mysteries of nature, and absolute disregard for human life, characterise the surgeon whose magisterial aphorism to his pupils runs: "When in doubt, operate. You may save life; you are certain to acquire knowledge."

Dr Slate is an old man now, but Benjamin Phillips lives to carry on his work, to unsex woman and maim men; to be a living testimony of manual dexterity and moral recklessness. He is the idol of his clinic, the prophet of the new school; his name is in all men's mouths, and he can ably defend himself with pen and tongue against the reproaches and attacks of his more timorous or more conscientious brethren.

So much for his public life: the brilliant, keen intellectual Benjamin Phillips as known to the world.

Then follow him home to 108 Brook Street when, his day's work done, he goes to take the rest he has so well earned.

108 Brook Street has more the appearance of Brunswick Place than of Portsdown Road. There is judgment and taste in the pictures on the walls, in the china in the cabinets. There is warmth and luxury in this snug bachelor retreat, and Bessie, the pretty parlour maid, promptly appears to relieve her master of his coat and stick. He is well served, well waited upon; his slippers are warmed and all his little comforts are attended to. Never again will the wiles of woman lure the doctor from his ambition, from his social or professional life, but something feminine and soft about him is a necessity, and if Bessie's services have other rewards besides her yearly wages? why, no one is the wiser, and Benjamin is happier.

284

This house is not haunted for him, and Mary is as dead to him as if she had never lived. But sometimes, when dinner is over and Bessie has gone to prepare him his coffee, the cosy chair and bright fire in his library will lure him to repose and in the dreamy slumber that steals over him Clothilde and Nita will be with him, and they seem to him then as mother and child, caressing him, proud of him, the foremost sharers in his honours, the most enthusiastic of his worshippers.

From this dream he wakes again to his loneliness, but Bessie is there with the coffee and the firelight flickers on her neat brown hair and saucy eyes, on her ruddy lips and white teeth, and Benjamin Phillips's loneliness has its consolations.

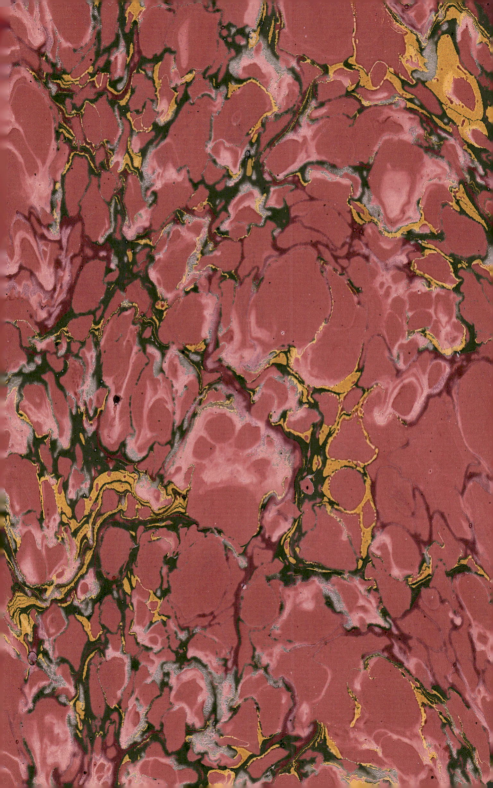

This edition of
A Maida Vale Idyll
consists of 300 numbered copies published by
the Keynes Press, London.
It has been designed by Sebastian Carter
and set, in Monophoto Modern,
printed and bound by
Cambridge University Press
on Fineblade Cartridge.

This copy is No. 72

The Keynes Press emblem
is a profile of Sir Geoffrey Keynes
engraved by David Gentleman
and based on the bust by Nigel Boonham
in the National Portrait Gallery